TEMPT ME

Dante took a step forward, his dark gaze connecting with hers, teasing her senses. If Hostess could bottle the look in Dante's eyes, they'd have world dominance over the snack food market. "I want more," he said.

"More?" Maria swallowed. "What kind of more?"

"Dinner. At my restaurant. You and me." His grin arched up on one side, exposing a dimple that made her knees weak. She'd always been a sucker for a man with a dimple in his grin. "No critics, no one else. Just a meal to remember."

Oh, damn. And she'd thought the Twinkies had been tempting. They had nothing over this offer. He was handing her an entire meal. Probably with him as the appetizer and the dessert.

He'd caught her at her weakest. Her willpower had fallen and wouldn't get back up. She wanted the Twinkies. She wanted the Cheez Whiz.

She wanted Dante.

BOOK YOUR PLACE ON OUR WEBSITE AND MAKE THE READING CONNECTION!

We've created a customized website just for our very special readers, where you can get the inside scoop on everything that's going on with Zebra, Pinnacle and Kensington books.

When you come online, you'll have the exciting opportunity to:

- View covers of upcoming books
- Read sample chapters
- Learn about our future publishing schedule (listed by publication month *and author*)
- Find out when your favorite authors will be visiting a city near you
- Search for and order backlist books from our online catalog
- Check out author bios and background information
- Send e-mail to your favorite authors
- Meet the Kensington staff online
- Join us in weekly chats with authors, readers and other guests
- Get writing guidelines
- AND MUCH MORE!

**Visit our website at
http://www.kensingtonbooks.com**

THE DEVIL SERVED TORTELLINI

Shirley Jump

ZEBRA BOOKS
KENSINGTON PUBLISHING CORP.
http://www.kensingtonbooks.com

To my husband, who stole my heart over a plate of steamers and an order of nachos at Faneuil Hall Marketplace all those years ago. Who'd have known I'd fall in love before the main entrée even arrived?

ZEBRA BOOKS are pubished by

Kensington Publishing Corp.
850 Third Avenue
New York, NY 10022

All Kensington titles, imprints and distributed lines are available at special quantity discounts for bulk purchases for sales promotion, premiums, fund-raising, educational or institutional use.

Special book excerpts or customized printings can also be created to fit specific needs. For details, write or phone the office of the Kensington Special Sales Manager: Kensington Publishing Corp., 850 Third Avenue, New York, NY 10022. Attn. Special Sales Department. Phone: 1-800-221-2647.

Zebra and the Z logo Reg. U.S. Pat. & TM Off.

First Printing: March 2005
10 9 8 7 6 5 4 3 2 1

Printed in the United States of America

The Devil's Seven-Deadly-Sins-in-One Manicotti with Ricotta

1 pound whole-fat ricotta cheese
1 egg
2 tablespoons chopped parsley, green as envy
½ teaspoon grated lemon rind
Dash of nutmeg
12 manicotti noodles, cooked until tender
1 cup pasta sauce, homemade and tasty as sin
½ cup freshly grated Parmigiano Reggiano—only use the best for yourself

Mix the cheeses, egg, parsley, lemon rind and nutmeg. Spoon into prepared noodles. Lick any excess from the bowl and your fingers . . . slowly, enjoying every bit. Don't worry about the salmonella thing. This tastes too good to be bad for you.

Come on, admit the truth, feel a bit of pride. Tastes like heaven . . . or even better, like temptation.

Drizzle the noodles with the sauce and admire the food for the scrumptious art that it is. Don't get angry about any mess it might make. Living in sloth can be very relaxing. Dust with extra Parmigiano, then bake at 350 degrees for 30 minutes, lusting after the dish while you wait. Remember, anything bad for you is best served *hot*.

Worry about the calories later. There's always tomorrow. Indulge today. Don't bother to share. Greed is good.

CHAPTER 1

Maria Pagliano was serious this time.

No-holds-barred, no-prisoners-taken, no-cheese-allowed serious. She had eight weeks to do what she'd never been able to do before—lose twenty-five pounds.

This time, she vowed, was going to be different. She wasn't going to cheat and fall victim to her own desires. But in order to stick to her plan, she needed a little help, which was why she had come here on a Tuesday night.

To a meeting of the Chubby Chums support group.

In the lime green basement of a tiny church in Boston's North End, a dozen or so people sat on folding chairs in a circle. Above them, a fluorescent light flickered and hummed like a pathetic disco ball. Maria crossed her legs, panty hose swishing in the quiet, trying very hard not to think about the lone manicotti from Guido's Italian Cafe sitting in her apartment refrigerator.

"Welcome, group!" A woman in tight jeans who looked like she'd never been tempted by a bowl of raviolis in her life stepped into the room and opened her arms wide, in an all-encompassing group hug. "And how are my Chubby Chums tonight?"

"We're peachy with light syrup!"

Maria looked around at the group, all laughing at their practiced pun. Had she accidentally stumbled into the Lunatics with Heart Support Forum?

The pixie leader's name badge said, *Hello, my name is: Stephanie,* with a smiley face and an exclamation point. Stephanie took a seat in one of the chairs, thrusting out her hands. The group copied her, becoming a human circle of joined palms. A portly guy—his tag declared his name was "Homer"—grabbed up Maria's left hand with a sweaty palm, giving her a smile that lacked a few teeth. "Jillie," a middle-aged sniffling woman, put down her stash of tissues to take Maria's right hand in a floppy fish grip.

Then, as if on cue, the group dropped their heads to their chests and began to recite: "God grant me the serenity to accept my goal weight, the courage to resist anything with more than three hundred calories, and the wisdom to check the fat grams before I open my mouth and insert a fork."

Goose bumps rose on Maria's arms. Bunch of lunatics. She should leave. But . . .

Mary Louise Zipparetto *had* gone from a size twenty to a size two, with the help of the Chubby Chums. Mary Louise had told her mother, who'd told Maria's mother, who'd told Maria over a cheese danish, that Mary Louise would be wearing a sleeveless Band-Aid of a dress to the class reunion to show off her new figure.

No way was Maria going to let Mary Louise be the best-looking woman in the Sons of Italy hall. All her life, Mary Louise had been the one to compete against. The first one to get an "A" in Mr. Marcetto's impossibly hard geometry class. She'd run for class president and won—two out of four years in high school. The other two,

Maria had taken the top spot and made Mary Louise serve as veep.

And now, Mary Louise was skinnier *and* planning on taking the spotlight at the reunion.

Over Maria's dead bruschetta-fortified body.

Maria straightened in her seat, yanked her hand away from Homer, who let out a sigh of disappointment, and started paying attention. Stephanie's hands danced around her head as she talked, dramatizing her clear joy at being among a crowd of wannabe-thin people.

"Let's get started with a little bit of sharing! Tell us the last food you ate today and then name an animal you'd most like to be."

Mary Louise Zipparetto. In a size two.

Starting today, Maria intended to leave the double digits behind for good. She'd been okay with herself as a ten, but as twelve edged toward fourteen, she'd begun to dread shopping. Getting dressed. Looking in the mirror. But most of all, she now dreaded dating and the inevitable getting naked part. For a woman who enjoyed sex as much as pasta, that presented a few problems.

Then the invitation to her ten-year class reunion had come in the mail, followed by a phone call that had sent her pulse—and her diet dedication—into overdrive.

Antonio Lombardi, captain of the football team in high school and God's gift to a sex-starved woman, had asked her if she was coming, and if she was still as pretty as the rah-rah cheerleader he remembered. He'd said something about letting him see her in *just* the pom-poms and she'd babbled some kind of agreement. It was, after all, Antonio, and she'd never been able to say no to him, not even on prom night.

Over the course of her life, she'd done every diet— the seven-day grapefruit plan; the all-the-meat-you-can-eat regime and the starve-yourself-until-the-dress-fits desperation diet, only to make a mad dash to Macy's and buy the next size up. Nothing had worked. Inevitably, she gave in to the first thing with tomato sauce and cheese, her diets failing faster than Michael Jackson's last album.

But now, there was no turning back. Hanging in her closet was a little black—and very expensive—dress from Saks in a size eight that she'd bought this afternoon. The dress, and the thought of Antonio eyeing Mary Louise at the reunion instead of her, kept Maria rooted to her seat.

"The last food I ate was a tofu burger for lunch, hold the bun, extra lettuce," said a slightly pudgy young woman in a tie-dyed shirt and frayed bootleg jeans. Her badge declared her name was Audrey, with a smiley in the curve of the "y." "And I'd most like to be a butterfly, because they bring beauty to the world."

"Sweet people are better than sweet treats!" shouted another woman. Others in the group echoed her, a human wave of trite phrases.

A young redheaded man with the body shape of an apple leaned forward, draping his arms over his knees. From across the circle, Maria saw he'd written "Arnold" on his name badge in pink marker. "I did good today, Chums," he said. "I had a protein bar for lunch and a power shake for dinner. I think this is it. I'll finally be down a pound this week!"

" 'Down a pound': a sign on your way to the finish line!" the group shouted. Arnold blushed and sat up a little straighter.

Stephanie-with-the-exclamation-point gestured toward Maria. "I see we have someone new. Welcome"—she leaned forward to read the name tag slapped on Maria's russet velour T-shirt—"Chubby Chum Maria!"

Maria wasn't so sure she liked being called a Chubby Chum. Nor did she like the way the group's heads all swiveled her way, like some mass *Exorcist* wave. "Umm . . . hi."

"New Chubby Chums are *awesome!*" said the group, smiling at Maria.

"Why don't you share with us, Maria? Tell us the last thing you ate and what animal you'd most like to be."

"I forgot to tell my animal!" Arnold cut in.

Stephanie gave him a patient smile. "We'll get to your animal after our new Chubby Chum has a chance, Arnold."

Everyone in the room waited, silent and expectant. Maria hesitated. She could lie. Say she'd had a salad with light dressing. But no, this was a *support* group. She was here to get serious and getting serious meant being honest. "I had a Guido's cheese manicotti for lunch."

A collective gasp went up from the people in the room. "But those are *fattening,*" Audrey said. "Why would you eat one?"

The tempting image of the manicotti appeared in her mind, as beautiful as if it were laid out in *Gourmet* magazine. Stuffed and swollen, cheese trickling out of the sides, tomato sauce drizzled over the top, Parmigiano Reggiano cheese dusting the top.

Guido's manicottis are better than an hour of sex. If Guido were smart, he'd use that in his next ad campaign.

She'd bought two of them this afternoon for lunch, before she'd bought the dress and thus, gotten serious. This time.

"Uh . . ." Maria scrambled for an answer. "Today's a holiday."

"And what holiday would that be?" Stephanie asked.

Her mind drew a blank. Then she pictured her day planner. Tuesday, March eighteenth. "Uh, Flag Day," she said. "In Aruba."

A heavy silence descended on the room, thick as a good Alfredo sauce. There was the squeak of a chair against the tile, then a slight cough from someone on her right.

"Maria," Stephanie said with the gentle tone parents used on slow-witted children, "did that manicotti give you satisfaction?"

"Well, yeah. It was from Guido's."

"Did it satisfy your soul?"

"It didn't hurt." But even as the words came out of her mouth, she had a feeling she was failing her Introduction to Chubby Chums test. She'd never been the kind of woman who felt out of place, or out of control, anywhere. But something about this group and their collective Borg-like minds had her off-kilter.

"Love yourself enough to eat healthy," Stephanie said. "Your soul will be filled when you reach your goal."

"I want to share my animal!" Arnold said. "When is it my turn again?"

"Arnold, Maria is struggling with her food choices. Let's give her some support and then we'll get back to you."

He slumped in his chair and pouted. "She shouldn't have had that manicotti. What kind of diet lets you eat manicotti?"

"I just started my diet this afternoon," Maria said.

Stephanie nodded, her lips a tight line. "After the manicotti, right?"

"Yeah."

"Did you tell yourself, 'Just this one more fix and then I'll quit?' Did you eat that cheesy pasta and say it was the last one, like you said with all the noodles before?"

"Yeah . . ."

"And do you feel guilty about that choice now?"

"Yeah . . ." At least her head did. Her stomach, however, twisted and grumbled, urging her to get out of this uncomfortable, cold chair and knock over anyone who got between her and the manicotti awaiting her at home.

"Guilt won't make you thin, Chubby Chum Maria. Only *you* can make you thin."

"If it's to be, it's up to me!" the group chorused.

"I want to be a teddy bear!" Arnold yelled. Then he flushed and shrugged. "Sorry, Stephanie. I really felt the need to share."

"That's okay, Arnold. We're here to support, not to judge." Stephanie patted his hand. "A teddy bear, though, technically, isn't an animal."

"But I want to be something cute and cuddly." Arnold's shoulders slumped. "So everyone will want to hug me, even if I'm . . . I'm f-fat."

"Oh, Arnold, *we'll* hug you, Chubby Chum!" The group surged forward, enfolding Arnold in a circle of platitudes and people.

Maria pushed back her chair and tiptoed out of the room. Screw Mary Louise Zipparetto and her Chubby Chums. She could do this on her own.

She was stronger than one manicotti. How hard could it be?

Vinny's Up-in-Flames GranGala
Flambé Chicken

1 pound boneless, skinless chicken breasts
1 teaspoon each salt and pepper
2 tablespoons extra virgin olive oil
1 small onion, quartered
2 portobello mushroom caps, sliced
1 cup dry white wine
2 tablespoons butter
4 tablespoons flour
2 tablespoons whipping cream
⅓ cup GranGala imported orange liqueur—the more flammable, the better

Heat the oven to 350 degrees. Feel the warmth as you season the chicken with salt and pepper and then brown it in a large skillet with the olive oil. Watch those flames. No sense getting all fired up too early in the process. Add the onions and mushrooms, stirring until the onions become translucent.

Add the wine, then transfer the mixture to a shallow casserole dish and bake, uncovered, for thirty minutes.

Take a break—Whew! That's a lot of cooking. If the boss is out, make yourself a hell of a mimosa with the GranGala and some champagne. Stand by your stove and feel the heat emanating. That's good, isn't it?

When the casserole is done, remove the chicken and vegetables, placing them on a warm platter. Time to light the burners again! Oh, I know. It's such an exciting moment. Try not to get too mesmerized by the flames. Mix the butter and flour into a paste, add it to the pan juices, then add the cream and simmer for five minutes. Put sauce in a nice dish for serving, so everyone, especially the boss, will be impressed and keep their attention on the plate, not the flame.

Now for the *real* fun. With *flames*. In a small saucepan, warm the GranGala over low heat. Ooh! Lighting another burner! Grab the serving platter and the liqueur, and get ready to set the place on fire. If you want a hell of a presentation, do it at the table. No one will ever forget *this* meal—guaranteed. Pour the liqueur over the chicken and vegetables and then—

Ignite.

Warning: Keep a fire extinguisher handy. And never, ever light the liqueur too close to someone you, or the boss, want to impress.

CHAPTER 2

Before he murdered his sous chef, Dante Del Rosso escaped the heat of the kitchen, bursting through the back door and into the cool March night. He leaned against the brick of the restaurant façade and took in a few breaths until the urge to hurt Vinny Ozello had subsided from a first-degree felony to a misdemeanor.

He sipped at a double shot of grappa, then closed his eyes, and waited for the alcohol to kick in. The spring air cut through his T-shirt, chasing a chill up his spine. He drank again. Unfortunately, no matter how drunk he got, he doubted he'd forget the titanic disaster of tonight.

For six years, he'd dreamed of seeing a review of his restaurant, La Vita Deliziosa, in *The Boston Globe*. With more than a hundred Italian restaurants in Boston, it had been a hell of a long wait.

And then, at half past six, George Whitman had strolled into Vita, asked for a corner table, and sat his thin white notepad beside his place setting. Dante had thrown the kitchen into overdrive, fussing over the veal scallopini, searing cutlets with all the care of a gem cutter honing a precious diamond, hovering over the sauce, ensuring it was precisely the right temperature, and then tinkering with the plate until the presentation was flawless.

Then Vinny, damn him, had to go and spoil the whole thing by lighting Whitman on fire.

Dante might as well hang up his hat now and get a job flipping burgers. After the review came out in Thursday's paper, no one would visit his restaurant ever again.

Especially after Dante had to hose down Boston's most critical reviewer with a fire extinguisher. He could see the headline now: *La Vita Deliziosa: A One-Star Inferno of Ineptitude.*

George Whitman was known for his scathing comments—and for never giving anyone a five-star rating. And yet Dante had worked for years to attract Whitman's attention because the slightest nod of the critic's approval would send diners streaming into the restaurant.

Well, he'd certainly attracted Whitman's attention. If he was lucky, he'd get off easy—with only a multimillion dollar lawsuit.

All his dreams, up in smoke. Literally. He'd worked for six years, trying to take what his father had started and turn it into something uniquely his. People were depending on him to make this restaurant work, and yet, despite the endless hours he put in, he still felt like he was pushing a Mack truck uphill. One of these days, his arms were going to get tired and the damned thing would run him over.

If he could just get a good review, some attention from people in high places, he'd thought . . .

Well, tonight had taken care of that.

Dante pushed off from the wall and crossed to the front of the building. He wasn't needed inside, at least not tonight. Or tomorrow night. Or the next night. Nothing like a little fire to clear the place and cancel the rest of the night's reservations.

In the sign over the restaurant, the light illuminating "Deliziosa" sputtered, then went out, leaving no pretty adjective to describe Vita. Seemed appropriate. Kind of like his life. One gaping, empty hole.

Cheers. He raised his glass, a silent toast, and then downed the rest of it in a single gulp, searing his throat. He was about to go back into the restaurant for a second grappa when he saw a woman exit the church across the street, her coat draped over her arm as if she'd dashed out of there in a hurry. She stopped under the street-light and scanned the road, probably looking for a cab.

"You won't find a cabbie here, not tonight," Dante called to her. "Not unless he's lost."

She pivoted, and he straightened, Vinny and the smoldering food critic forgotten. She had the shape of an hourglass, and shoulder-length dark hair with ringlets curling around her face like a frame. He stepped out of the shadows and into her line of vision.

She was as intoxicating as the grappa. No, hotter and definitely sweeter. He edged toward the sidewalk, now only separated from her by two narrow lanes of old, bumpy street, a leftover from the seventeenth-century city design.

Without her coat on, he had an unblocked view of shapely legs beneath a straight black skirt and a curvy chest pushing at her T-shirt. Her breasts jutted out seductively, as if they were introducing themselves to his gaze.

Hello, he thought. *Very pleased to meet you both.*

"There were a bunch of cabs outside when I came here tonight," she said. Her voice had the slight tinge of an Italian accent, telling him she'd grown up in a family that interspersed English with the colorful native tongue.

He pointed over his shoulder at Vita, the only business open after eight on the small North End side street. "No customers, no cabs."

"No customers? Did you file bankruptcy between dinner and dessert?"

He laughed, but the sound of it was a bit too bitter to be funny. "No, we just had a small fire."

She raised an eyebrow. "Fire?"

"Long story."

"Oh." He could see she wanted to ask, but didn't. Someday, over drinks maybe, he'd tell her. Hell, with a face and a body like that, he'd tell her his credit card account numbers, too.

They stood there a minute, in the uncomfortable silence of strangers who didn't quite know where to take the conversation next. Dante glanced again at her, standing in the soft pool of light across the street. His gaze traveled back down to his two new acquaintances.

He figured he better make a move before some Red Top made him into a liar and came cruising down the street, taking her away and leaving him with a bunch of regrets and an empty shot glass. He crossed the street, noting how her eyes widened when he approached. Yet, she didn't move, not so much as a flinch. One tough cookie. "You hungry?"

She shook her head. "No. No, not at all. Really."

He grinned. "Are you trying to convince me? Or you?"

Her face reddened and she paused a minute before speaking again. "Me, mostly. I'm on a diet."

"Why?"

She gave him an are-you-crazy look. "I think that's pretty obvious." She spread her arms wide.

Now that he was standing a foot away, he took his time perusing her voluptuous form. Much better close up. "Maybe you need a new mirror, because you look pretty damned good to me."

"Maybe you need glasses."

"Let me guess." He waved a hand toward the church behind her. "Chubby Chums support group?"

"Yeah, how'd you know?"

"They meet every Tuesday, Thursday and Saturday night from seven to nine. After the others have gone home, a couple of them head over to the restaurant for the all-you-can-eat pasta special."

"You're kidding me! Geez, and they bashed me for having manicotti for lunch."

"Ah, the food of the gods, isn't it?"

"*Oh, yeah.*" Her eyes rolled back and she smiled a contented smile that said the manicotti had been very, very good.

He hoped his was better. A lot better. Because he definitely wanted to see her smile that way after eating one of his meals. He gestured toward Vita. "Come on, I know the owner. He'll fix you something nice. I promise."

She shifted and turned on her high heels, causing her calf muscles to flex into little hearts, then release. *Lord in heaven.*

"I . . . I really shouldn't," she said.

He took a step closer. "I really think you should. You look like you've had a bad day."

Her lips, full and glossed with cranberry, curved into a smile. "A bad life is more like it. But . . ." She glanced over at the restaurant, then back at him. She slid her coat on. "No. Thank you."

"How about a salad? That counts as diet food."

She swallowed and he could see the longing in her eyes, like a child spying a new bike in a department store window. "What kind?"

"Whatever you want. The chef will take care of you, even custom-make something if you don't like what you see." He grinned. "On the menu, I mean."

Her smile turned flirtatious. "How can you be so sure?"

"Trust me."

"I don't even know you."

He put out a hand. "Dante Del Rosso."

She hesitated only a second, then took his hand. Her fingers were long and delicate, yet strong in their grip. Despite his better sense, he pictured her fingers grasping a very different part of his anatomy. His body temperature spiked like an August heat wave.

"Maria Pagliano."

He didn't let go right away. "Have a salad with me, Maria Pagliano. I've had a hell of a day, too."

She tilted her head, considering.

"Listen, I don't bite, my shots are up to date, and if you want a reference, my sixth grade teacher is listed in the phone book."

Maria laughed, a full, hearty sound that seemed to come from some well deep within her. "Okay."

As they crossed the street, the lights over "Deliziosa" came on again. Dante took that as a sign.

Actually, a damned good sign. Maybe his luck was about to change. As long as he kept Vinny away from anything flammable, things were bound to improve.

Dante glanced at Maria and decided they already had.

Dante's Taste-of-Heaven
Tortellini Temptation

2 tablespoons unsalted butter
2 ounces minced ground pork
2 ounces minced ground turkey
2 ounces finely chopped sausage
2 ounces minced mortadella
½ cup grated Parmigiano Reggiano
Pinch grated nutmeg
1 pound fresh pasta dough, made with your own two
hands
Salt and pepper to taste

In a large skillet, heat the butter over medium heat,
watching it melt while you're thinking of the beautiful
woman you want to impress. Add the meats and sauté
until cooked thoroughly. Remove from heat, add the remaining filling ingredients, choosing only the best quality
for her. If needed, dice additionally in a food processor
so everything is even and beautiful. Set aside.

On a lightly floured surface, roll out the pasta dough
(or use a pasta machine) to a thickness of ⅛ inch. Drop
½ teaspoon of filling along the length of the dough,
about two inches apart. Then carefully cut the dough
into squares with a pastry wheel.

With a pastry brush or your finger dipped in water,
moisten the dough around the filling. Don't overdo this
because you want it to be a perfect tortellini circle. Fold
the squares into triangles and press the dough to mold
around the filling.

Shape into the sexy curves of a belly button with your pinkie, pressing the ends together very well—don't want this to come undone; much better for *her* to do that when she eats this delight.

Allow tortellini to rest on a floured tea towel for at least an hour while you cook up something else with the pretty lady at your table. Later, boil in salted water, being careful not to crowd the tortellini.

Serve with a meat sauce and a good red wine. Cap the meal with a kiss and a promise of more dessert to come.

CHAPTER 3

As soon as Maria entered Vita, she knew she'd broken the first cardinal rule of dieting—never, ever surround yourself with the very temptation that had contributed to the problem in the first place. If Dante hadn't been holding her hand, she'd have turned and ran as far as her high heels could take her.

The aromas of the restaurant ganged up on her, teasing and tempting like a hundred dancing virgins in front of a sultan. Garlic bread, fresh Parmesan, simmering pasta sauce, sweet ricotta. Her stomach, which had settled into quiet complacency, roared to life, screaming *gimme, gimme, gimme*.

A portly man with a friendly face came around the mahogany lectern in the reception area, his hands extended in greeting. "Welcome to La Vita Deliziosa, the Delicious Life." The words rolled off his tongue with all the romantic beauty of her mother tongue.

She'd seen the restaurant a hundred times. The North End was, after all, a small place, but she'd never been inside. Clearly, she'd missed a stop on her culinary journey through life.

"Maria Pagliano, meet Franco Vaccaro, our maître d' and"—Dante smiled—"the one person who keeps me from getting into too much trouble."

"Ah, you not so much trouble," Franco said. "He has a temper, this one, and a head like a mule. But with a *bella donna* like you, he behave." Franco clapped Dante on the shoulder.

"Hush, Franco. You'll scare her away."

"Maybe, a good idea." Franco wagged a finger at him. "I know you when you were this high"—he raised his hand three feet off the ground. "Trouble, but with a smile that could charm the fishes out of the sea." Franco shook his head. "Even my Isabella, God rest her soul, she called him an angel."

"That's because I am one."

Franco's laughter was hearty and rich. "Ah, a devil more like. No, no angel here." Franco leaned closer to Maria and lowered his voice to a whisper. "He's a good boy, though. Like my own son. He treat you right."

"Whoa!" Dante put up a hand. "Don't start your matchmaking again." Franco gave an innocent, who-me? shrug. Dante turned to Maria. "Franco won't be happy until he sees me married and saddled with a dozen kids."

"He should meet my mother," Maria said. "She'd help fit you for the bridle."

"Marriage, it's not so bad," Franco said. "Good for the head and the heart. You should—"

Dante shook his head. "All I want is to get this pretty lady a meal."

Franco smacked his forehead. "Ah, *mio Dio*, I forget myself. I see a beautiful woman, my mind, it is a hole." He cleared his throat, then spoke again, his voice now as formal as his pose. "Your coat, *signora?*"

"Allow me," Dante said. Before she could move, his nimble fingers were at her nape, sliding the camel cashmere off her shoulders, down her arms and over her hands, smooth as a waterfall.

He lingered behind her, his aftershave teasing at her senses. If she backed up one step, she'd be pressed to his pelvis.

Now another part of her started shouting *gimme, gimme, gimme.*

Franco took her coat from Dante's hands and the two men stepped over to the coatrack, talking quietly. She heard the name Vinny mentioned, but the conversation didn't interest her anywhere near as much as Dante's rear profile.

He was wearing black jeans, and they fit him like the peel on a banana. Definitely a Grade-A rump. Maybe even A-plus, if there was such a thing.

God, when was the last time she'd had sex? She had to think for a minute, which told her it had already been too long.

January twenty-third. With Harvey Waite, the exterminator from Stoughton who her mother had introduced her to at Cousin Rosina's wedding reception. Foreplay had started at eleven P.M. and Harvey had finished at eleven-ten, leaving Maria still waiting at the starting line.

Needless to say, she had not gone out with Hog-the-Orgasm Harvey again. Since then, she'd had a two-month—well, she didn't want to call it a dry spell—just a period of no acceptable men on the planet.

This had caused her mother no end of worry and muttered impromptu prayers for the Lord to please give her daughter enough sense to settle down with a good Italian boy. After all, Maria was twenty-eight, and in her mother's mind, a hair's breadth away from her eggs drying up and her body falling all to hell, leaving her a lonely old maid who would never produce a grandchild to smother.

Maria wasn't looking for marriage right now—hell, she had trouble sticking to a diet, never mind a relationship. But lately, she'd had this constant, aching need she couldn't identify, making her wonder if there *was* something missing in her life.

Yeah, a good-looking man who didn't have sex by a stopwatch.

There *was* Antonio, who'd made it clear he wanted to resurrect the past when he saw her again—and Lord, if she were lucky, he'd start with a repeat performance of prom night. But he lived in California and she wouldn't see him until the class reunion in May. Good thing, too, because she fully intended to diet down to someone resembling the cheerleader he remembered. The way he'd said "pom-poms" on the phone had left her weak in the knees.

Clearly, two months without sex was one month and twenty-nine days too long.

Then, there was Dante. She'd seen the way he'd looked at her chest, like a barracuda spying a beefy scuba diver. He was definitely interested. He'd even offered to feed her, and in Maria's book, that practically equaled a marriage proposal.

Dante was a few inches taller than she, and walked with a confidence that said he was a man used to being in command. He had broad, powerful shoulders, tapering down to a lean waist, and powerful legs that flexed beneath the denim. The washboard of his stomach stretched at his T-shirt, and the bulge of his arms said he could lift a woman with ease.

And have a hell of a lot more duration than Harvey, who'd complained about his biceps cramping up halfway through.

Dante finished his conversation with Franco and returned, taking her by the elbow and leading her gently toward a table.

Antonio was hundreds of miles and two more, very long months away.

Dante, however, was right here. Right now.

Maria Pagliano was not a patient woman. She wanted a dress, she charged it. She wanted to eat, she grabbed the nearest available nourishment. She wanted a man, she told him. And Dante Del Rosso was definitely a wantable man.

He stopped and turned to face her. Dark hair, dark eyes, slightly olive skin, punctuated by a grin that seemed to tease and flatter her, all at once.

She swallowed when he came closer, resisting the urge to throw him on the floor and demand he end her nine-week celibacy.

"Hungry?" he asked in a voice that to Maria didn't mean salad.

"Starved." Her heart began to race. Franco had faded into the background. The restaurant was deserted, not even so much as a waiter to interrupt them. Around her, the scents of the food acted like an aphrodisiac, giving her a heady rush that propelled her toward him another step.

"Then I won't keep you waiting."

"Oh," she said, almost on a sigh. "Good." Her lips parted and her breath became ragged.

"Right here is a great spot." He motioned toward the vinyl banquette, handing her a menu.

Damn. He really *had* meant food.

She slid into the booth and opened the menu, wondering if she was due for her Depo shot again. Her hormones were completely off track, raging through her like an out-of-control train.

She glanced at her watch and realized she hadn't eaten in eight hours. Stomach first. Dante later.

But maybe . . . she should replace food with sex. Get a little exercise, keep the calorie count down while burning a few hundred. The idea did have merit.

Plus, that approach didn't come with unnecessary heart involvement, which was how Maria usually liked to handle dating. Get in, get what she wanted, then get out and never, ever get too attached. Ever since David the Gynecologist, she'd realized monogamy and men went together about as well as chocolate and tuna.

Dante had taken the opposite seat and was waiting for her decision, his hands clasped. His eyes were wide and deep, crinkled a bit at the corners, as if he laughed often. She liked that.

A lot.

"What do you recommend?" she asked. "Is the chef good?"

He smiled. "His food will take you on a journey you'll never forget."

She rolled her eyes at the hyperbole, then returned her attention to the menu. "How about the antipasto?"

Dante kissed the tips of his fingers. "Heaven."

Maria folded the menu and slid it to the side. "Then I'll have the antipasto and a Diet Coke." Not quite a low-calorie meal, but she figured the soda helped reduce the damage.

"No wine?"

She shook her head. The only thing Maria did in moderation was drink. Alcohol had a way of rushing straight to her brain, obliterating all common sense, and leading her to do incredibly stupid things, like go to bed with Harvey the Exterminator.

"I'll be right back." Dante left and returned a few minutes later with the most delicious-looking antipasto she had ever seen. Colors and tastes crowded the white plate like an array of butterflies.

Paper-thin prosciutto, creamy white provolone, thick sausage bits, deep red roasted peppers, plump marinated artichokes, mushrooms, pepperoncini, tiny green olives, stuffed cherry peppers and generous wedges of Parmesan. Maria held her fork over the plate, hovering, wondering where best to dive in and give her taste buds a culinary orgasm.

"Unless you want some botulism with your bill, I wouldn't eat anything in this place."

Maria turned and saw a short, white-haired man in a gray suit standing in the doorway, next to a tall, plump man in a darker gray suit. Mutt and Jeff, going to a funeral. Franco stood behind them, gesturing a wild apology to Dante for letting them get past him.

Dante scrambled to his feet and crossed to the men, putting out his hand to the short one. "Mr. Whitman. I didn't expect you to come b—"

"I'm here to slap you with a lawsuit." He waved a hand at his companion. "Meet my lawyer, Jerome F. Finklestein the Third, with the law firm of Finklestein, Finklestein and Jones."

Finklestein didn't clarify if he was the first or second said partner. He just dipped his head in greeting, his face about as cheery as Al Gore at an Ozzy Osbourne concert.

"What you did was negligent, Del Rosso." Whitman pointed a finger at him, his eyes narrowing. "You're lucky I didn't get killed."

"Vinny got a little overexcited lighting the flambé at the next table. It was an accident."

"He set my tie on fire."

"I'm very sorry about that."

Maria remembered him mentioning a fire in the restaurant. She hadn't realized he meant one of the *customers* had been ablaze.

"My daughter gave me that tie."

"I'm even more sorry, Mr. Whitman."

"And then, you sprayed me with a fire extinguisher." Whitman shook his head. "A fire extinguisher!"

Dante put his hands up in a what-could-I-do gesture. "Instinct. I saw fire, I reacted."

"My suit was ruined, you know," Whitman went on, his lawyer watching from the sidelines as his client did all the haranguing. "It wasn't just any suit, it was a Brooks Brothers."

"I'll gladly replace—"

"And to top it all off, I didn't get to finish my dinner." He made a sour face. "I don't like having my meals interrupted."

The two men were squaring off like rams in mating season. Maria slipped out of her seat, crossing to the trio. They paused, three pairs of male eyes immediately swiveling to the sole female in the room.

Actually, all they looked at was the scoop of her T-shirt. She could have had a monkey head above her breasts for all they noticed.

"Why not have something else to eat now? I suspect Vinny has gone home," she improvised.

In the years since she and her two best friends had opened Gift Baskets to Die For, Maria had realized her strength lay in saving the sale when it seemed unsalvageable. Working with two other women meant she could use her brain and be respected for it, instead of having all eyes on the acreage below the neck. Working with women had definite advantages over working with hormone-minded men. For a woman who'd never been taken seriously by a man, it was a damned good thing.

Then why was she helping this man? A stranger?

Dante glanced at her, his chocolate eyes sending a quiver through her stomach, and she knew exactly why she was coming to his rescue. Her brain had never been much for keeping her bed warm at night. But it did readily provide a few ideas for how Dante could return the favor. Her dry spell was about to end. *Oh, yeah.*

I'll worry about meeting a guy on an intellectual level after I've had an orgasm.

The men stared at her, mute, so she went on. "Try the sausage and cheese tortellini. It's"—she kissed her fingers as Dante had done earlier—"heaven on a plate."

"He'd probably poison me." Whitman glared at Dante.

"Nah," Maria scoffed. "How can you go wrong with tortellini? And oh, with that seasoned sausage and the mortadella. Ooh." She pressed a hand to her chest, drawing in a deep breath, as if inhaling the image. Six eyes watched her palm go up, down, up, down. Just as she'd expected. "Oh so tender and cooked perfectly, then served with that meat sauce and sprinkled with just the right amount of Parmigiano Reggiano." She knew she was lying, because she'd never tasted anything here, not even her antipasto, yet, but figured if the aromas were any indication, then everything in Vita was a mandible masterpiece.

"I'm not here to eat." Even as Whitman said the words, Maria saw his nose lifting toward the kitchen. He inhaled, then cleared his throat.

"Too bad," Maria said in a sweet, regretful voice. Dante stared at her, mouth agape, clearly not sure what she was doing or whether he should interrupt. Talk of lawsuits had stopped, though, and that was a good thing. "The garlic bread is incredible. Crispy, with just the right amount of crunch. And the cheese . . . Oh, Lord, it melts in your mouth."

Finklestein's stomach let out a growl. He flushed and pressed a hand to his abdomen, as if he could subdue the rumble with a steady palm. "Excuse me."

From the corner of her eye, Maria saw a young man's face peering out of the glass oval of the kitchen door. He was wearing a white chef hat, his eyes wide, brown, and worried. She was sure he was the aforementioned pyromaniac, Vinny. Dante caught her raised eyebrow and slid his gaze toward the doors.

He cursed under his breath.

"What'd you say, Del Rosso?" Whitman snapped.

Dante recovered quickly. "If there's anything I can do to make it up to—"

"You could stop jabbering and go get me some of that tortellini." Whitman motioned toward Finklestein's grumbling gut. "Make that two plates. And extra garlic bread."

"It will be my pleasure." Dante's whole body sprang into action, relief clear on his face. She had no idea who this Whitman guy was, why he was so important, or what Vinny had been thinking when he'd torched the guy's tie, but she could see this was important to Dante. Being in business herself, she could sympathize.

Franco stepped forward, extending his arm with a flourish. "Right this way, gentlemen. Best table in the house."

Maria headed back toward her antipasto, trying not to think about the tortellini. The sausage. The mortadella. The cheese on the garlic bread. If craving was a sin, she was definitely heading for hell.

"We'd like the pretty lady to join us," Whitman called after her.

Oh, no, don't tempt me, Maria thought. *I'm a weak woman.* "I've got an antipasto here."

"If the tortellini is as good as you say it is, you should have some," he argued. In his voice, she heard the sound of doubt, as if he suspected she'd lied. Dante was in the kitchen; Franco was busy filling water glasses.

With the manicotti at lunch, she was sure she'd already toppled her calorie count for the day. She'd also managed to not only flunk, but also ditch, her first support group meeting.

Her resolve wavered like a virgin in a room of Chippendale dancers.

Little black dress. Turning on the lights during sex. Mary Louise Zipparetto.

That settled it. She'd have the—

"Chubby Chum Maria!" Arnold's high-pitched voice shrieked from the doorway. "You never told us your animal!"

Maria's Running-from-Your-Troubles Frittata

3 tablespoons olive oil
¼ cup sliced green onions
¼ cup diced ham or prosciutto
2 ounces chopped mushrooms
6 eggs
Salt
Freshly ground pepper
¼ cup shredded mozzarella cheese

Heat the oil over medium heat in a large nonstick pan, avoiding all issues and any people who might want you to deal with issues. Stir in the green onions and mushrooms and cook for a few minutes, then add the ham, cooking until warmed through. This should buy you enough time to change the subject—or for the person who is interested in you to have moved on to another.

Beat eggs lightly in a bowl, then pour them into the pan. They're runny, just like your willpower. Season with salt and pepper, then mix the eggs quickly with the other ingredients.

Now, the hard part. Leave it all alone. I know, I know. Letting something sit is not part of your nature, but this time it will all be the better for your lack of input. Let cook for five or six minutes, until it's puffy and golden brown.

Then, using a plate and some dexterity (this is not something to do when you've been drinking heavily, trust me), flip the frittata onto the plate, then slide it back into the pan to cook on the other side for three to four more minutes.

Sprinkle with cheese and place under the broiler until cheese is melted and gooey, like the personal life mess you are trying to avoid. By now, hopefully your problems have gone home—or back to his restaurant—and your frittata is a lot more solid than your resolve.

CHAPTER 4

She'd managed to escape without having to classify herself as either a mammal or crustacean, thank God and all the saints. Maria slipped her arms into her coat, ignored the growling in her belly that told her she should have at least taken the time to eat before she made her mad dash from Arnold, and picked up the pace. At home, there was a fork waiting for her. And in her hands, her leftovers.

Who needed men when she had that combination in her kitchen?

"Maria, wait!"

That was *not* Arnold's voice—it was Dante's. She'd do well to keep on walking and not turn around. That man had "linguine in bed" written all over him.

Well . . . maybe stopping was a better idea than trying to outrun him. She was, after all, in heels. And linguine in bed wasn't *always* a bad idea.

Maria spun around, the Styrofoam to-go box from Vita in her hand. "I'm on my way home."

"I gathered that. But I couldn't let you leave, not yet."

"Don't you have a customer to attend to?"

"He's eating. I have a few minutes. Besides, if I stayed in the restaurant, I'd hover over the guy and if there's anything that's sure to piss him off again, it's a hovering chef."

She laughed. "I bet you're right."

"So why don't you help me pass the time?"

Damn, he had nice eyes. The kind that seemed to bore into a woman and read every thought she'd ever had. He'd be the type—she knew—to anticipate what she wanted in bed, just by reading the signals in her gaze.

The volcano in her pelvis began to stir.

Dante took a step forward, his gaze never leaving hers. "I'm sure we could find *something* to while away the minutes."

Antonio was the man she was supposed to be focused on. Antonio was the man she was starving herself half to death for. Antonio was expecting her to be ready and waiting, pom-poms in hand, when he arrived for the reunion.

But right now, she couldn't even remember what Antonio looked like.

From somewhere beside them, violin music began to play, an old Italian love song Maria had heard her grandfather sing to Nonna after a few too many grappas.

"See? They're even setting the mood for us."

She smirked. "I bet you planned that."

"Wish I could take the credit, but it's Crazy Carlo. He opens his window, year-round, and practices his violin. Damned good thing he's got some talent or I think the neighbors would kill him."

"Why the open window?"

"He says it lets in his creativity." Dante shrugged. "I think he just likes to put on a performance, whether it's eighty degrees out or eight."

Maria shivered in the chilly March night air and

drew her coat closer around her body. "Dedicated, or insane."

Dante laughed. "Maybe a little of both. Most people with a passion for something usually are." He took a second step closer, bringing him within inches of touching her. His eyes met hers, connecting across the short divide between them, increasing the heat in the small space. "Don't you agree?"

"Yes," she said, exhaling the word more than speaking it.

What were the objections she'd had to Dante again? Something about another man? A man far, far away, who was probably out with another woman right now, not even giving her a second thought. Then there'd been something about a diet.

Well, hell, she was holding an antipasto. She'd covered the diet thing. And Dante *did* need to take his mind off the difficult day he'd had. She'd be doing him a favor.

Yeah, that was it.

The violin music continued, the melody carrying along the air like hummingbirds around them. The vibrations of the sound intensified everything stirring within Maria.

"Dance with me, Maria," Dante said, his voice low and intimate.

"Here? In the middle of the sidewalk?"

"It's late, there aren't any cars. I can't think of a better place." He took her hands in his. He had a large, strong grip, firm around her own, as if he could hold her up, no matter the storm. "Or a prettier partner."

"I'm not very good."

"I'm not going to care." With his other hand, he took the Styrofoam container and put it on a stoop beside them, then wrapped his arm around her waist.

Had she really objected to his touch? She had to have been crazy. Thinking with a half-starved brain. Because Dante felt good. No, he felt *damned* good.

Crazy Carlo segued smoothly into an aria Maria had heard before. Veracini was the composer, she thought absently, then wondered why she even cared about the detail when Dante was right there gazing so intently at her.

He stepped to the right and Maria moved with him, their bodies pressing together with the movement. The volcano in her gut began to erupt into hot, molten arousal. The music, deep and heartfelt, swirled around them, like an ancient rhythm of desire. She tried to step to the left, to pull him with her, but he insistently moved again in the same direction as before, completing a circle.

His hand drifted down to the small of her back, pressing against the valley just above her buttocks. A nerve existed there, and he'd hit it, igniting something within her that Harry hadn't even been able to get a smolder on, despite his ten-minute effort at starting a fire with his stick and no kindling.

Dancing in the street in the middle of March was an insane idea. And yet, it was the exact kind of thing Maria knew her friends wouldn't be surprised to see her doing. She, of all people, was the least conventional, the one voted Most Likely to Do Something Unexpected.

This was about as unexpected and unconventional as a woman could get while staying fully clothed.

"It's a game, isn't it?" Dante murmured against her ear.

"What do you mean?"

"Dancing. I can feel you, vying for control at the same time I'm trying to lead, like the gentleman I am."

"*You* are not a gentleman."

"How do you know? You haven't given me a chance to prove it to you."

"I can feel it, right here." She pressed a hand against his chest, above his heart. His eyes widened and she knew who was leading whom right now. "You, Mr. Del Rosso, have ulterior motives."

He grinned. "I'd be a fool if I didn't."

"Spoken like a true gentleman." She smiled.

He leaned forward, his mouth against her ear. "Let me lead, Maria. And allow yourself to be traditional." The violin feathered up and down the notes, providing an undertow of emotion and sensuality to his words.

"I don't like tradition," she replied, trying to resist the melody and him.

"There's a reason traditions have been around forever," he whispered. "Because they work."

Then he took the lead anyway, circling her around a lamppost into the deserted street. The classical refrain brought them together, then apart, as Dante showed her the steps he was creating, mirroring the message of Crazy Carlo's passionate playing.

Dante swung her to the right, bringing his pelvis back against hers. Watch out Pompeii—Maria's hormones were about to overtake the city and drown all reasonable doubts.

"You're not a bad dancer," she admitted.

He grinned. "And here I thought you only wanted me for my pasta."

She spun away from him, but his grip on her was firm and he twirled Maria back into his arms, her back against his chest, her buttocks against a volcano of Dante's own.

Whoa . . . she needed a cold shower. Quick. "I can get pasta anywhere," she said.

Dante bent down and nuzzled against her neck. "Mine is special."

Hoo-boy. She'd bet it was. She was in trouble now. What had started as an innocent game, a flirtation in his arms, had become something much, much hotter— and with higher stakes than a bowl of spaghetti. "All men say that."

Dante twirled her out to face him again. They stepped to the side, swishing against each other beneath the quarter moon. "I'm not most men, Maria."

Crazy Carlo ended his song. The violin fell silent. The screech of a window being pulled down cut across the quiet of the neighborhood.

The moment was over, the spell between them broken. Pompeii retreated from an impending natural disaster to a simmering lava mass. Dante was still a linguine-in-bed guy and she was still a woman who had just left a diet support group. Trying his pasta, as he'd said, was about as smart as paying full retail when her credit card was already maxed out.

"You have a customer waiting for you." She stepped away from him and retrieved her food. "I think he's more interested in your pasta than I am."

Liar, liar, hormones on fire.

Maria left as fast as she could, before she made any other stupid mistakes where Dante was concerned. She'd rounded the corner and was a block from home when she heard the voices. This time a trio of male voices. Drunk male voices, singing an off-key and mostly jumbled version of an Italian love song.

She knew that pickled barbershop triplet. Her grandfather and his friends.

"Maria!" Sal Pagliano called when he spied her on the corner. "Come, sing with us."

"I'm on my way home, Nonno. You should be, too."

"I am, I am. We watch the game and drink to celebrate the victory."

Nicky Benedetto cocked his head. "Hey, wait a minute. Who won? I think we drank to the wrong team."

Nonno waved a hand in dismissal. "Doesn't matter. They win, we drink. Everybody happy."

Guiseppe Santo looked at Maria. "You look happy, too. You drinking tonight?"

"No, I was . . . out."

"With a man, I bet," Nicky said, elbowing Nonno.

Nonno looked at Maria, his hazy eyes suddenly going clear. He had the vision of a hawk when he spotted a lie—or an impending romance. "Are you falling in love?"

She let out a laugh. "Definitely not."

"Ah, too bad. Love, she is sweeter than the first sip of wine."

"Hey, if that's true, then why are we out drinking instead of home with our wives?" Nicky asked. He slumped against a lamppost and put the back of his hand against his forehead, pondering that question.

"Because our wives drive us crazy," Guiseppe said. "And a man needs a little room off the leash to play in the yard."

As much as she loved her grandfather and often laughed at the antics of his friends, *this* was exactly the kind of thing she wanted to avoid. Traditional men with traditional values that kept their wives behind an apron while they roamed the neighborhood. It was why she needed to avoid Dante Del Rosso, at all costs and all flavors.

Maria took her grandfather's arm. "Come on, Nonno. We'll walk home together."

"Be careful of that wife of yours," Nicky called after him as they walked away. "She might be mad at you."

"Ah, she's always mad at me," Sal said, grinning. "But a little of the Pagliano music and she'll forgive me before the moon is full."

Guiseppe snorted. "The wine has made you crazy, Sal. You're too old to last as long as the moon."

"I'm lucky if I make it long enough to hear Leno tell a joke," Nicky said. He shoved off from the lamppost and shook his head. "You, Sal, you always see Leno. The whole show, too."

"That's because I can last longer than the two of you

put together," Sal called over his shoulder, then turned back to Maria, a laugh in his face. "See what you get to look forward to when you're old and gray?"

Not if I'm lucky, she thought.

The other two walked away in the opposite direction, muttering their envy about Sal's endurance. Maria gave her grandfather a suspicious look. "Since when have you ever stayed up past ten o'clock at night?"

"Never." Nonno laughed and patted Maria's arm in the crook of his. "But those old fools don't know what I have up my sleeve."

"What's that?"

Sal leaned down and whispered in her ear. "A TiVo."

Mamma Pagliano's My-Daughter-Is-Never-Going-to-Get-Married Italian Wedding Soup

½ pound ground beef
½ pound ground veal
¼ cup seasoned bread crumbs, sprinkled with hope
1 egg, from a fertile chicken
1 tablespoon parsley
Salt and pepper to taste
4 cups chicken broth, made by a married mother who cares
2 cups spinach leaves, ripped into pieces like your no-grandchildren-yet heart
¼ cup grated Romano cheese

Combine the ground meat, bread crumbs, egg, parsley, salt and pepper in a bowl. Mix with love, all the while begging the Lord to bring a man into your daughter's life, and soon. Form into tiny meatballs, then bake for 30 minutes at 350 degrees. Bless the stove with the sign of the cross, then bring the broth to a boil and add the spinach. Cover and boil for five minutes, muttering a prayer for a happy marriage with enough steam to bring lots of grandchildren into the world. Add the cooked meatballs, dropping each one in with a whispered mantra for upcoming nuptials.

Stir in the cheese and serve to a good Italian boy who has marriage on his mind.

CHAPTER 5

"Sit, sit," Biba Pagliano said, gesturing wildly at Dante to get comfortable in her walnut kitchen chair. She laid a plate of toasted, cheese-encrusted bruschetta in front of him. "*Mangia.* You too thin. Eat."

Dante chose a thin slice of the Italian bread and took a bite. He'd only been in this house for three minutes and already knew it would be in his best interests to do as he was told.

Maria's mother was a formidable woman—not in size, but in presence. She didn't seem the type he should argue with. And well, hell, he enjoyed the attention. His own mother had gone to live in Florida after his father's death, starting up a new life of endless bingo games and horticultural club meetings. She'd forgotten everything from her life in Boston, including his birthday most years. He told himself it didn't matter. She'd never been the kind of mother who worried much about him, anyway.

Sitting in the warm Pagliano kitchen on a quiet Monday afternoon and being fussed over like a prodigal son was something Dante could get used to. He'd taken a chance, calling the first Pagliano he came across in the phone book. Maria hadn't been listed, but he'd bet one of the dozen or so families in the white pages would know how to find her. He'd struck gold by dialing her mother's house. As soon as she'd discerned it was an eligible male looking for her daughter, Biba had insisted he come right over, telling him Maria would be there that evening.

Biba bustled around the kitchen, her generous figure wrapped in a red-and-white-checkered apron, her gray hair tucked into a tight bun, her voice as lyrical as Mozart. She was a hummingbird, darting from this to that, back and forth from stove to guest, seasoning, tasting, arranging and then clucking over him like a hen with a straggling chick.

"I make you soup," she said, placing a glass of milk before him. "You feel better."

"I'm not sick, Mrs. Pagliano."

"Mamma." She pressed a hand to her bosom. "You are my Maria's friend. Please, call me Mamma." She turned back to the stove and her meatballs, now that she'd settled the issue of her name.

"Well, I wouldn't call us *friends*. Exactly."

Mamma Pagliano whirled around, a spatula in her hand. "No?"

"We don't know each other very well." Or at least not yet, Dante thought. He fully intended to change that.

In the last few days, he'd liquefied a batch of spaghetti by overcooking it and then forgotten to add the cheese to a lasagna. Instead of focusing on recipes, his mind teased him with images of her. With the feel of her in his arms, the sound of her laughter, the smell of her perfume.

"You know her well enough to come to my house, with flowers." Her gaze narrowed. "You like my Maria?"

"Yes, very much."

"Ah, good." She smiled. "Then I make a special soup.

Just for you." She hurried over to a cabinet and started hauling out ingredients and a large stainless steel pot.

"*O sole mio, Sta 'nfronte a te.*" A slightly slurred voice belted out the Italian love song, the tenor coming closer with each syllable. A second later, a large old man in a fedora burst through the back door. "Ada? Where are you, my beauty?" The old man lurched into the kitchen. "*Ciao,* Biba! My little bird."

"Oh, you. Drunk again." Biba swatted him with a dish towel. "She will be mad."

The old man grinned. "No matter. She loves me." He turned and noticed Dante. "Are you here to steal my woman?" He shook a bony fist at him.

"I'm here to see Maria."

The stern look transformed into a wide smile. "Welcome! I'm Sal. Her grandfather. You sit, Biba cooks. We all wait for Maria. I, however, sing for my love." And he launched into his song again.

The swinging door into the kitchen bumped open and a white-haired woman leaned in, her face pinched and annoyed. "Shush, old man. You'll scare the cat."

"Oh, the cat loves my voice. She knows I sing to my angel." He gave a flourish with his hand, indicating his heavenly match in the doorway.

The cat in question, a well-fed orange tiger, weaved past his legs and scooted out the cat door, wisely avoiding the scene.

Sal's wife waved a hand at him in dismissal. "You just want me to scratch your back."

"That and much more, my love." He winked at her.

"Go putter in your garden. I'm too busy for you now."

The older man crossed to the doorway, pausing by his diminutive wife. He placed a quick, smacking kiss on the back of her neck. She flashed him a look of irritation but Dante saw her smile when she turned away. "You crazy old man."

"Crazy for you, *mia bella*." He tipped an imaginary hat, then the two of them exited the kitchen, leaving Dante alone with Maria's mother again.

"My husband's parents," she explained. "Still in love. But they fight like two lions over one zebra." She laid the pan on the stove and started to light the burner, then stopped and turned back around. "Why you not at work?"

"That's exactly what I was going to ask."

Dante spun around in the chair. Maria stood in the doorway of the back entrance. She had her dark, full hair tucked into a comb-type thing that didn't quite grasp it all, leaving a few ends dangling and curling along her neck. She wore dark jeans and high-heeled boots, making her legs look like they reached all the way to her shoulders. A V-necked, deep turquoise sweater strained against her breasts, as if daring him to touch them. "Hi," he managed.

"What are you doing here?"

"Waiting for you." He got to his feet and crossed to her, stopping a respectable distance away.

She brushed past him and sat down at the table. "I can see that. Why?"

He'd anticipated her resistance. Fortunately, he'd come prepared. Dante reached past her and grabbed the bouquet of sterling roses he'd bought. "First, these . . ."

A shadow of a smile appeared on her face. She took the flowers and inhaled their soft, sweet fragrance. His gut gave a funny little twist.

"For this," he finished, handing her a copy of the Thursday morning paper. The page had been folded back to show the headline for the food section: *La Vita Deliziosa: A Four-Star Culinary Mecca.* "I wanted to thank you for your help the other night."

She looked up from the paper. "What did I do?"

"Convinced Boston's harshest food critic to give my restaurant a second chance. You're amazing. A true miracle worker." He smiled at her. "I should have brought you three hundred roses."

"Marry him," Maria's mother whispered in her ear. "He's a gentleman."

Dante's mind produced the image of a bridle and saddle. No way was he going to tell Franco about Mamma Pagliano. There'd be a conspiracy brewing between the two of them faster than he could change his socks.

Maria didn't respond to her mother's matchmaking. "That's who that guy was? George Whitman?"

"Uh-huh."

"And Vinny lit *his* tie on fire?"

Dante nodded. "Yeah, unfortunately."

She paused, reading over the critic's account. "Wow. 'Masterful meal.' 'True Italian atmosphere.' 'Chef with a magic touch.' " Her deep brown eyes met his and the twisting in his gut amplified. He found himself wishing Mamma would leave the kitchen and let him and Maria get some steam brewing between them, preferably with her on the counter. "Too bad all I got to try was the antipasto, huh?"

"Then let me introduce you to the rest of the menu," he said, meaning everything but food.

She shook her head, laying the paper on the table. "I-I—"

"Buon appetito!" Mamma Pagliano laid two stoneware bowls on the table before them.

Meatballs swam with bits of spinach in a clear, fragrant chicken broth. A sprinkling of Romano cheese decorated the top. "It looks delicious," Dante said, retaking his seat. "Thank you."

"Don't thank her and don't eat it," Maria said, pointing a finger at him. "Mamma, it isn't going to work."

"Hush." Mamma waved a hand at her and gave her a stern look. "It worked for Nonna. And your cousin Rosina. And for me. It's a good recipe."

Dante spooned up a bite, ignoring Maria's admonition. Eating the soup would put him on Mamma's good side, which could only help his cause with Maria. "It's delicious. What do you call it?"

"Wedding soup," Maria answered with a roll of her eyes and a frustrated sigh that told Dante she'd been down this soup road before. "My mother is convinced that if you eat her special recipe, you'll fall madly in love."

"Oh." Dante glanced at the innocuous-looking meatballs and spinach. "Really?"

"Look at Cousin Rosina." Mamma threw up her hands. "Married, and so happy. Soon, there'll be babies. The soup, it works." She motioned to Dante and Maria. "*Mangia.*"

It was only soup, Dante told himself, polishing off the bowl. He was a chef. He knew a bunch of shaped meat and fresh greens couldn't make anyone fall in love. He was eating it because he was hungry and because it tasted damned good with the bruschetta.

Maria left her bowl untouched in silent defiance. Mamma shot her a glare and pursed her lips in disapproval.

When he finished, Mamma's hands waved him out of his seat. "You and my Maria. Go outside. Talk. Maybe . . . kiss?" She smiled.

"Mamma!" Maria shook her head. "I'm not coming for dinner ever again."

Her mother ignored her and turned to the sink, humming "Here Comes the Bride."

Maria let out a chuff of frustration, then took Dante's hand and led him out the back door to the patch of grass that served as a yard in the crowded neighborhood. "Sorry about that. My mother—"

"Loves you very much, I can see." Dante shrugged. "I didn't mind. It's kind of nice to have someone fuss over me. All men love a woman who does that."

She let go of his hand abruptly, as if she'd just realized she'd been holding it. She wrapped her arms around herself. "It's cold out."

It reminded him of their late-night dance when she'd been cold, but felt hot as hell in his arms.

"That's March in Boston for you." He shrugged out of his leather jacket and draped it over her shoulders.

"Thanks. But won't you be cold?" Even as she said the words, she snuggled a bit into his coat. The action thrust her breasts forward, and before he could think better of it, he was drawing the jacket shut across her front, the backs of his knuckles grazing her chest.

"I'm not cold right now. At all." He released his grip on the coat, before he gave in to the urge to rip it and everything else she was wearing right off that delicious body and then show her a warmth of a very different kind against the brick wall.

"Thank you for the flowers."

"You probably saved my business Tuesday night, you know. The review came out Thursday morning and we've been hopping ever since."

"That's wonderful. Good for you." She stepped back as if she were about to say good-bye and go into the house.

Dante moved forward, no longer maintaining his respectable distance. The scent of jasmine teased at his nostrils, drawing him in like a siren song. "Why are you avoiding me?"

"I'm not."

"Yes, you are." He reached up and captured one of those stray ringlets in his finger, twirling the velvet tendril in a leisurely, sensual movement. "Is it my antipasto?"

She blinked. "Your . . . your what?"

He smiled. She wasn't as immune to him as she thought. "The salad, remember? Was it so terrible you decided never to see me again?"

"No, not at all. It was . . . delicious." She gulped. "I've just been thinking since I met you Tuesday night and . . . I don't think getting involved with you is a good idea."

He took a half step closer, the cloud of his breath mingling with hers. He trailed his finger down her jawline, along soft, smooth skin that glided beneath his touch like silk. Her eyes widened, her lips parted. He'd never wanted to kiss anyone so damned bad in his life. "Who said anything about getting involved? Why can't we just have mind-blowing sex? A few hundred times or so?"

She laughed, a rich sound that flowed from her like wine from a bottle. "Only a guy would say something like that."

He cupped her chin, tracing her lower lip with his thumb, slowly. Tenderly. The way he'd do it if it were his tongue instead of his finger. "You aren't interested in mind-blowing sex?"

"I . . . I wouldn't say that," she breathed.

"Good." And then, he decided to hell with waiting. With arguing about whether she was interested in him or not. He lowered his head, taking her cranberry lips with his, teasing at first, then not teasing at all when she moaned and opened against him, her arms spreading wide and reaching for his back.

She fit against him like butter on bread, her body molding to his in perfect harmony. He roamed his hands down her back, feeling the slight bump of her bra strap through the fabric of her shirt. His mind skipped forward, imagining his fingers undoing the hooks, her breasts spilling forward, his mouth tasting them as thoroughly as he was tasting her right now.

Her hands tangled in his hair, pulling him closer, demanding more. She pressed her pelvis against his, then away, the tease sending his brain into other stratospheres. She pressed, withdrew again.

She was as much of an aggressor as he. Lord, what fun that would be in bed.

"*Maria*. Oh, God, let's . . ." he whispered against her mouth, wanting to say much more. But he'd left his vocabulary somewhere between his fly and his brain.

With a start, she broke away from him, stepping back several paces and swinging his jacket off her shoulders. "I—I—I can't do this."

"What?" He wished like hell his body had an on/off switch. He definitely still felt *on* and it was damned hard to concentrate on anything but the memory of her body against his.

"I can't get involved with you." She handed him the coat and took another step back.

"Why not?"

"You wouldn't understand," she said. "It's complicated. I'm not even sure I can explain it to myself."

"Tell me." Hot desire still pulsed within him. He hoped she'd get to the explanation soon so he could show her the error of her argument and get her right back into his arms again.

"Well," she paused, then let the rest out in a rush. "Mary Louise Zipparetto, for one."

He raced through his mental little black book. "I don't know anyone named Mary Louise Zipparetto."

But she didn't hear him. She'd backed up another two steps, as if he were a chainsaw murderer about to carve her for dinner. "You smell like mozzarella," she said. "And you taste like lasagna. And . . . you haven't noticed a damned thing above my neck." She shook her head. "I'm sorry. I can't."

Then she turned and dashed back into the house, leaving Dante in the cold, stunned. Now he knew how the heel end of a loaf of bread felt. Rejected and crummy.

Women had left him for other men. One for another

woman. Most stopped dating him because he worked too much or didn't spend enough money or didn't drive a Lamborghini. Those were reasons he could understand.

But now, he'd been dumped because he *tasted* too good. What the hell had Mamma put in that soup?

Rebecca's Avoid-the-Subject Penne
with Pancetta

1 pound dried penne
4 tablespoons butter
1 onion, diced
½ pound frozen peas, thawed
1 ½ cloves garlic, crushed
6 ounces pancetta slices, rinds removed, cut into
bite-size strips, truth-tempting size
5 egg yolks
¾ cup heavy cream, the richer the better for eliciting all the details
1 ⅓ cups Parmigiano Reggiano, grated
Pepper
½ teaspoon saffron pistils, the color of a friend trying too hard to bluff that she isn't happy about
meeting someone new
Salt and pepper to taste

Cook the penne in salted boiling water until al dente
(about ten minutes, just enough time to start pumping
a good friend for details about a new man in her life).
Meanwhile, melt the butter. Sauté onion and cook until
softened. Add peas, garlic and pancetta, cooking until
pancetta is done but not crisp. Remove pan from heat
and set aside.

Try again for more information. If she still won't talk,
start in on the sauce. Put egg yolks in a bowl, add cream
and Parmigiano Reggiano. Grind in plenty of black pepper. Beat well to mix, hoping the action will distract said

friend and get her to do a little kiss and tell. After all, she needs a happy ending of her own and you can't help her if you don't have details. Right?

This is a mercy mission, not just a meal.

Drain penne, pour into pan and toss over medium heat until everything is evenly mixed. Add saffron, season with salt and pepper if needed. Remove from heat, add cream sauce and toss well.

Serve immediately. Makes a good dish for a friend who is trying to keep her mouth full so she can't talk about the sexy chef who has turned her world upside down.

CHAPTER 6

It was Tuesday morning and Maria had been awake for one hour, ten minutes and twenty-five seconds. Not once had she cheated on her diet. A miracle, too, considering her dreams had been about a sexy chef wrapped in nothing but linguine.

Her subconscious had better come up with a different image. Dante was off her list of acceptable men to date, whether he had good orgasm potential or not. Everything about the man was too tempting. From the way he smiled to the scent of his cologne—a mix of man and fresh tomato sauce—Dante was all wrong for her. Undoubtedly, he'd not just want to date her—he'd want to feed her, and next thing she knew, they'd be sharing lasagna in bed.

While Mary Louise Zipparetto was being fed celery sticks by a naked Mr. America.

Yesterday's kiss in her mother's backyard had been a momentary lapse of sensory judgment. Never again.

She got ready, then walked the few blocks to work, dodging the commuters speed-walking along Atlantic Avenue and the tourists creating pedestrian traffic snarls every time they paused to gape at the Big Dig transformation or to note how lost they were.

Finally, she walked into Gift Baskets to Die For. The little shop off of Atlantic Avenue had become a pretty successful venture, maintaining both the friendship of the three owners—herself, Candace Woodrow and Rebecca Hamilton—and a steady stream of work. Maria did sales and marketing, Candace kept the books and Rebecca was in charge of design. All of them had a hand in the cooking, though Rebecca was clearly the best at it. If there was one thing the trio had in common, it was a love for anything high in calories and fat.

Friendships based on food tended to last. The only disagreements the three of them had sprung up when the cookie jar got low.

"Something happened last night. I can tell," Rebecca said from her perch in the window as soon as Maria walked in the door. Rebecca had tape in one hand and spring decorations in the other, all designed to encourage the purchase of Easter Bunny bounty. She tore off a piece of tape and slapped it on the glass. "Come on, dish."

Maria sipped at her diet shake, staying silent.

Candace came around the counter, all thin and blonde, the complete opposite of Maria. If they hadn't been best friends, Maria would have had to hate Candace for being blessed with a metabolism that actually seemed to speed up with the consumption of chocolate. "Where'd you go Saturday night? You missed our standing movie date. Russell Crowe wasn't the same without you oohhing and ahhing in the background."

Maria hung her coat on the rack by the door and took her time putting her purse behind the counter. "Sorry. I, ah, had somewhere else to go."

Rebecca waggled a paper egg at her. "You met a guy,

didn't you? I swear, you're like some kind of magnet. If there's a Y chromosome within fifty feet, he zones in on you."

"It's the hips," Candace said, gesturing at her slim khaki-clad figure. "I wish I had some. I have the figure of a salamander."

Maria snorted. "Are you kidding me? I'm rhino woman."

"Hey, have a kid and then complain to me." Rebecca gestured to her stomach. "It's like there's a permanent airship under there."

Maria had no intention of discussing her hips with her friends. The grass was always greener on the other side of the dressing room door.

She'd gotten on the scale this morning, naked and sure her linguine resistance on Saturday had made a difference. It hadn't. Her weight was exactly the same as yesterday, not even an ounce of change. Hence the diet shake, which tasted about as appetizing as a jar of school glue but promised less than two hundred calories of nutrition.

"So, what's on the plan for today?" Maria said, changing the subject and reaching for the planner on the front counter. "Great! We have a few more of those hospital baskets to do." Last year, they'd teamed up with an ad agency to send gift baskets to all the new moms in Boston. The program had been so successful, it was being tested in other nearby cities, too.

Rebecca climbed out of the window and put the extra decorations into a box by the kitchen door. "Vogler Advertising's campaign with that formula manufacturer has really turned out to be a great year-round thing for our shop." She straightened, pressing a hand to her back. "Or it will be, as long as Candace keeps making Michael Vogler happy."

"Oh, he's happy." Candace sighed, one of those contented sounds that said Michael wasn't the only one getting his needs met. "Very, very happy."

"Wait till you get married and have kids," Rebecca said, emphasizing her point with a shake of some purple Easter grass, like a cheerleader for the losing side. "I can't remember the last time I had more than six minutes for sex." She covered her mouth and stifled a yawn. "Or the energy for more than four. Damn, I'm so tired."

"And then at three this afternoon—" Maria said, running her finger down the page.

Rebecca yanked the book out of Maria's hands and thrust it behind her back. "Oh, no, you don't. You'll have to get up earlier than eight to fool me. You're changing the subject. And I won't quit till I find out why. Where'd you go last night?"

Candace grabbed the glass dome off the cake platter on the counter and removed a glazed doughnut from the dish. "We have ways of making you talk," she said, waving the pastry in front of Maria's nose like a hypnotist's watch.

Maria shook her head. "Nope. Won't work. I'm on a diet."

Rebecca raised an eyebrow.

"I'm sticking to it this time. I have incentive."

"Incentive?" Rebecca asked. "What incentive?"

"Antonio."

Candace replaced the doughnut under its glass shrine. "Is that who you met last night?"

"No." Maria paused, fiddling with the top of her can. "That was Dante."

"Ah! I knew it!" Rebecca pounced forward. "You have that look."

"What look?"

"Like a cat with a chubby chipmunk."

"I do not." She took a sip of her shake and forced

herself not to gag on the taste. "Besides, Dante is totally wrong for me."

"Why? Does he have a criminal background?" Rebecca asked.

"No."

"A wife?"

"No."

"A husband?"

Maria laughed. "No, definitely not that."

"Then what?"

Maria let out a sigh. "He's a chef."

"Perfect!"

Maria danced her unsatisfying, bland, low-calorie shake back and forth. "Maybe in twenty-five pounds, but I can't date a guy who smells like Alfredo sauce. I'll end up cheating just by kissing him."

"What's so bad about that?" Rebecca asked. "I think you look great, exactly the way you are."

"That's what Dante said. I disagree." She finished the can and tossed it into the trash. "I'm really sticking to my diet this time. I joined . . ." she paused, then lurched the words out, "a support group."

"That's great!" Candace said. "One of our customers was just talking about a group like that. She said Mary Louise Zipparetto—"

"I know all about Mary Louise," Maria said. "She had great success with the Chubby Chums."

"Chubby Chums?" Rebecca bit back a laugh.

Maria nodded. "The group is more than a little strange, and they say these stupid phrases all the time, but I think it might help to have people to report in to, know what I mean?" Maria plopped onto one of the stools behind the counter and rested her chin on her hands. "And they seem to really care, in a weird kind of way."

"Are we talking tender group hugs here?" Candace asked.

"I haven't had that pleasure yet." Maria laughed.

Rebecca's eyes narrowed. "So where did you meet Dante?"

"After the meeting. He talked me into an antipasto at his restaurant. You know me, I'm a weak woman when it comes to Italian food. I left, though, before things got too crazy. Well, except for a quick dance in the street with him. *Then* I left." For now, she left out the details about his visit to her mother's house yesterday.

Rebecca shook her head. "You got it bad, girl."

"What do you mean?"

"I have never seen you run away from a man before."

"I didn't run away. I . . ." Maria thought, then realized she'd done exactly that. "Okay, maybe I did leave too fast. But—" She cut herself off when she noticed the perfectly matched Chanel getting out of a limo parked along the sidewalk outside the shop. "Oh-oh. It's Monica."

"Again? She was just here on Thursday to change her wedding theme from Elvis to Cher," Candace said. "She wanted peacock feathers in the chocolate centerpieces, for God's sake."

Monica Thurgood had changed her mind seventeen times about her wedding décor, ordering all new desserts, dresses and decorations each time. Last month, she'd had a "vision" of a Cinderella wedding, complete with chocolate mice. This past week, she'd talked about an Elvis-themed wedding, with the bridesmaids wearing blue suede shoes and polyester suits.

"Well, she's got a new idea now. She called me first thing this morning to warn us she'd be stopping by. Now, don't laugh when she tells you," Rebecca warned, biting her lip and suppressing a grin. "She's talking . . . trains."

"Trains?"

Rebecca nodded. "She said her fiancé has this thing

for anything railroad. He likes pretending he's the engineer and she's the wayward caboose, and they—"

"Don't!" Candace put up a palm. "I just ate breakfast."

"Have you met her groom?" Maria asked. "He's got the coordination of a cow. All I can see him doing is derailing her."

The bell over the front of the door jangled, interrupting them. Monica Thurgood waltzed in, complete with her Chihuahua child.

"Come along, Aphrodite," she said to the little dog, tugging on a Swarovski crystal–embedded leash. "We need to talk about Mommy's wedding."

Across the room, Candace's three-legged dog Trifecta barely lifted his head in acknowledgment of the diminutive canine companion.

"Monica, how nice to see you again," Rebecca said.

Monica laid her Coach purse on the counter and ran a hand down the front of her cream Chanel suit. "I know it's only been four days since I was here, but I had an absolutely brilliant idea when I was at the spa this morning, getting a pedicure for myself and Aphrodite."

"Another idea?" Maria said. "So soon?"

"Oh, you know me. An idea a minute." Monica let out a giggle. "My head is positively spinning with ideas for the ceremony and reception."

"You know we only have two months until the big day," Rebecca said. "Changing things at this point will—"

"Cost me more. I know. But Daddy said whatever makes me happy is worth any price." Monica picked up Aphrodite. "And Daddy loves his little girl, doesn't he, pumpkin?" She cuddled the dog to her face.

"So we aren't going with the Cher theme anymore?"

"Turns out Daddy is allergic to peacocks. The centerpieces would have given him hives." Monica shook her head, lips pursed. "Poor Daddy. He's never even been to a zoo, can you believe it?"

"That is a . . . a hardship."

"Anyway, I was thinking it might be more fun to have a train theme, because my Lester is so into locomotives."

"Trains, huh?" Candace managed. "Is he a collector?"

Monica twiddled her fingers at her lips, a faint blush coloring her cheeks. "More an . . . enthusiast, you could say."

"Choo, choo," Maria whispered into Candace's ear, covering the joke with a slight cough. Candace gave her an elbow jab.

"We can do trains," Rebecca said. "Let's go into the office and jot down a few ideas." She gestured to Monica, who followed along, Aphrodite taking quick dainty steps beside her.

Candace grabbed Maria's arm before they headed into the office. "You can't leave me hanging. Details. I need details."

"Nope. Not even under pasta torture." Maria grabbed the office door handle. "Besides, we need to get in here and help, so Lester can get cozy with Thomas the Tank Engine at his wedding."

"You are a bad influence on me," Candace said, laughing.

Maria gave her a quick one-armed hug. "Hey, we all have our missions in life."

Vinny's Osso-Buco-of-Tearful-Contrition

2 tablespoons of flour
Salt and pepper
4 veal shanks, supremely high quality
2 tablespoons olive oil
1 onion, minced (be careful not to cry as you chop)
1 celery stalk, minced
1 leek, minced
½ carrot, minced
2 cloves garlic, minced
1 ¼ cups white wine (pick an excellent vintage for apologizing)
1 ¼ cups chicken or veal stock
2 bay leaves
Zest of 1 lemon
1 14-ounce can chopped tomatoes
Salt and pepper

Gremolata:

2 teaspoons minced fresh parsley
Zest of 1 lemon
1 clove garlic, minced

Preheat the oven to 325 degrees. Season the flour with salt and pepper, then lightly dredge the veal. Shake off any excess and make sure everything is perfectly coated.

Put an ovenproof casserole on the stove. Turn on the burner. *Do not look at the flame!* This is no time for distractions. Heat the oil, then add the veal and the onion. Brown the veal on both sides. Keep your mind and eyes on your task; don't get sidetracked. Remember, this is your chance to make up for that other . . . ah, incident. Remove the veal and set on a towel to drain.

Add the other vegetables, stir and cook until softened. Then add remaining ingredients, seasoning to taste. Try not to cry over the pan, thinking about how you almost lost your job and how your rent is due and the air conditioner is broken . . . Pull yourself together now.

Focus. *Focus.*

Return the veal to the pan. Cover and cook everything for two hours or until veal is tender enough to be pierced with a fork, just like your sorry heart.

In a small bowl, combine the gremolata ingredients. Sprinkle on top of the osso buco. Serve immediately—

Before you do anything else stupid.

CHAPTER 7

Vita was a madhouse. If Dante didn't own the place, he wouldn't believe it was the same restaurant as last week. Reservations were being called in faster than Franco could answer the phone, diners were lining up outside the door, waiting for any available table.

The review had worked a miracle. Perhaps he should nominate George Whitman for sainthood.

"Ah, your papa would be so proud," Franco said, coming alongside Dante at the reservation desk. "All his life, he wanted this."

Dante nodded. "Too bad it never became a hit while he was around."

Franco waved a hand. "He's around. He's in the flowers, the air, the smells from the kitchen. Your papa, always he be a part of this place."

Dante's gaze traveled over the dark wood paneling, the cranberry upholstery and the delicate wall sconces. His father had chosen every element in Vita. When Dante had inherited the place, he'd talked about changing this, lightening up that. But it had all been talk. He hadn't done much more than update the menu and add a few plants to the foyer. From the ceiling to the diamond-patterned carpet, Vita was still his father's vision. "You're right, Franco."

The maître d' nodded. "Of course I am." Franco picked up the grease pencil, his hand hovering over the laminated seating chart. "What about the other beautiful addition to Vita?"

"What other addition?"

"The vixen who created a miracle in the dining room. And stole your heart."

"She didn't steal my heart. She's a pretty girl, and yes, she helped me smooth over things with Whitman, but—"

"But nothing. Don't you lie to Franco. I know love when I see it."

"You are getting old. You need glasses."

"I need nothing but a tux for a wedding." He winked and arched a hinting brow at Dante. "And you, *mio amico*, need a wife. You work too hard, worry too much, live too little."

Franco should have been a champion dart player. He'd hit that particular bull's-eye with unerring accuracy. Dante had kept Vita the same as it had been when his father owned it, but that also meant living the life his father had. All-consuming, workaholic. No time, no energy, no room in his day planner for a date, never mind a wife.

"You *really* need to meet Maria's mother. You two could create your own marriage mafia."

Franco's eyes widened. He pressed a hand to his heart. "*Mio Dio!* I thought you were scared to speak that word."

"What word? 'Mafia'? Oh, come on. It's not the twenties."

Franco scoffed. "You think I worry Jimmy Hoffa is

going to come through our door? No, not that word. The 'marriage' word."

"What's wrong with it?"

"My mamma, God rest her soul, she had the sight. She tell me, 'Franco, those who speak of marriage, they want it. They say the word and it happens. Just like that.' " He snapped his fingers and a chill ran down Dante's spine. "Say it and before you know it, you are a Mister."

"I'm already a Mister," he told Franco, hedging at a real answer. Dante did want to get married someday. Not to replicate the nightmare marriage his parents had had, but to find the traditional life that had always eluded him. A wife, a couple kids, a home.

For now, though, that dream would have to stay on a shelf. Vita was his family.

"You need to find your beautiful butterfly and introduce her to your flower," Franco said. He did a little dance with his shoulders to punctuate the sentence.

"Franco!"

"You think I got to be an old man by living the life of a monk? I know about *amore*"—he winked—"if you know what Franco means."

"There are people waiting to be seated."

Franco sighed. "And each day, your heart, she grows more lonely. Someday she shrivel up like a rotten tomato. Die in a dark place. Alone."

"I have to get back to the kitchen. Vinny shouldn't be left unattended."

"When you end up pushing your own wheelchair around, don't come crying to Franco."

"Gee, thanks for the pretty picture of my future." Dante left and headed into the kitchen.

Dante would never admit Franco was right. Doing so would open up an entire can of matchmaking worms. If he knew Franco, the man would be camped out on

Maria's doorstep, chatting up Dante's assets until she caved and agreed to date him. In another life, Franco would have made a hell of a hostage negotiator.

Today, he had the restaurant to worry about. All this good fortune could be gone tomorrow. Another place in town could get a better review, take the limelight off Vita and leave him struggling once again. Too many people depended on Dante for him to direct his attention anywhere but within these two thousand square feet.

"I didn't touch the oven once," Vinny said when Dante entered the kitchen. Behind him, the swinging door slapped softly back and forth, slowly coming to a stop. "I didn't even look at the flames. I swear."

"Good. Did you get the veal braised?"

"As even as Pamela Anderson's tan."

"Risotto started?"

"Simmering like an August day." Vinny gestured toward the plates lined up along the stainless steel counter. "And I've got ten orders up, ready to go."

"Great." Dante slipped on his chef hat and tied his apron around his waist. "I'm counting on you, Vinny. Don't screw up."

"I won't." He toed at the floor. "I just want to say—" and he started to sniffle.

"Don't start, Vinny. Come on, we've got work to do." Dante gave him a light jab in the shoulder. "Buck up."

"I gotta say it, Boss. Please." More sniffles.

Vinny had an emotion control problem. He felt everything in extremes. He didn't laugh, he guffawed. He didn't get angry, he blew up. And he didn't sympathize, he broke down into sobbing. "Go ahead, but don't get yourself all worked up."

The sous chef nodded and swallowed hard. "Thanks for-for-for—" and he dissolved into tears, draping his head and arms across Dante's shoulders.

Dante patted at the younger man's back. "Vin, you're gonna make the rice salty. Don't cry."

"You're the only one who would give me a job," he mumbled through the tears, "and after all I did, you let me keep my job, and my kid needs shoes and now, she's gonna have them." And then he was off again, tears racing down his face.

"Vin. Vin. *Vin!*" Dante waited until Vinny had lifted his head and met his gaze. "It's all right. I forgave the fire thing—well, let's say I got over it. You concentrate on cooking. You're a good chef; stick with that."

"Yeah, Boss. I will." Vinny swiped at his eyes with the back of his hand. "You ever need anything, though, a car, a new stereo, a TV, you come to the Vin-man."

"You promised me," Dante said, pointing at Vinny's chest, "you'd give up that life when you came to work for me."

"I did! I got friends who have friends, you know. And I'll take care of you, the way you took care of me."

"Then stir the risotto before it sticks to the pan."

The kitchen door swung open and Rochelle, his head waitress, bustled in, an empty tray balanced in her hand. "Shit, it's busy out there. My ass is burning." She shoved her hip against a counter and heaved a deep breath, running a hand over her tight, nearly shaved black hair.

"Hey, Rochelle," Vinny asked from his position by the risotto. "How's that TV working that my cousin got you?"

"The remote eats batteries like they're candy, but it's good. My ma says she never knew the people on *General Hospital* came in colors other than green."

"Good. You need a stereo, you come to me. I'll—" He cast a quick glance at Dante. "I'll, ah, get my cousin to hook you up."

"Yeah, sure, Vin." Rochelle stretched a kink out of her back, then reached for the plates of food and began covering them with silver warming covers. "What the hell happened to this place? I like busy, but this is ridiculous."

"Enjoy it while it lasts," Dante said. "George Whitman could find another 'delight' tomorrow."

"Well, he better not do it too soon. Ma's meds went up again. Damn doctors prescribe things like money grows on the freaking moon. They must think I got some unlimited trust fund." She shoved herself upright again and started loading the covered plates onto her tray. "Honey, I ain't even got trust for my man, never mind no fund."

With the risotto back under control, Vinny discreetly headed off to the storage closet to replenish some of the spices. Dante could hear him still sniffling a little in the back room.

"Isn't Medicaid picking up the increase?"

Rochelle turned and gave him a face that told Dante exactly what she thought of Medicaid. "Hell, no. It don't pay to get old. Soon as I hit sixty-five, I'm jumping off the Tobin Bridge to celebrate my retirement. Toot a damned horn the whole way down." She raised the heavy tray to her shoulder. "Three hours I argued with Medicaid today. It was like trying to get a nut out of a squirrel. Far as I'm concerned, they can kiss my black—"

"Before you go pissing off the federal health plan," Dante began, reaching into his back pocket and withdrawing his wallet, "how about you let me give you a hand?"

Rochelle's smile wavered for an instant, the only emotion she'd betray. She was a tough woman, his head waitress, and she rarely let down her guard. "Now you know I can't take that, honey. You already paid for that nurse when the damned hospital sent Ma home three days after her hip operation. You've done enough, and then a bag of chips."

Dante shrugged. "It was nothing."

"I told you not to do it. And you did it anyway."

"Can't have my best waitress worrying all the time." He cleared his throat. "It's bad for business." He thrust five twenties at her. "Here, take these. It'll help tide you over for a few days."

She was already shaking her head. "Boss, I can't."

"Consider it a tip." He tucked the money into the pocket of her apron before she could refuse. "Bring me a glass of water later and we'll call it even."

"But—"

"Now get those dinners out there before you ruin my four-star rating and I have to fire you."

"You've never fired anyone in your life." Rochelle tossed him a tender, fleeting grin, then shifted the tray on her shoulder and turned toward the door. "You're a damned softie," she said. But her words lacked their usual punch.

For the rest of the night, Dante busied himself with keeping the diners happy. He barely had a second to breathe, and when he did, his thoughts strayed to Maria. Then back to the restaurant. How could he even think of dating her? He already had enough on his plate.

Dante had responsibilities. Too many of them to take time out for his own needs.

He'd have to settle for dreaming about Maria instead. And drooling in his sleep.

Maria's Talking-Margherita Pizza

1 pound peeled plum tomatoes
1 pizza dough, rolled out
1 pound fresh mozzarella, sliced thinly
10 to 12 basil leaves, torn into strips
4 tablespoons grated Parmigiano Reggiano
Salt and pepper
Extra virgin olive oil

Preheat the oven to 475 degrees. Puree the plum tomatoes to make an extra fresh sauce, then spread the tomatoes onto the prepared dough, just to the edge. Don't want it bubbling over and burning, spoiling the whole thing. Layer mozzarella in a tempting, overlapping circle around the pizza. The more the better is always a good philosophy. Scatter basil here and there. No need to make this into a piece of art—listen to the cheeses calling to your taste buds. They're getting impatient, so get a move on.

Sprinkle the pie with Parmigiano, salt and pepper. Drizzle with oil. Ah, a culinary Mecca all on one baking sheet.

Put the pizza in the oven and bake for 15 to 20 minutes or until the crust is golden brown, the cheeses are bubbling and you are at the absolute end of your waiting rope.

If you can't stand to wait that long for a pizza, mug someone else's delivery guy in the hall and abscond with their order.

CHAPTER 8

Moisture pooled in Maria's mouth, heavy on her tongue, urging her to open up and just taste one itty, bitty bite. A morsel. A mouse nibble.

The food was, after all, in her own kitchen cabinets. That made it practically kin.

She'd had two diet shakes, one low-fat snack bar that might as well have been dog kibble, and nothing else today. After working all day at the shop, surrounded by cookies, chocolates and candies, she was damned near suicidal with hunger by the time she left for home at five.

Stupid diet, anyway. All it did was make her want to cheat.

Look at the yummy treats in those kitchen cabinets. One won't hurt. You've been so good today. Give in. Just this once . . .

She jerked a hand forward and reached into the cabinet to retrieve something forbidden and very, very illegal in the weight loss rulebook—Twinkies. Bliss in a box.

The phone rang. Maria jumped away from the cabinet, clutching the box to her chest. She picked up the cordless, pressed "Talk" and uttered a greeting.

"Maria," Antonio breathed into the phone, "are you decent?"

Every sense in her body went on high alert, as if his voice had pressed a magic button in her vagina. The box of Twinkies tumbled out of her hands and onto the counter.

"Depends on the day of the week," she managed.

He chuckled. "I'm going to be in town next weekend. How about a sneak preview before the reunion?"

Her loins cried yes, but her hips reminded her they had a long way to go before they'd look like an hourglass instead of a goblet.

Damned Twinkies. She grabbed the box off the counter and threw it into the trash.

"I wish I could, but . . ." Oh, why couldn't she have started her diet earlier? Like two years ago? That way she'd be ready anytime Antonio said "bed." "I'll be out of town. Uh . . . catering convention."

"They have those?"

"Oh, yeah. All the time." *Whenever I conveniently need one.*

"Well, I hope you think of me when you're looking at all those pastries and pans."

She glanced at her trash can and gave the Twinkies a silent wave good-bye. "Oh, I will. More than you know."

"I'm heading into a meeting so I'll catch up with you later," he said. "But before I go, tell me one thing."

"What?"

"Do you still like skinny dipping?" He chuckled, a deep, throaty sound that echoed naked and raw in her ear, then he clicked off the line.

It was all she could do to hang up the phone. Maria crossed to the trash, drove a fist through the box of Twinkies and stood there, watching the flap swing back and forth, feeling great satisfaction.

She did have willpower. Really.

Then she caught a glimpse of her kitchen cabinet, still open from her earlier snack foraging. Pop-Tarts, Doritos, Cheez Whiz in a jar, Ritz Crackers and a box of Italian cookies stared back at her.

Eat us. You know you want to.

"No. I'm sticking to this diet."

Oh, come on. One won't hurt. Just a bite.

Her mouth watered, her stomach growled. *Traitors.* She spun on her heel and dove for the refrigerator. Maybe there was a salad or an orange in there.

Uh, no. Big mistake.

Inside was an entire block of Fontina cheese, the still-leftover manicotti from Guido's, a lone ricotta-stuffed cannoli that she'd resisted as dessert at Mamma's the other day but had not been able to escape the house without, a stack of rum balls she'd brought home from the shop—

She slammed the door shut. The fridge rattled in place, clearly annoyed that she'd peeked and run.

That's what she should do—go for a jog. Exercise instead of eat. Burn off the calories rather than shoving them into her mouth. Yeah, except, well, she hated to exercise. Hated it more than her annual gyno checkup, hated it more than getting her legs waxed, and hated it more than listening to her mother bemoan the lack of grandchildren in the Pagliano family.

The smell of pizza wafted down the hall of her apartment building, tickling at Maria's senses, urging her to dash into the corridor, yank the pie out of the delivery boy's hands and eat it before he recovered from shock. Those damned shakes hadn't filled her up. She might as well have had two hundred calories of air.

Maria had her hand on the doorknob when the bell rang. Could he be delivering the pizza to her? Some kind of psychic pizza service that sent over a margherita pie to the truly desperate and starving?

Oh, God, please let it be so.

But standing on the other side of her door was the exact opposite of the man she wanted to see.

And worse, he didn't even have any food in his hands.

"Hello, Dante." She leaned against the jamb and inhaled the retreating scent of tomato sauce, cheese and basil. "How'd you find out where I live? No, wait. Let me guess. Mamma thought you could use my address."

"She gave it to me when I left. Rather . . . forcefully." He smiled and for a second, Maria forgot about the pizza.

"That's my mother. Always willing to go to great lengths to see the continuation of the family line."

Dante chuckled. "I stopped by to apologize."

"For what?"

"For showing up like that. I shouldn't have gone to your mother's and ambushed you."

"That's okay, you made Mamma's day. Gave her hope that she won't die without grandchildren."

He grinned. "Has she set a date?"

"Knowing Mamma, the church is already booked and the priest has been paid in advance." She straightened, crossing her arms over her chest. Dante's gaze went with the movement. Clearly, apologies weren't the only thing on his mind. "Tell me you aren't here to propose."

"No." He put up both hands, warding off the words. "*Definitely* not."

Gee, he sure knew how to make a girl feel wanted. Not that she'd wanted him to propose, but still, it would be nice if he did. Then she could reject him and add a notch to her ego. The battle with the Twinkies and Antonio's skinny dipping question had pretty much destroyed any self-esteem she'd had when she'd woken up this morning.

"Shouldn't you be at your restaurant right now?" Maria asked.

"I have an hour and a half until it starts getting busy. I left Vinny in charge."

"You did? But I thought—"

"Don't worry. Franco's in the kitchen with him, a fire extinguisher at the ready. If Vinny gets the slightest bit overzealous with the pilot lights, Franco will foam him down."

She laughed at the image of Franco hovering over the pyromaniac sous chef. "So you came all the way over here, right before your dinner hour, merely to apologize?"

He took a step forward, his dark gaze connecting with hers, teasing at her senses. If Hostess could bottle the look in Dante's eyes, they'd have world dominance over the snack food market.

Maria reminded herself to breathe.

"I want more," he said.

"More?" She swallowed. "What kind of more?"

"Dinner. At my restaurant. You and me." His grin arched up on one side, exposing a dimple that made her knees weak. She'd always been a sucker for a man with a dimple in his grin. "No critics, no one else. Just a meal to remember."

Oh, damn. And she'd thought the Twinkies had been tempting. They had nothing over this offer. He was handing her an entire meal. Probably with him as the appetizer *and* the dessert.

He'd caught her at her weakest. Her willpower had fallen and wouldn't get back up. She wanted the Twinkies. She wanted the Cheez Whiz.

She wanted Dante.

In the back of her mind, she could still hear the foods in the cabinet. *Eat us. One quick bite. Do the diet tomorrow. Eat—*

"Actually, you could give me a ride," Maria said quickly. "I'm going that way and could save some walking."

"You want to go to Vita? Now?"

"No! Not now." Twenty pounds from now . . . maybe. She cast another glance at the smorgasbord of color in her kitchen—

Maria, we're here. Waiting in the cupboards—

"I . . . I have another place to go," she said, grabbing her coat off the hook, then scooping up her keys and purse from the hall table. Before she could change her mind and make a headlong dash for Doritos, Maria stepped out of the apartment and shut the door. Firmly. "Let's go."

"Where?"

The pizza guy came striding back down the hall, his bag now empty, but still holding the scent of its earlier cheesy gift.

"Away from temptation," Maria said. "Far, far away."

Then she glanced over at Dante's profile and realized she'd just exchanged one temptation for another.

Oh, shit.

Dante hadn't intended to go to Maria's apartment tonight. He should be kicking himself for leaving the restaurant when he should be cooking.

But the slip of paper Mamma had given him with Maria's address on it had been burning a hole in his pocket all day. Whenever he'd had a second, he'd slipped his hand into the gabardine trousers and touched the edges of the note, as if he could touch Maria by fingering her street address.

Clearly, he needed mental help. Or a hobby.

"I didn't picture you as the Honda type," Maria said, interrupting his thoughts.

"Oh, yeah? What type am I?"

"Ferrari. Lamborghini. Porsche. Something that screams 'man on the road.' "

"Man on the road?" He glanced at her, eyebrow arched. "Is that how you see me? Some beer swilling, horn honking, guy on a power trip behind the wheel?"

She considered him. "Well, maybe not the beer swilling part."

They came to a stoplight and he turned slightly in his seat, facing her, their gazes connecting across the short divide of the car's interior. "I own a Honda because it's good on gas, easy to park and gives me more money to put back into the restaurant. I like wines, not beer, and will go to great lengths to taste an excellent merlot. I hardly ever honk my horn because the city is noisy enough. And my power trips are all over my linguine, not the size of my engine."

She cocked a grin at him, a tease in her eye. "Is that because you only have a four-cylinder under your hood?"

"I have enough horsepower, trust me."

"Yeah, well, it's not about how many horses you're running. It's about what you do with them." She reached in her bag and pulled out a compact and a lipstick tube. "And in my experience, most men are good at mechanics but suck at finesse."

He should have had a witty rejoinder. Some kind of sardonic remark that would put him back in charge of the conversation. But when she swiveled the cranberry color up from the gold tube and slid it slowly along her bottom lip, pouting it out ever so slightly. . . .

He forgot his native tongue. Hell, he forgot he even *had* a tongue.

She tipped the lipstick up to point the bows of her lips with crimson. Her tongue darted out, sliding across the front of her teeth. He thought of his mouth on hers earlier, of the sweet yet hot taste of her, pulsing against him, igniting a roaring in his gut he hadn't felt in a long time. If ever.

The blare of the car horn behind him jerked Dante's attention back to the road. Good thing, too, because he'd almost taken out a defenseless grandma pushing a metal cart filled with groceries.

"Having a little trouble driving?" Maria asked.

In the rearview mirror, Grandma flipped him the bird.

He cleared his throat and focused on the road. "My mind wandered for a minute."

"Uh-huh." She smirked as she slipped the lipstick and compact back into her purse.

He banged a right on Prince Street. Only a couple more blocks until the restaurant came into view and Maria would slip out of his grasp. Again. She intrigued him, this woman who conducted business with the gustiness of a man yet had the vulnerability of a woman in her eyes. "Come to dinner with me."

"I can't." Her stomach let out a rumble and she pressed a palm against it, as if trying to keep it under control. "I really can't."

He couldn't let her go like that. She'd hooked him but good. She'd helped him, then refused to have anything else to do with him. He could see the want in her eyes, though she kept telling him something very different.

That push-pull was sexy as hell. An Olympic challenge if ever he'd seen one.

"Then I'll come to dinner with you. Name the night. Mamma told me I'm welcome anytime."

Maria laughed. "Mamma's getting out her tape measure to fit you for a tux. If you know what's good for you, you'll get a restraining order against her."

"Why? I like your mother." He'd reached the restaurant and parked in front of it, still hoping Maria would change her mind. "I happen to enjoy being fussed over, cooked for and appreciated."

She let out a sigh that sounded a lot like disgust. "Most Italian men do."

"Oh, is this some kind of he-man comment? Like maybe I should quadruple the hair on my chest and order you around from the Barcalounger?"

"You wouldn't be the first to try."

"Ooh, I sense bad relationships there."

"I'm single, twenty-eight, and Italian. Bad relationships come with the DNA."

"Mamma seems happily married. She said your grandparents had been together forever, too."

She shrugged. "For some people, it works out."

"But not for you?"

Maria had her hand on the door handle. He'd pushed too hard. "Thanks for the ride," she said.

"Come by the restaurant later and I'll treat you to a glass of wine." He put up a hand to head off her objections. "It's a glass of wine. Not a lifetime commitment."

She considered him for a moment, then opened the door and stepped out of the car. "Maybe," she said softly before closing the door and crossing the street.

He watched her go in his mirrors, with the swiveling stride of a woman who had hips and an innate sexuality. Damn. Even the way she walked was a promise.

Mamma mia. If anticipation were a sin, he was heading straight to hell.

Arnold's Spread-the-Love Mozzarella and Tomato Bruschetta

3 loaves ciabatta, plenty for sharing
1 cup sun-dried tomato paste
Sliced low-calorie mozzarella, as much as you need
for all your chums
2 teaspoons dried oregano
3 tablespoons olive oil
Salt and pepper

Preheat the oven to 425 degrees. Cut the ciabatta on the diagonal into 12 to 15 slices. Discard the heels. No one needs those party poopers anyway.

Spread the sun-dried tomato paste on one side of each slice. Arrange the mozzarella slices over the paste. If you want, use cookie cutters to personalize the mozzarella into appropriate animal shapes. Just remember, they'll get all melty in the oven and take on blob shapes. Don't do this with anyone who might be easily heartbroken to see their cat become a mat.

Dispense hugs to all your chums, then put the toasts on baking sheets. Sprinkle delicately with oregano, salt and pepper if desired, then drizzle with oil. Bake for five minutes. Let the toasts settle a bit, while you chat and shore up your chums in their hour of need.

Remember, eating together makes for friends in all weather. Hug a Chubby Chum today!

CHAPTER 9

"Chubby Chum Maria! You came back!" Arnold opened his arms and strode toward Maria, welcoming her into the circle of his embrace.

He moved so fast, Maria didn't stand a chance.

"Couldn't make it on your own out there, huh?" asked one of the men standing by the coffee urn. His potbelly extended past his Boston Red Sox T-shirt, giving her a not-so-appetizing peek at flesh and belly button hair beneath the dark blue cotton. "It's a big freakin' world of food, isn't it?"

"Now, Bert, that's not a very supportive statement," Stephanie said. The group's leader had on a bright pink "I'm proud to be a Chubby Chum!" T-shirt and matching ball cap. She was as perky as usual and zipping around the room, talking as she gave out welcoming air kisses like a human Pez dispenser. "Maria is here because she needs a shoulder, not a wagging finger."

Arnold stepped back, finally releasing Maria. "I know what animal you are! I figured it out just this second!"

"And what animal is that?"

He cupped a hand under his red goatee. "A chin-chilla!"

"A-a—what?"

"Chinchilla. You know, elegant fur on the outside and a sweet heart on the inside." Arnold drew her close to him again, murmuring something about chinchillas and teddy bears being great cave companions.

No one had ever described her like that. It didn't sound so bad, come to think of it.

Sort of.

"Well, thank you, Arnold," Maria said, extracting herself for a second time, "I think," she added under her breath.

He beamed. "You're welcome." He wrapped an arm around her shoulders and gave her a quick squeeze. "Now you're part of the Chubby Chum family, for sure."

"All right, group, let's get started." Stephanie clapped her hands together. "We have a lot of calories to atone for."

The Chubby Chums shuffled into the basement room, each taking a seat in the circle. As soon as they were seated, Stephanie led them in the group's version of the serenity prayer.

This time, Maria managed to squeak out "the wisdom to check the fat grams before I open my mouth."

As she said the words in concert with the others, she had to admit it felt a little like when she'd gone to Girl Scout camp as a kid. Included. Warm and fuzzy. Except without the sticky mess on her fingers from the s'mores she'd stuffed in her pocket for late night devouring.

"Now, let's talk about our food issues for this week," Stephanie said. "Arnold, why don't you start?"

He heaved a sigh, then pressed a palm over his mouth and choked back a half-sob. "I wasn't strong enough, gang," he said. "The Twinkies beat me. I could hear them calling me: 'Arnold, you want us. We're so light and fluffy. Arnold, have one. Just get to the cream filling and we'll leave you alone.' " He slumped a bit in his chair, dropping his face into his palms. "I caved. I-I-I ate one—"

"Oh, now, Arnold. One isn't so bad," Stephanie said.

"One economy-size box from the wholesale club."

And then he was really sobbing, his shoulders shaking, his head going back and forth in his hands like a palm tree caught in a summer storm.

"Oh." The leader pursed her lips, then forced them into an encouraging smile. "Well, today is a new day, right?"

He sniffled. "Yeah. I guess so."

"Arnold, be strong. You can do it." Stephanie turned to the group. "Does anyone have anything to say to help Arnold?"

"Yeah, don't buy the fuckin' Twinkies," Bert muttered.

"I know!" Audrey said, shooting up a hand and speaking at the same time. "You could eat an apple at the same time as the Twinkies. Take a bite of apple, then a bite of Twinkie, then a bite of apple. That way, it's not so bad."

"A way to get your cake and eat it, too?" Stephanie asked.

"Oh, that's so clever! Yes, exactly." Audrey nodded her head, then took out a small notebook and pencil from her purse. "I've got to write that down."

"Audrey, it may not be the best way to diet. What we want to do is avoid those bad foods altogether."

Audrey's face fell. "Well, can I still do the apples part of my idea?" She held up her notebook. "I already wrote that part down."

"Certainly. Group, what do we say about fruit?"

"Fruit's the secret to fitting in your skinny suit!" several people shouted.

Maria put her hand up a few inches, not really committing to giving input, half hoping no one would notice.

Stephanie had the eyes of a hawk, though. "Maria, did you have advice for Arnold?"

"Probably knows some Twinkie holiday in the Czech Republic," Bert grumbled.

Maria gave him a glare, then cleared her throat. "I just wanted to say I know how Arnold felt. I had a hard time throwing out my box of Twinkies today. But I did it. I stuffed them into the garbage and left the apartment."

"Have you been back yet?" Bert draped his arm over the empty chair beside him. His belly protruded a little bit more, as if introducing itself into the conversation.

"Well, no."

He snorted. "That's the real test. Show me a full box of Twinkies on garbage day and then I'll believe you're on a freakin' diet."

Stephanie gave him a sour look. "Bert, that's not very supportive."

He shrugged. "I'm not in a supportive mood."

"A bad mood leads to too much food." She wagged a finger to emphasize the point.

"You gotta have the right attitude to get rid of your fat-i-tude," someone piped up.

"Chubby Chums make you forget the Yum Yums!" another person shouted.

The platitudes were flying like pudding cups in a food fight. But oddly, this time, instead of driving Maria crazy, they felt almost . . .

Comforting.

She could almost see the appeal of this group. As quirky as they were, they were sort of like a family. Granted, the dysfunctional kind you only let out of the closet on major holidays, but a family all the same.

And, they seemed to understand what she was going

through. If she could cut through the rhymes and get some real diet advice, then she might be able to stick to this thing and get the weight off before Antonio could say "skinny dipping" again.

Or before Dante came over for Sunday dinner.

Now where the hell had that thought come from? Dante was *so* not her type. He was *Mamma*'s type, i.e., available, Italian, Catholic and breathing. Maria's standards were a little more exacting. For one, she didn't want a man who made a living with food. It was hard enough working in the gift basket shop all day. Temptation ran rampant in the boxes of truffles and delicate handmade chocolates.

Being with a man who could actually cook would be her undoing. Then she'd have him at her disposal three meals a day. *And* snacks.

She could just see the scale, the arrow waving between her goal weight and cow weight like a seesaw with two chunky kids battling for control.

The Chubby Chums continued tossing advice and rhymes at each other. An impromptu group hug sprung up, encircling Arnold with lots of Chubby Chum love. Only Maria and Bert refrained.

"You all are the best friends a teddy bear could ever have," Arnold said.

"Oh, we love you, too, Arnold," the crowd said in unison.

Love. That was Maria's whole problem. Too many people telling her she needed to fall in love, like a relationship would bring world peace and predictability to her Friday nights.

She shifted in her seat and realized what the biggest problem was with Dante. He made her feel off-kilter. Out of control. Maria Pagliano was a woman who always had the upper hand when it came to men and relationships.

She called the shots. *She* tossed them out when they were jerks, like Commodus with his downward thumb at the gladiator fights. That way, her heart remained unbroken.

She'd learned that particular lesson from David the Gyno, thank-that-bastard-very-much. When she'd caught him with Bambi the Stripper on their dining room table—the one she'd sweated over, sanding and polyurethaning it for three straight days while David babbled on and on about their future as a couple—she'd felt her heart shatter like ice falling off a roof.

Never again. No man would get that close, or get his butt near her eating area again.

"Okay, group, let's talk about our goals," Stephanie said, dispersing the group hug like a cop kicking the pigeons on Boston Common out of his way. "Remember, make them realistic. If you put the moon too high in the sky—"

"You'll only end up chomping pie," the group chanted back.

Stephanie put up a thumb. "That's right. Now, let's share our visions for the week ahead. Close your eyes, picture yourself and tell the group where you'll be in a week."

If miracles were possible, Maria would be in a size eight and swimming au naturel with Antonio.

"I've got it!" Arnold said. "I've got my vision!"

"Go ahead and share, Arnold."

"In a week, I see myself surrounded by all my friends here, feeling the love." He clutched his chest for emphasis.

"Yeah and still feeling like a damned whale," Bert muttered. "Love don't make anybody skinny."

Damn straight, Bert, Maria wanted to say, but didn't. Arnold was, after all, having an emotional moment.

Arnold cast Bert a little look of horror, then shrugged

off the comment. "Words don't have any calories, so they can't hurt me," he said. "Or my waistline."

She'd have to remember that one. Finally, a tip she could use. Audrey was busy writing it down, her pencil scratching across her notepad faster than Paul Pierce blazing down the Team Green court.

"Bert, what's your goal for next week?" Stephanie asked.

"To buy some freakin' Twinkies." He got to his feet and scratched at his belly. "You got me cravin' them now. Anyone want to make a run to Cumberland Farms with me?"

Audrey was on her feet in a second, joined by three other Chubby Chum diet defectors. "Do they sell apples there, too?" she asked, tucking her notepad away.

"Dunno. I never make it past the snack foods." Bert loped off toward the door, the others following behind like a gaggle of hungry baby geese.

"This is a support group!" Stephanie cried. "You can't walk out in the middle of a meeting."

"Sure we can," Bert said. "We're supporting each other's need for some freakin' junk food." And with that, he was gone, his mutiny leaving only a few lost souls, Maria included, clinging to their chairs with the steadfastness of women riders on the T clutching their handbags.

"Well," Arnold said, straightening his shoulders and letting out a dramatic breath, "I'd say Bert's animal is a jackass."

Dante's Mind-on-One-Thing Chicken Breasts with Chianti

4 boneless chicken breasts, skinned
¼ teaspoon salt
Dash pepper
3 tablespoons olive oil
2 ounces sausage, casing removed, meat crumbled
¼ cup fresh bread crumbs
¼ cup grated Parmigiano Reggiano
½ shallot, minced
1 egg
1 tablespoon chopped fresh parsley
1 teaspoon chopped fresh thyme
1 medium red onion, sliced in rings
2 tablespoons pesto (red or green)
1 ¼ cups Chianti
1 ¼ cups water
4 ounces red grapes, halved and seeded

Mix first nine ingredients in a bowl, keeping your mind on your task, not the woman who has got you preoccupied lately. Slice a pocket in each chicken breast and spoon in two tablespoons of filling. Tie with kitchen string to hold together. Season with salt and pepper.

Heat oil in a heavy skillet. Brown chicken breasts, watching the pan, not looking in the dining room for a pair of sexy eyes and an even sexier pair of . . .

Well, you're *supposed* to be cooking.

Remove the chicken. Add the onion and pesto to the pan and cook until onion is softened. Then add the

Chianti and water. Stir and bring to a boil, much like your blood already is with the thought of the hot woman waiting for you.

Don't lose your concentration now—you're almost done. Return the chicken to the pan. Reduce the heat (in the pan, not in you). Cover and simmer for 30 minutes or until chicken is cooked through.

If you have the patience of a saint, or of a man who just had a cold shower, transfer the chicken to a plate and keep warm. Simmer sauce until slightly thickened and reduced. Add grapes. Season with salt and pepper.

Serve by feeding bites to her, one succulent morsel at a time. Or if she isn't there, do the next best thing—fantasize.

CHAPTER 10

Around nine, the dinner crowd petered out, giving Dante a little breathing room. "I'm heading outside," he told Vinny.

"You are?" Vinny's voice squeaked in surprise.

"Yeah. I need a break."

"But-but . . . you never take breaks."

"Well, I need one now." He headed out the back door before Vinny could ask more questions. He knew he was being grouchy, but better to be thought a grump than a man looking for a woman who likely wouldn't be out there looking for him.

Maria. Even the thought of her name caused a weird hitch in his chest. It wasn't just desire, it was something more. Some indefinable connection, as if he'd finally discovered what he'd been missing out on all these years—

Then lost it again.

He ducked around the corner of Vita, hoping like hell she'd be out there again, searching for a cab. The Chubby Chums were meeting again tonight, he knew, from the sign he'd seen outside the church on his way in to work. Would she be there? Inside, debating the merits of lettuce over linguine?

But the spot under the streetlight outside the church was empty. Dante sighed and leaned against the brick façade.

Against his hip, he felt the thrum of his cell phone. Dante unclipped the Motorola, flipped it open and barked a hello into the mouthpiece.

"What kind of greeting is that for your mother?"

"Sorry, Ma. It's been a long day."

"It's Tuesday, you know. You didn't call."

"Whenever I call you, you're never home. I talk to your answering machine more than I do you." His mother had a better social life than he did, between the card club, bingo hall and horticultural society meetings.

"Well, still. A son should call his mother on a regular basis. Even if she isn't here to answer the phone."

Dante bit back a sigh. "Can't argue with that logic."

"Exactly. I'm always right, you know." On the other end of the phone, Dante could hear the swish of water. He could picture his mother, tanned and fit, sitting at the edge of her pool, dangling her feet in the water while she sipped a martini and chatted into the fitted earpiece that connected to her cordless phone.

"The restaurant's been busy. The *Globe* critic came out and gave it a four—"

"You're still holding on to that thing?" His mother sighed. "Why?"

"Because Dad left it to me."

"That doesn't mean you have to keep it, you know. Your father left me with an ugly house in Dorchester and an El Dorado that ran like crap. I dumped that thing first chance I got and sold the house to some idiot who called it a great starter home. Yeah, a start and an end if you aren't careful."

"Ma, Vita isn't a house. Or a car. It's a legacy."

His mother's bitter laughter rippled across the phone line. She'd hated every day his father had spent at the restaurant, as if she'd resented the care and attention he'd put into the place. Sometimes, Dante wondered if maybe his mother had been jealous of Vita, the dining room another woman taking his father's attention away. She'd refused all those years to move closer to the North End, as if actually setting foot in the neighborhood would show tacit approval of his dream. So they'd lived outside of the city and Dante's father had made the trek in and out every day, multiplying his hours with traffic and commuters.

"Some legacy," Carolina snorted. "I thought you wanted to be a lawyer. What happened to that?"

"I help people with their legal issues." Bailing Vinny out and giving him a job counted. He'd never even made it to law school. His dad had gotten cancer during Dante's senior year and from that summer on, he'd made the daily commute from the house in Dorchester to Vita with his dad. At first, just to help, then later helming the restaurant.

"Listen, Dante, I don't give you much advice because, well, that stopped being my job when you turned eighteen." She paused and he heard the sound of her taking a sip of the martini. "Listen to me on this one. Dump that albatross and live your own life. Come down to Florida. Buy a bingo hall. You'll be rich."

"Ma, I don't care about being rich."

"Did I dial the right number?" she said. "Who doesn't want to be rich? Money solves everything, believe me. That and a hefty life insurance policy." She laughed again, the sound deeper and throatier now that the martini was kicking in.

Across the street, the door to the church opened and

Maria came down the stairs, flanked by a skinny blonde on one side and a wildly gesturing apple-shaped red-headed man on the other.

"Ma, I gotta go." He'd long ago given up the dream of having a connection with his mother.

For just a moment, though, he longed for the family Maria had. A kitchen filled with warmth, jokes and laughter, not fights and resentment.

"I'm talking to you, Dante."

"I'll call you tomorrow. I promise." He started toward the street, his gaze never leaving Maria. She hadn't noticed him yet. The blonde woman had walked away from the group, leaving Maria and the man on the bottom step. Maria was laughing at something the redhead said and a flare of crazy jealousy went through him.

"Sell that dive, Dante. While you're still young enough to have a life."

"Bye, Ma. Have a good night."

"Oh, all right. Have it your way. I'm heading out with the girls for singles night at the community center, anyway. Maybe I'll find a better ship to hitch my dinghy to." His mother let out another laugh, then disconnected.

Dante slipped the phone back onto the clip on his waistband and then jogged across the street, stopping a few feet from Maria. When she saw him, she cut off her words mid-sentence.

"Dante! I didn't expect to see you tonight."

He grinned. "I'm only across the street."

"I know."

The redheaded guy looked from Dante to Maria, his brows jerking up and down like Groucho Marx. "I think I'll go home now, Maria. And leave the chinchilla to the fox." He gave her a little two-fingered wave. "Ta-ta!"

"Chinchilla? Fox?" Dante asked when they were alone again.

"Don't ask." She bent over a little, buttoning up her knee-length chocolate brown leather coat.

And hiding that glorious body. Damn.

"So, you want to take me up on my offer?"

"Nope. Got my motivation fix in there." She straightened and pointed a thumb toward the church.

He stepped closer, fingering at the lapels of her jacket. The leather was butter soft, well worn. Almost like a second skin. "One glass of wine won't hurt you."

She smirked, shaking her head, already saying no. "You sound like my kitchen cabinets."

"What?"

"Never mind."

"I'll make it easy on you. You can drink ice water and I'll have the wine." His hand traveled up to touch her chin. "Maybe enough for both of us."

She inhaled, her coat rising and falling, the air between them stilling with the suspense of waiting for her answer. "You're a bad influence on me."

He grinned. "I'm trying my damnedest."

She bit her lip, considering, and he held his breath, hoping. "I can't go into the restaurant. I'm not that strong yet."

To him, she seemed very strong. Maybe the strongest woman he'd ever met. Certainly with the guts of a guy, given the way she'd handled Whitman. But if she didn't want to go into Vita, he wasn't going to push the issue. She had, after all, just left the Chubby Chums and was probably doing her best to stick to the diet she clearly didn't need. "Then name the place. And I'll be there with my best Chianti."

"Aren't you forgetting something?"

"What?"

"Your restaurant. You don't close for another, what, two hours?"

He chuckled softly, his gaze connecting with hers. "Every time I look at you, I forget where I'm supposed to be."

Her eyes widened, twin dark pools reflecting the amber light above. "Damn, you're good at this."

"What?"

"Bullshitting a girl."

He cupped her chin, lowering his mouth within kissing distance. The scent of her perfume teased at his senses. "You're wrong," he murmured. "This isn't bullshit at all."

Then he closed the distance between them and captured her mouth with his. She tasted of coffee and sweetener, like a specially brewed cappuccino. A surge of want erupted within him and he had to hold himself back from pressing her down to the stairs and taking this a hell of a lot further than kissing.

She reached up and cupped the back of his head, long, delicate fingers pressing at nerve endings that seemed to lead straight to his groin. Her lips moved against his with the kiss of an expert, as if she *knew* him, knew what would feel perfect, knew exactly how to add fuel to a fire already roaring.

And then her tongue, curling in against his, teasing him into compliance, begging his to come out and dance. He groaned and ran his hands up her back, pressing her chest to his, inhaling her, tasting her, wanting everything that came with Maria.

She tore away from him, her velvet-soft cheek against his, her breath coming hard and fast. "Be at my apartment as soon as you're done at the restaurant. And don't bother with the damned wine."

Then she was gone, striding away fast in the dark night, as if she might change her mind if she stayed there a second longer.

Holy shit. He should take breaks more often.

Mamma's If-Wishes-Were-Son-in-Laws
Lady's Kisses

10 tablespoons butter, softened like your wrinkled,
still-waiting hopes
½ cup confectioners' sugar, sweet as you'd be to
your grandchildren (if you had some)
1 egg yolk
½ teaspoon almond extract
1 cup ground almonds
1 ½ cups flour

Filling:

½ cup almonds, finely ground
1 tablespoon almond paste
1 cup chocolate chips

Cream butter and sugar with an electric mixer until
it's as light and fluffy as your long, drawn out, continued hopes for a marriage in the family. Beat in the egg
yolk, almond extract, ground almonds and flour. Chill
for two hours, until as firm and cold as your daughter's
dateless heart.

Preheat the oven to 325 degrees. Line baking sheets
with parchment paper. Break off small pieces of the
dough and roll into 40 petite balls, making a wish over
each one for happily ever after. Place the balls on the
baking sheets, spacing two inches apart. Bake for twenty
minutes.

In a food processor, grind almonds and almond paste

for filling until they are as fine as your daughter's character. Melt chocolate chips and spread on cooled cookies, then dip halves into almond mixture, and press two cookies together to make a sweet sandwich. They're a beautiful creation, almost a work of art.

Mate the two halves like a perfectly matched couple. Serve as a hint to a solo daughter with space in her heart for a good man.

CHAPTER 11

She didn't need a diet. She needed psychiatric help. A one-on-one with Dr. Freud. Maybe the economy-size bottle of Prozac and a little electroshock therapy would help her figure out why she'd invited Dante over.

Maria smoothed her skirt over her knees and paused at the hall mirror to fix lipstick that didn't need fixing. There was no need for analysis. Her Dante-driven reasoning—or lack thereof—had been fueled entirely by her hormones.

She wanted him. And like the Twinkies, Maria saw, grabbed and consumed.

Unlike the Twinkies, the desire for him couldn't be shoved in the garbage can and forgotten beneath the plastic lid. When she'd looked at him, and long after she'd walked away, she'd only felt this searing flame of want. And when he'd kissed her—

At that moment, nothing else mattered but having Dante. The sooner the better.

Maria paced the small kitchen of her apartment. She wouldn't have to wait long. It was nearing midnight and before she knew it, he'd be on her doorstep, wanting to resume where they'd left off.

Oh, yes.

Oh, no.

Her doorbell rang. She stopped mid-step and wheeled around. He was here. And damned if her heart didn't react like a jackrabbit in heat.

Just before she opened the door, Maria straightened her back and took a deep breath. No way was he going to see her as the eager one. She opened the door, flashed him a calm, I-don't-need-to-have-you-in-my-bed-more-than-I-need-to-breathe smile and said, "Hi."

He stood there, in dark jeans and a white shirt unbuttoned at the neck, that lopsided grin on his face, and her composure slipped to the floor like a pair of panty hose that had lost their elasticity.

Damn. All she wanted to do was tear off his clothes and drag him off to her queen-size.

"Hi, yourself," he said.

"Uh . . ." The words she meant to say went right out of her head.

His grin widened. "I'm sure the hall's available for socializing, but your apartment might be a bit more private."

"The hall?" She blinked, then the connections in her brain began clicking, neurons fizzing and popping like crazy. "Oh, oh, yeah, of course. Come in."

"I thought you'd never ask." He entered the apartment and made the room seem too small. He wasn't a large man, but he had a presence that filled her space.

It said there was a man in her apartment. Not any man. *Dante.*

He withdrew his arm from behind his back. "I brought a bottle of Chianti Classico, anyway. I didn't want to be rude and show up empty-handed."

"You could have shown up with nothing and I would

have been fine with that." She took the bottle from him, cradling the cool glass in one arm.

"Nothing?" He arched a brow.

She couldn't resist. "The neighbors might have a problem with a naked man in the hall, but personally, I think every building should have one."

He smirked. "Depends on the man."

She allowed her gaze to roam over his toned V-shape. "And how he looks naked."

"True."

She laughed. Her heart hadn't resumed anything resembling a normal pace, but at least the teasing had eased the tension between them. And ratcheted the temperature up a few thousand degrees with all those thoughts of naked and Dante. Two words that when put together, did really funny things to her gut. She turned away from his gaze and headed toward the kitchen. "Let me get some wineglasses."

He followed her into the kitchen, making her damned glad she'd kept on the skirt. She could feel his eyes on her legs, watching the swish of her skirt against the bare skin. Her slides clicked against the tile, followed by the answering clack of his shoes. She paused at the counter and reached into the cabinet, withdrawing two delicate gold-rimmed wineglasses.

When she pivoted, he was there. So very much there. Her gaze went straight to the warm, golden skin exposed by the open buttons on his shirt. A simple triangle, nothing more, but it hinted at the ridges and planes that lay below.

And stirred a whole other appetite within her.

Who needed Twinkies with something like that in her kitchen?

"Corkscrew?"

"Please," she murmured.

"Excuse me?"

"Oh, you meant the wine."

"That's usually what that tool is used for, yes."

Maria pivoted on her heel and flung open a kitchen drawer, rummaging in it for the wine opener. For a second, she couldn't even remember what it looked like.

This was never going to work. Never had she been so discombobulated by a man.

"Isn't this what you want?" Dante reached past her and pulled the wine opener out of the drawer.

"Oh, yeah. I just, ah, have something in my eye"— blink, blink—"and missed it."

"Uh-huh." He smirked as he inserted the corkscrew into the top of the bottle, screwed it down and popped off the top. The wine let out a soft pop when the cork was released and the scent of Chianti filled the air between them.

With an easy, practiced hand, Dante reached for a glass and poured, twisting the bottle at the end before tipping it upright, never spilling a drop. "For you," he said, handing her a glass.

When she took the goblet, their fingers brushed and the simmering tension between them perked into a steady boil. "Thank you."

"My pleasure."

The way he said it made her think of pleasures far beyond the wine. Oh, this was wrong. In too many ways to name.

He poured his own glass, then raised it to hers. "To a taste of something delicious."

Their glasses clinked. He smiled and sipped. "And I'm talking about the alcohol. Of course."

She took a sip. The wine was divine.

But damned if his smile wasn't better.

Not to mention the scent of him. Every Italian delicacy under the sun seemed to emanate from his skin, his clothes, his hair. He was like a buffet waiting to be sampled. A nibble here, a nibble there, and before she knew it . . .

She should get rid of him. Just as she had the Hostess snack foods. Any dieter knew the first cardinal rule: eliminate the temptation. Otherwise, her willpower didn't stand a chance.

Hell, she'd already lost that battle. The minute Dante's lips had met hers, Maria's willpower had deserted her for a vacation in the Bahamas. For a moment there, he'd had her thinking commitment—maybe even marriage—wouldn't be such a bad idea if it meant being with a man like him every day.

That he was a man who could be trusted. Who'd stay true to the words that came out of his mouth and not undermine them behind her back.

Crazy thoughts. She'd been down that road once before with a man who had pled a damned good case, then perjured himself at the same place setting where she'd served him gnocchi.

She reached forward, setting her wineglass on the counter. "Listen, about what happened earlier . . ." she began.

"Don't tell me you're already regretting that kiss?" His voice was deep and teasing.

"Well . . . yes."

"Why?"

She sighed. "Because you're the kind of man my mother likes. Not the kind I like."

He seemed surprised. "Just because I ate her soup?"

"No. Because you're responsible. And nice. And mature. And Italian."

He shook his head. "And that makes me a bad man . . . why?"

"Because you're the kind of guy a woman falls in love

with. She gets all wrapped up in him. Her every thought centers around what he's doing. Where he is. Who he's with."

"Yeah? So?"

"And then it turns out to be a big, fat, one-sided lie."

"Whoa!" He put a hand up. "Am I sensing some left-over baggage you're dumping off at Dante National Airport?"

"It's not baggage. It's reality." She leaned forward, into his space, connecting her gaze with his, telling him in no uncertain words she was looking for truth. "Do you want to get married right now?"

"Are you asking me? Or just talking hypothetically?"

"I don't have a white gown in my closet. Nor do I have any kind of urge to hitch myself to someone who's going to tell me when to be home and how much to spend at the Stop & Shop. So, no, I'm not asking. It's entirely hypothetical."

His gaze traveled up and down her frame. A flush ran through her body that had nothing to do with the alcohol. "You'd look good in white."

"That's not what we're talking about."

"Why not? That could be my new favorite subject. Maybe even make it a category on *Jeopardy*. Ways to Describe Maria Dressed *and* Naked."

"I bet you'd knock yourself out on the video clues."

Once again, his gaze slid over every inch of her like a heated visual caress. Damn. It had suddenly become August in her apartment. "I might need CPR from Alex Trebek," he said.

"Now that would be something I'd watch."

"Gee, glad to know my getting mouth-to-mouth from a game show host would interest you." He leaned toward her. "A guy's gotta take some pretty desperate measures to get your attention, I take it?"

"No. Not at all. He just has to be the opposite of Mamma's Dream Date."

"Well, for your information, I don't want to get married this minute."

"Well, good."

"But I do someday," he said, moving closer, his words soft, as if he were sharing a secret. "I want a house and a bunch of kids and a wife who smiles when I walk through the door."

"One of those traditional lives, huh?"

"What's wrong with that?"

She looked away. "Everything."

A woman lost her identity, her self in that kind of life. She'd seen it in generation after generation of Pagliano women. That particular buck stopped here. With her.

"You seem scared of marriage, which surprises me," he said.

"Surprises you?"

"You stood up to George Whitman and his lawyer. Not many men would do that, never mind women. And yet, the mere mention of a little gold ring has you running for the Berkshires."

She took a sip from her glass. "I'm not scared of anything."

His gaze sought hers, probing. "Now who's bullshitting who?"

She drank again, giving him a noncommittal shrug.

Dante smiled and drank from his own glass, then turned a slow circle around her apartment. She could see he knew he was right but wasn't going to rub it in.

"Hey, what's that?" He crossed past her and into the living room.

She pivoted, following his line of sight. "A chess set. Gathering dust."

"Do you play?"

"I play all kinds of games."

He turned, smiled at her. Something went liquid in her gut. "I bet you do."

She grabbed up the wine and took a gulp.

"So you do play chess?" he asked again.

"I used to."

"And why not anymore?"

She laughed. "The men I date don't come over to play games involving my brains."

Dante considered her for a long, heated second that seemed to last forever. "They don't know what they're missing."

"They don't care is more like it." She gestured to her breasts. "Most men never see past these. I could have a bobblehead for all they know."

"Well, I—"

She put up a hand, cutting off the sentence before he could finish. "Oh, no. Don't even try it. When we met, your eyes couldn't have been more glued to my chest if you'd slapped them on there yourself with some Elmer's."

"You're a voluptuous woman. You can't blame a man for looking."

"Oh, *please.* I have two large pieces of my anatomy that serve very little purpose in life except to drive men crazy. That's not attractive. That's a generosity of skin. And men stop right here." She pressed on her chest.

Dante's gaze stayed with hers. "Then you're dating the wrong kind of man."

"Well, I guess that leaves only gay men in my dating pool."

"No, I think you just need to pull from the deep end." He crossed to her, took her glass from her hand, then took her other hand and led her to the chess table. "Have a seat."

She arched a brow at him. "You want to play *chess* with me?"

"I do, indeed." He pulled out her chair at the small gateleg table against the living room wall.

"Being all chivalrous now, are you?"

"I figure I might as well be nice before I whup you on your own chess board." He watched her sit and marveled again at how different Maria was from anyone he knew. A woman who was smart, sexy *and* played chess? Dante had definitely died and gone to Man Heaven. He took the seat opposite her and ran a hand along the crackled surface of the table. "Nice piece of wood."

"Thanks. I salvaged it myself last year. Had a hell of a time getting the old finish off but I think it looks a lot better now than it did painted pink with flowers."

"You did this?" She could use power tools, too? This wasn't just heaven, it was utopia in female form. He fingered the edge again. "Great job."

"Thanks." Maria opened the drawer on her side of the table and pulled out the chess pieces. "It was part of a . . . refinishing frenzy I had for a while."

"Had?"

"Yeah."

"What happened? You run out of furniture?"

"No. Another woman imprinted her ass on my dining room table."

"Oh." He considered that piece of information for a moment. "That would do it."

"Yeah." She brought out the last of the pieces. "Black or white?"

"Black. For the bad guy. I can't have you keeping me on a pedestal forever." He grinned.

"I don't have you on a pedestal."

He reached over and started taking his pieces and placing them on the corresponding squares on the board. "Oh, yes, you do. You think I'm some kind of choirboy destined to become every mamma's dream son-in-law."

"Not every mamma's." She set her bishops in place. "Just mine."

"A match made in heaven," he said.

"Or hell. Since your name does mean 'devil' in Italian."

He smirked. "Think of me as a study in contrasts."

"If I think of you at all," she said blithely, sliding a pawn forward. "Your move."

He took a sip of wine, considering the board.

"It's just a pawn," she said. "Not a lifetime commitment."

Dante met her gaze. "What if we raised the stakes a little?"

"Meaning?"

"Loser gives the winner a massage."

She cocked her head. "Uh-huh. Typical male thinking. And of what body part?"

He grinned. "I'll be fair. Make it loser's choice."

She wagged a finger at him. "You'd probably lose on purpose."

"I never lose on purpose. My male pride couldn't take the hit."

Maria sipped at her wine and met his teasing gaze. "Nope. This is my apartment. My chess board. Thus, my rules." She gestured toward him with her goblet. "You lose, I choose the part of my body you massage. I lose and I *still* choose the part of your body to massage."

Even as the words left her lips, though, Maria wasn't so sure it wasn't a losing proposition either way. The word "massage," combined with Dante's hands on her skin, well . . .

That wasn't losing, was it?

Nor was it staying away from him. Uninvolved. If anything, it was ratcheting up the connection, ten notches at once.

Dante grinned. "Doesn't sound like I really win either way."

"Exactly." She smiled, took a sip of wine. "Your move."

He slid a pawn forward two spaces.

Maria leaped her knight over its pawns.

"Gutsy move," Dante said. "For a girl."

"You ain't seen nothing yet, buddy."

He advanced a second pawn. She countered with one of her own. "Where'd you learn how to play?" he asked.

She shrugged. "I screwed the chess team in high school."

He hesitated, his fingertips on a pawn, his dark brown eyes studying hers. "I don't believe you for a second."

She drew herself up a little, blinking in surprise. "Really?"

"Well, hell, yes, you're a beautiful woman but not a stupid one." He drew out his bishop and aimed it toward her knight. "Or a loose one. You have more character than that."

Maria didn't say anything for a long moment. She didn't move any pieces, didn't sip her wine. When was the last time a man had observed anything about her besides her looks? Particularly something about her character?

"My grandfather. Not Sal, but my mother's father, who died when I was fifteen." She said it softly, with a shrug, pretending the answer was no big deal. "He liked chess. I was the only one who could beat him once in a while. And who didn't mind when he left his teeth on the table."

Dante almost felt bad taking advantage of her reminiscent state. Almost. But this was chess, after all, and, outside of the restaurant, he took few things in life as seriously as he did chess. He slid his bishop forward and scooped up her knight.

She cursed under her breath. "That won't happen twice." She slid her own bishop out to take his.

Damn. She'd thought three steps ahead of him. Clearly, he'd met someone who took the game even more seriously than he did. "You-you—"

"What?"

"You took my bishop."

She grinned. "That's the objective, Dante."

He paused, his hand halfway to a piece on his side of the board. "Say that again."

"That's the objective? What, do you want me to rub it in?"

"No. Say my name."

"Why?" She smiled. "Did you forget it?"

He rested his arms on the table, his attention now off the game and on her mouth, wanting to see the little slip of her tongue when it formed the vowels in his name, the slight opening of her parted lips. "I like the way it sounds when you say it."

"Your move," she reminded him.

She hadn't said his name. With a twinge of disappointment, he reached forward and started to slide a pawn up two spaces.

"Dante," she said, her voice deep and throaty, a caress that tingled through him with the force of a tidal wave.

The pawn tumbled to the board, teetering on its side.

"Oh, am I distracting you, *Dante?*" She gave him a look of wide-eyed innocence.

He smirked. "You don't play fair."

She gave him an answering grin. "I hate to lose."

"A woman after my own heart."

"Not your heart," she said, moving her rook forward two spaces, "just your king."

Dante's Hot-and-Spicy Rigatoni-to-Remember

½ pound pancetta, diced
¼ cup olive oil
1 onion, chopped
1 red pepper, chopped
3 cups canned Italian plum tomatoes, strained
4 cloves garlic
⅛ teaspoon red pepper flakes
Salt
½ pound rigatoni, cooked al dente
8 to 10 basil leaves
3 sprigs parsley
⅔ cup Pecorino cheese, grated

Sauté the pancetta over a medium flame, keeping the heat up in your own kitchen, too. Don't back down now, she's beginning to cave. Add the oil, the onion and the pepper, sautéing until onion is translucent. Now add tomatoes, garlic, red pepper flakes and a pinch of salt.

Set things to simmering—in the pan and with the woman. You've got a good half hour to get her temperature up, but be careful not to let anything boil over.

Pour sauce over cooked rigatoni. Sprinkle with basil, parsley and grated Pecorino. Serve immediately. It'll be sure to add a little bite to things.

CHAPTER 12

One hour and the entire bottle of Chianti later, Maria had Dante against the wall. "Checkmate," she said.

"I refuse to give up that easily." He bent over the board, looking one way, then the other, studying every angle like a mouse hoping to find a cranny to escape past the cat.

"Besides your king, you have three pieces left on the board," Maria said. "Or should I call them eunuchs?"

"Hey, pawns can be very effective warriors."

"Face it. You lost. To a girl."

He studied the board a moment longer, then tipped his king in defeat. "You're good."

"No, I'm *very* good."

Dante leaned forward, his gaze locking with hers. The wine had softened everything between them and when she looked at him now, a slow, burning want churned in her gut. The kind of comfortable sexy feeling that grew after years together. Not hours.

"At everything?" he asked.

What was it about this man that made her want to settle down and play house? Or at the very least, play bedroom and skip all the boring parts?

"You'll never know." She arched a brow and leaned back, determined to break the connection, yet not doing a very good job of it.

"Wanna bet?"

She laughed. "You've already lost to me once. You went down in flames that would embarrass Napoléon. And now you're challenging me again?"

The smile that curved across his face melted her resolve like butter on angel-hair pasta. "I'm a glutton for punishment."

No. She wouldn't do this. He was all wrong for her. Already he had her thinking about white picket fences and comparing him to illegal foods. Next she'd be kissing him between bites of three-cheese lasagna. And Mamma would be getting the calla lilies in order like soldiers going to war.

Antonio was the man she wanted. A man who didn't require a commitment, a key to her apartment or one to her heart.

"You're a man who has kept me up past my bedtime." She faked a yawn, got to her feet and pushed her chair back under the table.

Dante rose, came around to her side and took the wineglass from her hands, laying it beside her victorious queen. She could feel the tension building between them and knew what came next would undo her resolve as quickly as a whiff of Guido's manicotti.

But try as she might, she couldn't step away. Couldn't back up. Could barely remember to breathe. Dante was in control of her emotions, her actions.

Everything.

She watched, mesmerized, as his hand came back up to her chin. He trailed a finger along her jaw in a touch so gentle it could have been a whisper. Everything within her, kept on a tight rottweiler-worthy leash during the game, erupted in pandemonium like zoo animals suddenly freed by a renegade chimpanzee.

"You don't look sleepy," he said.

"I'm exhausted."

"You may be good at chess," Dante said, his finger now toying with her bottom lip, "but you really stink at lying."

She opened her mouth to his touch, wanting more, wanting to take that finger in and taste him, to consume him like all the foods she'd denied herself these last few days.

He was watching her with those hypnotic chocolate eyes, that dimple beside his smile, all saying he knew the effect he had on her and he was enjoying having the upper hand.

Damn him. That was why she stuck to men like Antonio who filled her bed for a few hours and nothing else.

Because *she* had the upper hand then. She was the one who teased and tempted. And who said it was over when it was obvious the relationship had become more drain than fun. When she, in short, had had enough.

But this time, she couldn't get enough. Heck, she couldn't even begin to get a taste.

His finger slipped into her mouth, just a fraction of an inch, tipping at her teeth, and she couldn't hold back anymore.

Her tongue zipped forward to taste the tip of his finger, her teeth holding it lightly there, a hostage in her mouth. He tasted of salt and warmth and—

"Dante," she groaned, her mouth parted now, asking for more than a finger to satiate the appetite within her.

"Maria," he said, his voice just as husky and full of want. He leaned forward and for one brief, frustrating second, kissed her. Then he pulled back and broke the contact between them. "Do you regret *that* kiss?"

"Oh . . . no," she breathed.

"Then we have a problem."

"A problem?"

He gave her a lopsided grin. "Yeah. You're falling for me, like it or not." He kissed her again, hot, sweet and short—much, much too short. "And that means your Mamma might just be right about me."

Then he was gone, leaving her with a fire in her belly and an unasked question still on her lips.

Thank God the lone leftover Guido's manicotti was still in her fridge. She needed that and a damned good vibrator if she was ever going to get to sleep tonight.

Papa's Simple-Answers Cookies and Beer

1 six-pack Samuel Adams beer
1 package biscotti

Open the beer. Take a drink, then flip channels until you find the Celts, the Knicks or two men beating the hell out of each other. Take another drink, then switch the channel because there's another goddamned commercial for Depends on.

Call for your wife to bring biscotti. Eat between sips and flips.

Kick back in the recliner and count your blessings. Life is damned good.

CHAPTER 13

Early the next morning, before she headed to work, Maria's doorbell rang. "Couldn't take losing, could you?" Maria said as she pulled open the door, expecting Dante and finding—

Malcolm in the Middle.

"Are you Maria?" the kid said, his face all toothy and acne-riddled. He looked like he'd picked up his driver's license on the way over.

"Yes." She narrowed her gaze. She had no weapons nearby, but then again, this skinny teen wasn't big enough to take her on. As a size almost-ten, she could take him, should he try anything funny like trying to commandeer her TV for a PlayStation party. "Why?"

He shifted from foot to foot, a blush creeping up his collar and blooming in pale cheeks, seeping into his blond hairline. "I hear you're looking for a man. And uh"—he drew himself up to his full five-foot-eight height, letting out a John Wayne–type gust of testosterone— "I'm a man. Well, almost. I'm eighteen in six weeks."

"Who told you—"

No. She wouldn't. She *couldn't* have.

The teenager gave her a smile that had given some orthodontist a Benz. "Gerry at Paulie's Grocery said you were pretty hard up. Being as old as you are and all."

"I am not old and I am not hard up," Maria said, her fingers tightening on the door. "And you can tell Gerry that if he helps my mother anymore, he'll get a zucchini up his—"

But Malcolm in the Middle was already gone. Maybe the impending wrinkles on her face had scared him away. It was either that or the thought of losing his virginity to a member of the squash family.

That night, as soon as she got off work, Maria headed over to her mother's house. She timed her arrival to miss the calories of dinner but still catch her mother in the kitchen, where she was easiest to pin down for a conversation.

"Mamma, this has to stop," Maria said.

Biba hurried around her kitchen, stacking dinner dishes in the sink, then filling it with soapy water. Nonna stood to the left, drying the finished plates. "Stop what?" Mamma asked, all innocent.

"Trying to marry me off like I'm some reject from a leper colony."

"I am not."

"Then why did a seventeen-year-old boy show up on my doorstep this morning, offering to take this 'old lady' out for a spin?"

From her place by the sink, Nonna snickered.

"I did nothing," Mamma said. "All I did was talk to Mary Louise Zipparetto's mamma in the checkout line. Maybe some snoop overhear."

Mary Louise Zipparetto. Everything bad in Maria's life could be traced back to that one name.

"Did you say anything to Gerry?" she asked.

"I only make conversation." Mamma scrubbed at the plates in the sink. "It's rude not to talk to the bag boy. He packs my bags so nice. Cans always on the bottom."

"He does a good job," Nonna piped up. "Never an egg broken."

"Mamma, I don't need you advertising for a husband for me when you redeem your double coupons."

"I'm only helping."

"Why won't you listen to me?" Maria sighed and dropped into one of the kitchen chairs. "I am not going to get married. *Ever.*"

Mamma clasped her hands over her ears, soap dripping from her fingers and onto her shoulders. Then she dropped one hand to her chest and made the sign of the cross, fast and furious. "The devil has ears, you know."

Maria rolled her eyes. "Mamma, all single people do not go to hell."

Mamma choked back a sob and laid a rooster serving bowl carefully into the sink, sniffling as she did. "Never will I hear the laugh of my grandchildren."

"And never smell the diaper of one, either. *Che puzza!*" Nonna pinched her nose. "Those plastic ones hold a lot of stink."

Clearly, she wasn't getting anywhere here. Maria left the kitchen to go farther up the chain of command.

"You should marry a good Italian boy," Papa said, settling into his worn black leather La-Z-Boy and flinging out the recliner base like a warrior girding up for couch potato battle. "Like your mamma did."

"Papa, I'm not interested in getting married."

"Biba! Bring me a beer." Papa grabbed up the remote and turned on ESPN. "Why the hell not?"

"I'm happy alone. I call my own shots."

"Take out your own trash. Change your own oil."

Papa flicked the channels, running through every sports show known to mankind in a fifteen-second blitz. "Sleep alone in your bed. And die alone, too, with no children around to wipe the drool off your chin."

"I also come home when I want. Spend what I want. Answer to no one but me."

Her mother bustled in with an open Samuel Adams and a glass. She put them down on the metal TV tray beside Papa, smack dab in the center of the impressionist painting of Boston Common. He gave her a kiss on the cheek and a pat on the butt. *"Grazie."*

Mamma smiled at Papa, gave Maria the cold, you've-disappointed-me-again shoulder, then headed back to dishes and dinner cleanup. As long as Maria could remember, it had been this way. Dinner was served precisely at six. Papa would get home from his shift at the phone company, eat, murmur his appreciation, then retreat to the recliner for a beer and the game. Didn't matter what team or what sport—he watched them all until the beer kicked in and he fell asleep in the chair. When Mamma finished cleaning up, she'd work on her quilting for a while, then nudge him awake so the two of them could climb the stairs to bed.

Not the life of romance and passion Maria wanted. That kind of predictability would make her run screaming and naked down the Callahan Tunnel.

She'd almost fallen into that trap with David and learned pretty damned quick she wasn't cut out for "married life." Especially when he'd slept with that stripper on her dining room table. If that's what being committed to someone was like, she'd much rather *be* committed.

Papa took a swig of beer, ignoring the glass. Mamma always brought him the glass, and he always ignored it. It was as if Mamma hoped someday he'd grow into civilized behavior.

"What Mamma and I have is good," he said. "Like pasta and gravy. It goes together, and doesn't give you too much heartburn." He tipped the bottle in her direction, Sam Adams nodding agreement.

"Nothing against you and Mamma, but I just don't want what you have."

"You're breaking your mamma's heart." Papa scratched at the stubble on his chin, considering her, the Celtics temporarily forgotten. "A girl who says she doesn't want to get married either goes into the convent or starts wearing those army shoes. You know . . ." He lowered his head, hinting at an answer he didn't supply.

"No, I don't. What are you talking about?"

"Those type of girls wear the boots because they're buttering their toast on the wrong end of the loaf."

Maria let out an exasperated sigh. "Just because I don't want to get married doesn't make me a lesbian."

Papa leaned back in his chair, the beer back at his lips. "Just as long as you're shopping in the right bakery."

Mamma hurried in again, this time with a rooster-decorated plate of biscotti. She put them on the tray, then topped the dessert delivery with another peck on Papa's cheek. "Dessert for you."

"Ah, you always know what I like." He kissed her back. "See, this is marriage," he said to Maria. "Two people who know each other so well, they never have to say a word."

"Except . . ." Mamma quirked a brow.

"*Ti amo.*" Papa grinned and gave her another kiss.

She whispered the same words back, holding his gaze for a long, private second, then left, still avoiding her disappointing daughter.

Maria tried not to grimace as Papa dove for his nightly beer and almond cookies snack. The combination was disgusting, but Papa had the stomach of a goat and never seemed to notice the odd juxtaposition of sweets and hops.

A second later, her grandfather followed the scent of the cookies down the stairs and into the living room. Nonno took the seat opposite the TV tray, grabbing a couple of cookies from the plate. "You watching the game?" he asked Maria.

"Nah. We're talking about Maria not wanting to get married."

"Ah." Nonno nodded. "Has your mother made the soup yet?"

The damned soup *again*. "I'm not going to get married just because of something I ate."

Her grandfather shrugged. "Your Nonna's mamma, she made me the soup. I proposed the next day." He nodded. "The soup, it works."

Maria lowered herself to her knees beside her father's recliner. "Papa, you *have* to talk to Mamma for me. She won't listen to a word I say and she keeps trying to fix me up with Dante. Not to mention every single man under the age of eighty in the North End."

"I remember him, the day he come to see you. He seemed like a good man, that Dante," Nonno said. "They don't grow on clotheslines, you know."

Papa changed the channel again. "Damn! You idiot! Get that shot, you—"

"*Papa!*" Maria waited until her father's attention left the Knicks and came back to her. "She's getting desperate now. She told Gerry, the checkout boy at Paulie's Grocery, to keep an eye out for a husband for me."

"Your mamma cares about you." Papa slammed his beer down on the table. Sam spewed a few drops across the metal surface. "*Merda!* What's that coach doing? Sleeping?"

Maria ignored the rhetorical question and pressed on. She'd had no luck getting through to her mother. Her grandfather seemed to be on Dante's side, and Nonna had never been able to convince Mamma to do anything. Papa was her last resort.

When Papa laid down the law, it stayed there, like a road of steel. If he told Mamma to back off, she would.

There were, Maria had to admit, some advantages to a traditional Italian marriage. Though she'd never opt for one, not if it meant being a chicken under a rooster who couldn't be bothered to peck up his own kernels.

"Papa, Gerry is *seventeen*. Mamma gave him my address. Every senior from Sacred Heart has been at my door this week, asking me to the prom."

"You'd look nice with a corsage," Nonno said.

"Mamma means well," Papa changed the channel, this time settling on a boxing match. "*Madonn!* Get off the ropes! You have the brains of a flea!"

"Papa. *Papa!*"

He flicked a glance at her. "What?"

"You have to talk to her. I don't need her help finding a husband. I don't even want a husband."

"Jab! Use your jab! No. The right! Get him with your right!" Her father's face had started to turn red.

"Your blood pressure," Maria warned. "Remember what the doctor said."

Papa scoffed. "That doctor should watch Lennox Lewis once in a while. Then he'd see why I have high blood pressure." He punched a fist forward. "Uppercut! Get the chin!"

"Papa, about Mamma—"

"Your mamma means well," Nonno said. "And she knows you better than you know yourself."

"Get off the ropes!"

Maria rose. It was no use. "I'm going now. Enjoy the fight." She turned to leave.

Papa grabbed her arm. "I'll talk to your mamma," he said. "But it won't do any good."

"Why?"

"Because she's right. Your mamma's a smart woman. A very smart woman." He nodded. "And she knows what's good for you."

Maria shook her head. "Marriage is *not* what's good for me."

Mamma hurried in with a second beer, made her delivery, then went back to her kitchen.

Papa picked up the frosty new Sam Adams with his free hand and took a sip. He kicked back a little farther in the recliner and replaced the beer with the remote again. "I don't know why not. It's pretty damned good to me."

Franco's Deception-in-One-Dish
Milanese Veal Chops

2 ounces pancetta, cubed
¼ cup unsalted butter
4 veal cutlets, tender like a lying tongue
¼ cup bread crumbs, as fine as your tall tale will be
Salt and pepper
1 cup dry white wine, to soothe the lies on your
palate
1 onion, minced
1 carrot, minced
1 celery stalk, minced
2 tomatoes, peeled, seeded and chopped
½ cup chicken broth, clear as your conscience
Lemon wedges

Cook the pancetta in the butter until golden brown
and *magnifico*. Dredge the veal in the bread crumbs. Shake
off the messy extra. No need to clutter your mouth with
clumps. Brown the veal in the pan, then season with salt
and pepper.

All the while, cook up an *interessante* story to bring
two lonely hearts together. You aren't lying, you are . . .
creating a happy ending. It's a good thing.

Remove the veal to make room for the vino. Deglaze
the pan with wine, then cook the onion, carrot and celery until the onion is as gold as the halo over your head
for doing such a good deed for your friends.

Bring the veal back and marry it with the vegetables.
Add the tomatoes, cover and let everything be happy

together for oh . . . an hour and a quarter or so. Long enough to come up with a story to send one running into the arms of the other. Your swans will find each other across the pond because the power of *amore* is stronger than a silly, stubborn mind. Be sure to check on it from time to time, adding a tablespoon of the chicken broth or so, to keep your sauce from drying up

Serve hot, with lemon wedges for a little tartness. Like your lies, this dish has layers of truth beneath the surface. When they dig in, they find it. And they find each other, in their happy smiles.

And everyone will say Franco, he was right.

CHAPTER 14

Franco bustled around the tables, straightening place settings, fixing the flowers in the vases and tilting candles upright. "We miss something."

"What?" Dante looked up from the table where he sat planning the next few nights' menus and specials. And trying not to think about the unfinished business between Maria and him.

For nearly two weeks, he'd left her alone. Hadn't even checked to see if she was across the street. He'd thought after what had happened in her apartment, and on the church steps, that she'd make a move next, because he'd left all his balls in her court.

But—

"A sweet. We need something sweet."

Yeah, he needed a sweet. Another sweet kiss like the one he'd started—and like an idiot, not finished—in her apartment. He'd thought he'd be leaving her with something to think about. A few regrets, a steam of desire. Instead he'd left himself in a constant state of agony.

He shifted in his seat and went back to the menu.

"We have desserts on the menu," Dante said, wishing Franco would go away and leave him to his misery. "I was thinking of adding a walnut and ricotta cake to—"

"No, no." Franco waved a hand at him. "Something . . . *ma petite.*" He pinched his fingers together.

Dante eyed the maître d'. Franco rarely gave input on the menu. In fact, Franco was usually pretty content to stick to his job up front and leave the rest to everyone else. All of a sudden, he was spouting dessert ideas? "What have you got cooking?"

"Me?" Franco raised a brow and shrugged a shoulder. "I cannot cook."

"You have something in mind, though. Quit dancing and tell me what it is."

Franco directed his gaze at the place settings instead of his boss, as if perfecting the flair of the napkins was infinitely more important. "I know a shop that makes perfect little cookies. Just right for an after dinner delight."

Dante considered this. "Instead of mints? Or chocolates like the other restaurants do?"

Franco nodded. "A little Vita Deliziosa to go."

Dante nodded, then went back to the menu, crossing out the fish for Tuesday and substituting a veal. Carlo's Fish Market hadn't been up to its usual freshness standard, not since Carlo had gone on the lam in Italy with the maid. While wrapping a swordfish—and nearly beating the poor dead *pesce spada* into unrecognizability with the plastic wrap machine—the usurped wife had told Dante she'd be gunning for Carlo with a tuna as soon as he landed at Logan. Until Dante could find a new fishmonger—or Carlo solved his two-honey housekeeping mess—Dante was going to stick to non-swimming menu items.

Above his shoulder, he could feel Franco waiting for an answer. "I'll look into it."

"No need to think." A box appeared in front of him, open to reveal several chocolate thumbprint cookies that had raspberry jam in their centers. The scent of the jam wafted up to greet him, teasing at him to take a bite. "Try."

Dante sighed and pushed the menu to the side. "Persistent, aren't you?"

Franco didn't answer.

It certainly wouldn't hurt to eat one. He hadn't had time for breakfast or lunch yet today. Dante put his pen down and picked up a cookie, taking a taste. "Not bad. Where'd you get them?"

"Oh, nowhere." Franco fluffed at a carnation in the center of the table.

Dante closed the lid on the box. Imprinted in gold script were the words "Gift Baskets to Die For." Franco was a matchmaker with all the stealth of an elephant trying to sneak up on a kitten. "Maria's shop?"

"Oh? Is that who works there?" He fluttered a finger at the flower's tip.

"She co-owns it."

"*Interessante!*"

"Franco, you're the worst liar I know."

"Franco does not lie." He bustled over to the front desk and straightened the pile of menus. "Much," he added in a mumble.

Dante took another nibble of the cookie. "They *are* good."

Franco bustled back. "The best."

"They *would* make good thank-you gifts for our customers," Dante said.

"*Magnifico.*" Franco kissed the tips of his fingers.

"And I do know one of the owners."

"And you have to see her many times to work on these. To make them perfect." He grinned.

"You never give up, do you?"

"Me?" Franco took a cookie from the box and bit into it. "I like cookies, nothing more." Then he walked away, humming a Dean Martin song under his breath.

Dante returned to his menu but his mind was no longer on the Milanese Veal Chops. He tossed the pen to the table and got to his feet. Franco was right, though damned if Dante was going to admit it and eat crow for a month.

It was time to add a little sweetness to his Vita.

Rebecca's Take-a-Chance-on-Your-Heart Stuffed Artichokes

6 large artichokes
1 teaspoon lemon juice
3 slices day-old bread, ground into bread crumbs
3 anchovy filets
2 cloves garlic
2 tablespoons capers, rinsed and minced
3 tablespoons fresh parsley, chopped
4 tablespoons olive oil
Salt and pepper
6 tablespoons olive oil
6 tablespoons water

Just like with a man, remove the outermost spiny leaves of the artichoke to get to the best layers beneath. Cut off the stem and the tips of the tallest leaves, then hollow out the inner bristly "choke." Now you have the best of the artichoke, without all those silly walls it puts up to keep from getting hurt.

Put the prepared artichoke in a bowl of water deep enough to cover them, adding the lemon juice while you're working on the stuffing. Preheat the oven to 375 degrees. Mix the bread crumbs, anchovies, garlic, capers, parsley and four tablespoons of oil together. Season with salt and pepper. This is the stuffing that will bring out the best of your artichoke. It's like the final ingredient you bring to the perfect match for your heart.

Drain and stuff the artichokes. Place them stuffed side

down in a roasting pan, close enough to snuggle together. Mix the oil and water and drizzle over them. Trust me, this will be wonderful.

Cover tightly with foil and bake for an hour. When it's done, the artichokes will have tender hearts, filled with flavor and bursting with joy. Everyone deserves a happy ending, especially when it's waiting right under their noses.

CHAPTER 15

Hell, Maria had decided, was a constant diet, filled with nothing but vending machines stuffed with diet sodas and lettuce. She walked over to Gift Baskets in the early Friday morning April sunshine, avoiding the Big Dig construction and a few hoots from the orange-vested workers. She picked her way past the pothole puddles and faux Rolex vendors hoping to convince the tourists a bargain could be found under the old Central Artery.

She shouldn't have walked to work. She should have traveled in a bubble. The constant smells of the bakeries, the rolling cart vendors, the breakfast restaurants—all nearly undid her.

Three weeks of hell. And seven damned pounds to show for it. That wasn't enough to make a dent in the way her panty hose fit, never mind her pom-poms.

A businessman strode by her, a six-pack box of Dunkin' Donuts in his hand, and she nearly tackled him out of need.

Finally, the shop came into view. Maria ducked inside and shut the door, backing herself up against the glass, lest she be tempted to run back outside and assault the doughnut-bearing investment banker. "I can't be alone out there," she said.

"Crime up in your neighborhood again?" Rebecca asked.

"No. Damned bakeries are increasing their aroma output."

Rebecca nodded, her brown ponytail swinging in emphasis. "That'll do it. Maybe you should take to wearing a gas mask."

"Oh, that would be attractive."

"You could call it smog apparel. Start a new trend. Make millions."

Maria came away from the door and crossed to the coatrack. She hung up her coat, then stowed her purse behind the counter. "And retire someplace where no one can cook and the only food product is salad fixings?"

"When you're rich, everyone loves you, even if you're as big as the Prudential building."

Maria joined Rebecca at the counter and helped her set out the new display of gift items for spring. "So you're telling me I should get rich instead of thin?"

"Come on out back, and while we talk, help me with this basket order so we can both get rich."

Maria followed Rebecca and the two of them set to work on a birthday basket for four-year-old Timothy Barnes. The eighteen-inch parental guilt gift was just big enough to hold the mother lode of toys Timmy's mom had purchased, along with candies and treats. Rebecca was delivering it to Timmy's classroom later that afternoon, timed to induce proper classmate envy and one-upmanship in the swanky Charlestown neighborhood where the Barneses lived and competed with the Joneses.

"You're doing great," Rebecca said to Maria, handing her a stuffed Steiff teddy dressed up as an aviator.

Maria tucked the bear in front of the "Happy Birthday, Timmy" sign and added four boxes of toy cars on either flank. "This isn't exactly rocket science. Just a few toys and some cookies. We do these all the time."

"I didn't mean the basket, silly. I meant your diet. It's showing, in your face and hips. You're looking good."

"You notice a difference already?" She hated to admit it, but the Chubby Chums had been a help. Maria had gone to all three meetings last week and despite Bert's Eeyore-on-suicide-watch perspective, she'd found enough motivation to stick to her diet.

"Of course. You're gorgeous to begin with, but now you're starting to make us all look like Macbeth's witches on a bad day." Rebecca laughed good-naturedly. "The mailman about killed himself handing you the mail yesterday. Most days he dumps it on the counter and backs out fast, giving the rest of us ordinary folk a little grunt."

"It was only because Lester had on his glasses yesterday. The man is, what, sixty-four?"

Rebecca wagged a toy drumstick at her. "Men's hormones are the last thing to die, believe me. The heart, the brain, the liver. All of those can quit ticking and the testosterone just keeps going."

Maria twisted some blue satin into a bow and secured the decoration with a piece of thin floral wire. "Well, there's only one man I'm looking to impress."

"That Dante you mentioned?"

Hearing his name caused a catch in her breathing. He'd been on her mind, in her dreams, ever since that Tuesday night with the chess game. And the wine. And the kiss . . .

He'd been right, damn him. She hadn't been able to forget him. But that was only because he was a good kisser. Not because she had some masochistic need to tie herself to one man forever.

"Dante has made it clear I'd impress him in a tent and flip-flops." Maria shook her head. "No, I have my sights set on Antonio. We knew each other in high school."

"An old flame—"

"With a big torch."

Rebecca laughed. "That's the best kind to reunite with." She unrolled a large sheet of plastic and wrapped it around the finished basket while Maria turned the gift and helped her. "So, dish. When are you seeing him?"

"He's in town this weekend, but . . ."

"But you're avoiding him because you have no need for wild sex?" Rebecca pressed the back of her hand to Maria's forehead. "Are you ill? Maybe I should get you over to Mass General."

"I just don't feel"—Maria waved vaguely at her shape— "ready."

"What? I've never known you not to feel ready for a man." Rebecca grinned and leaned closer to Maria. "Besides, when the lights are off, everyone looks ten pounds thinner."

Maria laughed. "You have a point." She grabbed her cell phone off the counter and flipped it open, scrolling through the recent calls until she got to Antonio's number. "All right. I'll call him. Give myself a little treat for the weekend."

And get my mind off Dante once and for all.

Rebecca withdrew a cookie from the leftover pile on the counter and wagged it at Maria. "And if it doesn't work out with Antonio, there are always cookies. Fat-free, of course."

Antonio's deep greeting carried through the cellular connection and Maria forgot the dessert in Rebecca's hands. "Hi, Antonio. It's Maria."

"I thought you'd never call," he said. "I'm in Boston. Alone. That's no way to see a city."

"What part did you want to see?"

"What's the view from your bedroom window?"

She swallowed. Who needed Guido's when there was Antonio? Damn. She thought of the half-assed attempt by Harvey the Exterminator to make something happen in her bedroom four months ago. "Where are you?"

"Where do you want me to be?"

The bell over the front door rang and Rebecca headed out to the shop. Now that she was away from Rebecca's encouraging glances, Maria's belief that she really would look slimmer in the dark disappeared.

"Maria? Can we get together tonight?" Antonio asked.

"I can't. I'm—" She racked her brain for the excuse she'd given the last time but came up empty. Living on rabbit food and air didn't seem like a good enough reason not to see him.

"Don't say no. See me tonight for dinner. Drinks. Anything you want. We can catch up or"—he let out a low chuckle—"make some new memories."

Maria glanced down at herself and shook her head. In ten more pounds, maybe. "Antonio—"

"You know, I've always thought you were a smart woman," he said. "If we go out tonight, we can talk. I can get your ideas. Pick your brain and maybe"—another sexy laugh traveled through the phone lines—"more than that."

"You think I'm smart?"

"The brains of Einstein and the looks of Aphrodite. Perfection in one woman."

A man who wanted her for her mind, not just her body? Was that possible? Rekindling the flame with Antonio on an adult level fulfilled fantasies they didn't even run on the Playboy Channel. For a second, she allowed herself to think about the best of both worlds—being in bed with him and being appreciated for her mind.

Then she went back to being in bed with him. *Mamma mia.*

She took in a breath. "I don't look *exactly* like Aphrodite anymore."

"Ah, you will always be beautiful to me." She could almost hear him smiling on the other end. "Come, go out with me. Don't say no. You'll break my heart."

"You're such a cliché."

"I'm Italian. It's in my blood."

She laughed. "You're a hard man to resist."

"I try. So will you be there?"

Maria considered for a minute. If she unearthed the stomach flattening, aka sausage casing, underwear from her lingerie drawer, wore all black and put on high heels to make her legs look slimmer, then she might be able to pass for a size ten. In dim light. She'd leave her hair down and not eat anything over two hundred calories for the rest of the day. "It's a date." She sputtered out her address.

"No. It's a pleasure." Then he was gone, leaving her with a smile on her face.

Maria hung up, breathless, then headed out to the front of the shop to find Rebecca. "I need a Diet Coke and a trip to Victoria's Secret."

Rebecca laughed. "Sounds like you have a date tonight."

"Am I too late?"

Maria wheeled around. Dante stood in the doorway, Candace beside him, the open door against her hip. For a moment, he seemed so much realer—more manly—than Antonio ever had.

A crazy thought. It was only because Dante was here and Antonio was not.

"Too late for what?" Maria asked.

"To ask you to a picnic for two on Castle Island."

"I've already made plans."

Dante took a step closer, his gaze on hers. "If those plans change—"

You and Mamma will fit me for a ring and a house on a cul de sac.

No, thank you.

"I know where you are." She cocked her head. "Why aren't you there right now?"

He held up a small white box of cookies from the shop. "These. I want them."

He wasn't here to see her. She'd just made plans with another man, so why did she feel disappointed?

"We have a dozen of those in the case," she said, slipping into business mode.

"I want more. Much more."

"We can get another few dozen baked up tomorrow."

He shook his head. "More."

She paused. "Are we talking cookies?"

"Of course. Aren't you?" His grin looked about as innocent as a monk at a Vegas slot machine with a roll of quarters up his puffy sleeve.

"You have a sudden sweet tooth or are you ordering these for something special?"

"Franco thought they'd make great after dinner treats for our customers. I tried one and have to agree. You could attach a card advertising your shop to them." He grinned. "You kiss me and I kiss you."

"Isn't the phrase about scratching backs?"

His grin turned devilish. "I don't have that kind of itch."

She thought of that kiss at her door and something inside her melted.

"You, ah, might want to see a doctor about that."

He put the box of cookies into his inside jacket pocket. "So, are you up for a rematch?"

"Rematch? Of what?"

"Our chess game. I believe you owe me a chance to win back my dignity."

No. She was *not* going to go there again. Too much temptation. She had Antonio, after all, and that's who she wanted. She pulled out an order pad and scribbled the restaurant's name and address at the top. "Business first. Total humiliation later."

Dante leaned against the counter. "I'll need enough cookies for every diner we have each night." He did a few quick mental calculations and gave her a number.

Maria nodded, making notes in the columns. "You could try our Chocolate Treasure Cookies for special customers. They've got like a roll outside and chocolate on the inside. People call them our "surprise is inside" delights. They're great for customers with birthdays or engagements, anniversaries, things like that."

"Good idea."

"And if you have customers who come in regularly, you could put together a little gift basket"—Maria crossed to the workbench and withdrew a square four-by-four-inch dark cranberry basket with gold trim—"like this with some cookies in it. Once in a while send them a special gift as a thank you."

Dante considered the basket, turning it over in his palm. "There are a few people who have been coming to Vita since the day it opened. That would be a nice way to really show them my appreciation."

"Building goodwill is always a good idea."

"You're absolutely right." He smiled. "You're a smart woman."

Two men in one day to say that. Must be something in the smog today. If she heard it any more, she'd be signing up for Mensa.

"Thanks."

"I mean it. You know your stuff. I'm not just talking

about what you did with the food critic either. These ideas are the kinds of things that will make Vita a bit different from the other restaurants. Set us apart, give us that touch people remember. Make it live up to its name." His gaze softened and he put the basket back on the counter. "And my dad's vision."

"Well, good." Maria swallowed, wanting to touch him, to somehow show she'd heard the emotion in his voice, but not quite knowing how to do that. She opted to do nothing because it was easier than saying words that would build any more of a connection with him. "I'm glad I could help."

"So," Dante said, his voice changing in pitch back to normal tones, "how do I do that with you?"

"Do what?"

"Build goodwill." He twirled the basket on the smooth Corian surface. "I think it's going to take more than some wicker and a few cookies."

"Why do you keep trying? I told you, I'm not interested."

"In me? Or dating?"

"Both."

"Bull." He gestured to her cell phone. "You made a date for tonight."

"With a man who has no use for marriage and doesn't expect anything out of me."

Dante gave her a lopsided smile. "Now where's the fun in that?"

She wasn't going to answer that question. Not now, not later. Not until she was seventy-five and no one cared if she was married.

She didn't want commitment and predictability. Both were traps that sucked in her heart and made her trust. Then, when she least expected it, she'd find another woman under the man who "loved" her because Maria hadn't been enough for him.

She put on her professional face, totaled up his order and raised her pen to the date section. "When would you like the first delivery?"

"As soon as you're available."

"Sorry. Not my department." She gave him a pleasant, noncommittal smile. "Rebecca is the ambassador of goodwill. And good cookies." Maria tore off the order sheet and handed it to Dante. "She'll take care of you."

He took the paper, folded it and put it in his shirt pocket without looking at it. "You wouldn't be avoiding me, would you?"

"Of course not." But even as she said the words, she knew they were a lie. She was in charge of sales. She could both assign and personally take over an account. Neither Candace nor Rebecca would care. She told herself it was easier this way. Distance herself from him now— before all the wine and linguine reeled her into the exact web her mother wanted to weave for her daughter.

He leaned in close, the look in his eyes half tease, half desire. And maybe, a flicker of disappointment, too. "Like I told you before, you're a really bad liar. And I intend to prove it to you."

Then he was gone. And Maria knew she was in trouble. Dante was as stubborn as her mother.

If Biba Pagliano and Dante Del Rosso ever joined forces, Maria would be a goner.

Nonna's Theory-of-Men Tri-Colored
Fusilli with Vegetables

1 red onion, sliced
3 cloves garlic
Olive oil
1 big zucchini
Thyme
Marjoram
1 pound fusilli
Basil leaves
Salt and pepper
1 large red pepper
1 large yellow pepper
2 tomatoes, chopped
Fresh parsley
Grated Parmigiano Reggiano

Don't be asking me for measurements now. I cook the old way—throw it in by instinct. It's how you should choose a man, too. Trust your nose; it'll tell you if he's a good choice or if you should put him on the curb for the pigeons to crap on.

Dice your onions and garlic, then saute them with the oil. Next, slice the zucchini into little sticks. Sauté it with some thyme and marjoram in the same pan. Dip a ladle in the pasta water, drop it into your pan, then cover and simmer your zucchini till it's as tender as a man's true heart. If he isn't nice to you, you don't need him. Life's too short for men with no manners for a lady.

Cook the fusilli until al dente. Meanwhile, add lots of basil, a bit of oil, some salt and pepper to your zucchini. Go with your instincts. They'll tell you the right choice to make. In life and in cooking.

Dice your peppers, sauté them for a bit in a separate pan, just to soften their hard shells (like a man who needs a swift kick from a woman to get his smart ass in gear), then add the chopped tomatoes. Salt as needed.

A little seasoning is always a good thing. Like a good fight adds spice to a marriage. Keeps him on his toes and doesn't let him get too comfortable in his damned chair.

Stir in the drained fusilli and zucchini, cover and cook for another minute or two. Serve with the Parmigiano on the side. That's the only thing your man should have on the side—a little cheese.

If it doesn't work out, then toss the whole thing and start again. It's just a meal, not a marriage. With a man, you need a bit more patience and a hell of a big sense of humor.

CHAPTER 16

She had to go in there..It was either that or play subway sumo wrestling with the other five o'clock commuters to get over to Downtown Crossing and pray she could find something that fit—and she could afford—in twenty minutes, then hop back on the train for home.

Antonio was coming at seven. She didn't have enough time for T games.

Maria stood on the sidewalk outside her mother's house off of Hanover Street and debated. Inside was a killer black dress she'd stored in her old bedroom. The kind of dress guaranteed to make Antonio sweat.

But another very dangerous thing lurked inside. Her mother's quilting club.

She squared her shoulders and vowed to march in there, grab the dress out of the back bedroom and—

Sneak out the back door before those women could get their matchmaking paws on her.

She made it as far as the front hall. "Maria? Is that you?" her mother called from the dining room table. "Come, say hello."

"Mamma, I'm late. I need to grab a dress and—"

"You come in. Say hello." When her mother spoke in that tone, arguing with her was about as productive as trying to take a bone from a pit bull.

Maria poked her head into the dining room as little as possible. "Nice to see you, Mrs. Tamburo and Mrs. Benedetto. Hello, Nonna."

She didn't pull her head back fast enough. Rosa Benedetto was the first to put in her ante. "Maria, my Nicky is out on parole next week, you know."

"Great." Maria tried again to leave but Mamma came up beside her, blocking the way. She bent over, ostensibly looking for thread in the little sewing caddy beside the doorway.

"You always liked Nicky," Rosa said, arching a brow. "He has the eyes."

"What eyes? I never see no eyes," Lucia Tamburo said.

"The eyes. The kind women like," Rosa said.

"Women like eyes that stay at home. Not go roaming around the neighborhood like a tomcat in heat," Nonna said. She snipped the end of the thread on the pastel baby quilt she was making as a good luck charm for newlywed and as-yet-not-pregnant cousin Rosina. "He got eyes like that?"

"He's been in jail for three years. He's gonna look at his woman, believe me." Rosa put down her sewing and gave Maria a nod. "He always like you. Whenever I go see him at Cedar Junction, he say, 'Mamma, how's that Maria? She was a looker.' "

Mamma found a spool of black thread and straightened. "How he going to support my daughter with the jail on his record?"

"Mamma, I'm not marrying Nicky. I'm only here to borrow—"

"Are you saying my Nicky isn't good enough for your daughter?"

"Beggars can't be choosers," Lucia said with a shrug. "Not at her age."

"I am not that—"

"Rosa, you know trouble hangs around Nicky like pigeons around a bakery." Mamma took a seat across from Rosa and picked up her wedding ring pattern quilt.

Rosa thrust a fist onto her hip. "Nicky is not trouble."

"Then why is he in jail?" Nonna asked. "Three years is no vacation."

"He didn't take that car. He borrowed it. How you expect him to get to work with no car?"

Mamma waved a hand and let out a mutter of disagreement.

"God gave him two legs," Nonna said. "And a subway system."

"Nicky can't ride the T." Rosa heaved a sigh. "He's color blind."

"Maria should date my grandson," Lucia piped up. "He's very good with color. You should see how he decorated the ladies' bathroom at the Sons of Italy hall. The boy knows his pinks." She emphasized the point with a needle.

Maria knew the only way to end this. Offer herself up for sacrifice. "Actually, I have a date tonight."

The heads of all four women in the room swiveled faster than a lazy Susan on a power drill. "You do?" they said in concert.

"Yes. That's why I need the dress. I don't want to be late."

Mamma jumped to her feet. "We get the dress."

"I can get it myself. It's in my old closet."

"I help you; make sure you get the right one." Mamma was fast on Maria's heels now, her hand at her daughter's back, lest she escape without providing details.

They headed up the stairs to Maria's old room. "Who is this boy? What does he do?"

"Mamma . . ." Maria warned. "It's just a date. Nothing more."

"Do I know his family?" Her mother put a finger to her chin. "Is it Angie Giovanni's boy? He's no good, you know. Never calls his mother."

"It's not him." They had reached the top of the stairs. The door to Maria's old bedroom was three feet to the left. "Mamma, I can get my own dress."

Her mother didn't take a hint well. She opened the door for her daughter and entered the room, taking a seat on the old twin bed with the pink ruffled comforter. "Where is he taking you? Somewhere nice?"

"I don't know. We didn't talk about it yet."

Her mother tsk-tsked. "Not a good sign. A man should warn a woman. Let her be ready."

Maria opened the closet door and rummaged past the size sixes. Shoved the size eights aside. Took a longing glance at the tens before digging past them and finding the black dress she was looking for. Long, sleek, shiny.

And best of all, with a ten percent Lycra count.

"Make sure he opens the door." Mamma reached back and fluffed the two pillows, even though they had gone unused for the better part of eight years. "He treat you nice, or he answer to your papa."

"Mamma—" Maria bit her tongue. She could stand here and argue chivalrous conduct for an hour or just nod her head and escape unscathed. "He'll hold the door. Or he'll answer to me first."

Mamma rose and crossed to her daughter. She patted Maria's cheek. "That's my girl. So strong."

"Thanks, Mamma."

Her mother's face took on a stern look. "But don't

be so strong you act like a man. Ask for help with the car, the sink." She nodded. "Men, they like that."

"I'm not some damsel in distress who needs a man to help me out of the castle." Maria shifted the dress in her arms. "I can change my own oil, fix my own faucet, even pay bills without any help. I don't need a man to fix anything."

Mamma's soft brown eyes met hers. "Ah, but you do, *cara.*" Her palm rested again on Maria's cheek, but this time in a quiet, gentle touch. "To fix your heart."

Antonio's Tempting-Maria Wine-Stuffed Apples

½ cup golden raisins
½ cup dried cherries
1 cinnamon stick
½ cup sugar
Pinch of grated nutmeg
Grated lemon zest
¾ cup water
¾ cup Marsala wine
6 tart apples
3 tablespoons butter

Ah, apples. The fruit of temptation. Start by combining everything but the butter and the apples. Let this spicy stuffing sit for an hour while you whisper the sweet words she wants to hear.

Preheat the oven to 375 degrees while she's getting hot, from the magic of your touch and your words. Wash and core the apples, being sure not to cut through the bottoms. Wouldn't want your stuffing to leak out too soon, now would you? Divide the delectable mixture between the apples, filling the hollowed cores just as you'll fill the empty void in her Friday night.

Arrange the apples in a buttered dish. Pour the remaining wine mixture around them, then top each with a little pat of butter for additional richness.

Bake for 40 to 50 minutes, basting with the wine mixture every few minutes. Serve hot, with a dish of cold ice cream on the side. The mixture of sensations is guaranteed to set her palate on fire while the wine will sweeten the way for you.

And she'll be putty in your hands once again.

CHAPTER 17

Maria heard Antonio before she saw him. The red Ferrari came zooming down her street, breaking the speed limit three times over. When he stopped outside her building, the tires squealed in protest.

She headed downstairs to greet him. He stood outside the car, holding the passenger's side door open with all the flourish of one of Bob Barker's girls.

"Maria," he said in a dark, deep tone that made her name sound like the title of a really good porno.

And all comparisons to game show help disappeared.

Antonio's black hair was slicked back from his head, emphasizing his dark eyes. He wore a white collarless shirt open at the neck and tapered black dress pants that showed off his trim, tight abs.

Oh, Mamma.

She came around the car to his side. "Hi."

A long, slow smile stole across his features. "You haven't seen me in years. Can't you come up with a better greeting?" Then he leaned forward and brushed his lips against hers.

The Fourth of July fireworks over the Esplanade had

nothing over a kiss from Antonio. He was good. No, he was damned good. And she remembered all over again why she'd offered to be his love slave back in high school.

"There," he said, ending the kiss, "that's how you say hello to an old friend."

"I can't wait to see how we say good-bye."

He chuckled and wrapped an arm around her, easing her into the car. "Patience, *bignole*, patience," he said, calling her "cream puff," just as he had all those years ago.

He came around the other side and slid into the driver's seat of the Ferrari, then put it in gear and roared forward. Maria's silky dress slid against the cream leather seat. She braced herself with a hand on the dash.

"Am I going too fast for you?"

"A little."

He chuckled. "You haven't seen anything yet." And he depressed the accelerator again, commanding the windy streets of Boston with the skill of a teenager at the helm of Mortal Kombat.

A few minutes later, they arrived at a ritzy downtown restaurant. Antonio pulled up to the valet, handed over the Ferrari, then joined Maria on her side. Together, they walked into the restaurant, Antonio's arm slipping in against her waist.

"You look beautiful," he whispered in her ear.

She glanced at him to see if he was lying, but his gaze was clear. "Not the same as in high school."

"Better," he murmured. "More of a woman now."

Whew. It was warm in here. She might have to get home and get out of this dress soon.

Antonio nuzzled against her hair.

Very soon.

The diet had been a success, even with only a few pounds of loss. As had her almost calorie-free day. If she could just refrain from eating tonight, too, she'd be okay.

Otherwise, Maria knew the first big bite she had would make her explode at the seams like an overfilled Mylar balloon.

Within a few minutes, they were seated and had ordered. Antonio asked the waiter for a martini and a bottle of Soave.

"I don't really drink," Maria said.

"Don't worry," he told her, leaning forward, his hand grasping hers. "I'll be joining you." When he looked at her like that, refusal didn't seem to be an option.

At least with the menu she managed to stick to her resolution. She went with the skinless chicken topped with roasted vegetables with a side salad.

For dessert, she'd have a bowl of Antonio. With whipped cream and extra chocolate sauce on the side.

After the waiter left, she watched him sip his martini, and told herself this was exactly what she wanted. A date with a sexy man. A no-strings, no expectations evening. A fun time in bed and a kiss good-bye in the morning.

She didn't want someone else's slippers on her bedroom floor. Another's towel hanging on her shower door. Someone else's coat taking up the second hook by the door.

Been there, done that. Only an idiot whacked her head against the same wall twice.

Antonio put his glass down and reached for her hand. "It's been a long time, Maria."

She sipped her wine. The Soave went down smooth and easy. "More years than I care to count. Makes me feel old."

"Oh, you aren't old. You're just better." The smile that crossed his lips told her the exact kind of better he was anticipating.

"And you're still the same flirt as always."

"I do my best to live up to my reputation," he said, grinning. They exchanged small talk until the waiter came by, depositing their meals with a minimum of interruption.

Worried about potential Lycra stressing, Maria picked at her chicken, leaving half her plate untouched. What she had eaten was delicious and it took tremendous self-restraint not to dive across the table and suck down Antonio's lobster casserole. She stuck instead to beverages, especially the wine.

Wine held virtually no calories and beverages, she reasoned, didn't boast the same dress-straining properties as solid food.

From his side of the table, Antonio flirted just enough to let Maria know he was still interested. Very interested.

Clearly, he hadn't noticed the extra pounds. Or maybe he had, and didn't care.

And why did she care what he thought so much, anyway? If he were that shallow that he would reject her over a dress size, then Dante was right—she needed to start pulling from the deep end of the dating pool.

Maria bit into a sliver of chicken and swallowed that thought. Dante, right? Well, she certainly wouldn't tell him that.

"What's on your mind, *bignole?*"

"Oh, nothing," Maria lied. "Just lost in the company."

Antonio shoved his empty plate to the edge of the table, placing his silverware in precise straight lines atop the white china surface. "Do you remember those days in high school?"

She took a gulp of her wine and caught his gaze. "Oh, yeah."

"They were fun, weren't they?"

She smiled and took another long sip, trying not to look at the half-eaten dinner, which had been so delicious . . . too delicious. "Lots of good memories."

Antonio removed his napkin from his lap and folded it into precise quarters, then laid it on the table to his right. "And do you remember, in English class, how you'd help me sometimes?"

"Do your homework is more like it," she teased. "Did you ever read a word of Shakespeare?"

"Only the sex scenes." He grinned.

"Just what I thought. You missed a lot of great literature."

"I was too busy staring at you. I couldn't keep my mind on all those silly plays."

She flushed and took another sip from her goblet. When she placed it on the table again, Antonio drew the bottle out of the marble wine caddy and refilled the glass. "I wasn't going to have any more wine," she said.

"Life is about indulging," Antonio said, pouring. "Drink deeply of it."

"Now *that* sounds like Shakespeare."

"See, I learned something while I was staring at your legs." He grinned and signaled to the waiter for another martini. Then he steepled his hands and directed the full force of his gaze on her face. "I have a . . . proposition for you."

She picked up her glass to sip again, and realized she was more tipsy than she thought. Heat flooded her face and flushed against her chest. Maria lowered the goblet to the table without drinking. She should have eaten more. She felt so . . . empty inside. It had to be the beverage dinner.

"The way you say it, it sounds illegal," she said.

"No, no, nothing illegal. Just a little . . . help." He smiled.

The waiter came by with Antonio's second martini. "Can I interest you in dessert?"

"No," Antonio said. "We have plans for dessert." And he sent Maria a wink that made the flush on her chest flame red.

And yet, the empty feeling seemed to multiply. She

reached for her goblet and drained it, trying to fill whatever was missing.

It didn't work. It did, however, make the room start to spin in a very interesting way.

The waiter nodded. "I'll be back momentarily with your bill."

Antonio reached for his wallet. "Let me settle this and then we'll talk back at your place."

The wine had settled into her like a comfy blanket and she leaned against the soft chair, a happy grin on her face. "Sure."

By the time they got back to Maria's apartment, the happy feeling had begun to wear off, replaced by one of exhaustion. She slumped against her leather sofa, trying her best to maintain decent posture so the Lycra wouldn't have to do the work of Hercules to hold her body in the dress. "So . . . what was this idea you mentioned?" Some of the words kind of blurred together in her head. Had they come out that way, too?

Antonio took the seat beside her on the caramel love seat, turning so that his arm draped over the back of the couch and his fingers toyed with her hair. Ah, that felt good. Sort of like a scalp massage by dwarves. Maria smiled.

"I don't want to talk about work now," he said, his voice all deep and throaty, coming to her as if through a tunnel. "Not with you looking so beautiful."

She smiled. "I take it you don't want me for my mind, then?"

Antonio chuckled. "Since when has that ever been my focus?" He reached out a hand and cupped her breast, his thumb rolling over the nipple through the fabric with an expert touch that said he'd done it a hundred times before and knew what would make her turn on like a spigot.

But for some reason, this time it didn't work. Maybe

it was the wine. The heat of the room. The fact that she'd barely consumed three hundred calories all day.

"Maria," Antonio whispered, moving his face closer and his hand into a more aggressive grip.

"Antonio—"

"Ah, baby, I love the way you say my name." Then he closed his eyes and kissed her.

She felt—

Nothing. His kiss, which had seemed so wonderful before now felt about as exciting as hanging Nonna's girdle on the clothesline. There was no answering zing from her hormones. They'd all gone on hiatus.

Or maybe, David had broken her heart so damned well that it had turned off the connection to her libido, too.

Dante, her mind reminded her, made her hormones stand at attention. *Dante* awakened those nerve endings. *Dante* succeeded where Antonio—

"No," she said against his mouth, then pulled back, the room a wild kaleidoscope. "I'm sorry, Antonio, but I can't do this. Not tonight."

His hand moved up to cup her face as gentle as he would handle a butterfly. "What's the matter, *bignole?*"

"I-I—don't feel so well," she managed. And she didn't.

Her stomach, filled with more wine than food, rebelled against her. She could feel it rolling and pitching, a ship caught in a hurricane. She scrambled backward, trying for purchase on the leather sofa, but the silky dress was having none of that. The fabric was made for sliding off easily, not helping her get to the bathroom before—

Too late. Her dinner and her wine made a return appearance on Antonio's pants.

"Oh, my God," she said, "I'm so sorry, Antonio. Let me—"

He was already backing away from her, fast as a germophobe encountering a flu sufferer. "No, let me. You're obviously not, ah, well." He glanced at his pants, bit back a look of disgust, then gave her a wobbly smile. "I'll get cleaned up and leave you alone."

Maria moaned and flopped back against the sofa. Big mistake. Like a greased pig, she slid off the love seat and landed with a thud on the floor.

She lay there, figuring it was the only safe place to be until her stomach settled, and vowed never, ever to go on another diet.

In the morning she would play Megabucks. At this point, becoming a millionaire was her only hope of ever getting laid again.

Vinny's True-Love-is-Hot
Deviled Chicken

½ cup olive oil
Zest and juice of one lemon
2 cloves garlic, minced
2 teaspoons red chilies, minced
Salt and pepper
4 chicken breasts

When you're in love, there's no denying the heat you feel for your lady. It's like a flame that won't go out. Sort of like a butane burner that's on all day. Geez, if someone would invent one of those . . .

No. We're talking about a good woman here. She's the heat in your heart, so serve her this chicken and she'll feel the warmth, too. Combine the oil, lemon rind, juice, garlic and chilies in a large, shallow dish. Add salt and pepper to taste, depending on how much more spice you want. Heat is good. In everything.

Mix well, creating harmony in one place, as you have with your lady. Add the chicken breasts, turning to coat evenly. Cover and marinade in the refrigerator for at least four hours. If you can stand the wait, let it sit overnight. Me, I'm not that patient. When I got something to say, man, I gotta get it out or I'll burst.

Anyway, when it's done marinating, broil or grill the chicken until cooked thoroughly. Ignore the flames of the stove. You're thinking about the love of your life here so it's important you keep your mind on her, not the way the fire kind of licks up at the pan, reaching for—

Damn. That was close. Serve the chicken with a diamond ring and a bended knee proposal and you'll be sure to keep your love on high heat forever.

Zebra Contemporary

If the FREE Book Certificate is missing, call 1-800-770-1963 to place your order. Be sure to visit our website at www.kensingtonbooks.com.

FREE BOOK CERTIFICATE

Yes! Please send me FREE Zebra Contemporary romance novels. I only pay $1.99 for shipping and handling. I understand that each month thereafter I will be able to preview 4 brand-new Contemporary Romances FREE for 10 days. Then, if I should decide to keep them, I will pay the money-saving preferred subscriber's price (that's a savings of up to 30% off the retail price), plus shipping and handling. I understand I am under no obligation to purchase any books, as explained on this card.

Name _____

Address _____ Apt. _____

City _____ State _____ Zip _____

Telephone (___) _____

Signature _____

(If under 18, parent or guardian must sign)

Thank You!

Offer limited to one per household and not to current subscribers. Terms, offer and prices subject to change. Orders subject to acceptance by Zebra Contemporary Book Club. Offer Valid in the U.S. only.

CN035A

ll..l..l..ll...lll.l.l..ll.l.l.l.l..ll.l..l.l..l.l.ll..l

Zebra Contemporary Romance Book Club
Zebra Home Subscription Service, Inc.
P.O. Box 5214
Clifton , NJ 07015-5214

PLACE
STAMP
HERE

CHAPTER 18

Dante came into work Saturday afternoon after a sleepless night spent dreaming too much about a woman who didn't want him. He grabbed up his apron and wrapped it around his waist. He'd concentrate on work. That plan had always worked in the past.

It better damned well work now. Because he didn't have a backup.

"How's it going, Vinny?" he asked.

"All under control, Boss." His sous chef grinned and went back to slicing red peppers, laying them in a roasting pan for broiling.

"Are *you* staying on track?" Dante asked as he crossed into the walk-in refrigerator and pulled out a sheet of chicken breasts to marinate.

"I got my mother on my back again, but I'm okay." He shrugged. "She thinks I should marry Theresa."

"Well, do you love her?"

Vinny finished the peppers and then drizzled them with olive oil. "I had a kid with her. So, yeah."

The entire kitchen staff was buzzing with pre-dinner chores, so Dante whisked the marinade together, then coated the breasts himself, flipping them and moving on without losing a second of time. He liked doing the cooking himself, rather than delegating.

The management part of running the restaurant had never been his favorite part of the job. Too much worrying about juggling the balls of employee morale, benefits, marketing and business development. He'd much rather be getting his hands into the anchovies and artichokes. "You either love a woman or you don't, Vin."

Now done with the peppers, Vinny grabbed a stack of garlic cloves. He slammed the side of a butcher knife against the pile, then peeled them like a mother undressing quadruplets for a bath. "I better. I got her pregnant again."

"Theresa's having another baby?"

Vinny stopped peeling to beam an expectant father smile across the stainless steel kitchen. "By Christmas. Told her not to put anything under the tree but my son."

"You know it's a boy?"

Vinny nodded. "I got intuition."

Dante finished the chicken breasts off with an extra dusting of dried red chilies, then returned them to the cooler. He didn't comment on Vinny's psychic abilities. "How's Theresa feel about getting married?"

"She hung a wedding gown on my side of the closet. First thing I see whenever I get out a pair of shoes."

"I'd say she's in favor of the idea." He sprayed disinfectant over the prep area and cleaned it. "What are you going to do?"

"Man, I don't know. Marriage . . . that's, like, forever."

"That's the point."

Vinny lowered his knife to the counter and hung his head. "Theresa really loves me. No matter what I do, she always takes my idiot ass back. And I do some pretty dumb things."

"You? Nah."

Vinny sniffled. "Theresa says the same thing. She's so-so—"

And then he lost it. Vinny's chest heaved and his eyes started leaking. "She's too good for me. I don't deserve a wife like that."

Dante groaned. Not again. He left the rag on the counter, crossing to his emotional employee. "Vin, come on man, pull yourself together."

Vinny shook his head, wiping his eyes on his hunched shoulders. "Aw, shit, Dante, I do love her."

The new line chefs were watching Vinny's outburst with wary nosiness. They continued chopping and prepping, but at a slower, quieter pace than before.

"Then marry her," Dante told Vinny, draping an arm over his shoulder.

Vinny looked up, his eyes watery pools. "You think I should?"

"If you love her, yeah."

Vinny sniffled again, hard and loud, then nodded. "Okay, I will. But . . ."

Dante eyed him. "What?"

"If I propose, it's gotta be perfect. Theresa deserves the best, you know. If I screw it up, she's going to remember that forever and then . . ." Vinny's shoulders shook again, "I'll never forgive myself."

"Vin, you'll do fine."

"I don't know. I think I need to practice."

"Practice what?"

"Proposing."

Dante gestured toward the counter. "I think you need to practice chopping garlic. I need another forty cloves in the next ten minutes."

"Just once. Please? Let me see how it sounds?"

"How what sounds?"

"My marriage proposal. Will you listen to it?"

"You want to propose . . . to me?"

"You're the whole reason I'm marrying Theresa. I mean, you introduced us, you gave me this job here, and you helped me see my true heart. You should be a part of it." Vinny's large brown eyes had now turned pleading.

"All right," Dante grumbled. "Do it quick and do it quiet so the kitchen help doesn't hear."

Vinny nodded. He cleared his throat. Twice. Then drew himself up, squared his shoulders and—

Dropped to one knee at Dante's feet.

"Vinny, get the hell up," Dante whispered.

"I gotta do this right, Boss. Now, give me your hand."

"No. I'm drawing the line there."

"Fine. I'll just pretend." He cleared his throat again, extended his left hand in the general direction of Dante's. "You are the greatest thing in my life," he began, his voice starting to crack. "You make my eggs right and you do that little thing with your tongue—"

"Vin!"

"Okay, okay." He sniffled and started again. "You're the ricotta to my lasagna and without you, I'd be"—a sob escaped him—"this tasteless lump of dough." He lifted his watery eyes to Dante's. "Oh, baby, will you marry me?"

All activity in the kitchen had ceased, now silent as a convent. For a second, a weird feeling ran through Dante. What would it be like to be in Vinny's shoes? To love a woman so much that he'd humiliate himself in front of an entire kitchen, just to get a marriage proposal right? To be so overcome by the thought of proposing that it left him a sobbing, damp mess?

Granted, it didn't take much to make Vinny sob, but still . . .

When was the last time he knew anyone who loved someone else that much?

Much less himself?

Someone across the room cleared their throat and Dante realized he was standing in the middle of a very odd, romantic tableau. "Vin, get up," he muttered.

"You didn't answer me."

"Get back to your garlic or I'll fire you." He glanced at the other cooks and the two waitresses, standing in the stainless steel room like statues. "Get back to work, all of you."

No one moved. Apparently they'd all heard from Franco that Dante's bark was about as harmful as a Pekingese's. "Vin, Theresa's going to say yes."

Vinny sniffled. "How do you know?"

"Because if I were a woman, I'd be sobbing all over the diamond right now."

"You mean it?"

"Yeah." Dante tipped his head toward the counter. "Now, back to the garlic. Please? I have a restaurant to run. I can't be getting married in the middle of the dinner hour."

Though, for a minute there, the idea of getting married hadn't seemed so crazy at all. Just as long as his intended life partner was a lot more attractive—not to mention the opposite gender—than his sobbing sous chef.

And maybe . . .

Had a name that reminded him of marinara sauce.

Mary Louise's Meal-of-Nothing
Mozzarella, Tomato and Basil Salad

2 large tomatoes, sliced
10 slices fat-free, reduced calorie mozzarella cheese
10 leaves fresh basil
2 teaspoons extra virgin olive oil
Reduced sodium salt
Pepper

Arrange tomato slices and cheese on a pretty plate with enthusiasm. The smaller the plate you choose, the more food it looks like you're getting.

Decorate it nicely with the basil, slipping the leaves in here and there, almost like you're making yourself a little flower.

Sprinkle with the olive oil and dust with a little salt and pepper. Eat only half of what is on the plate and save the rest for another day, so you can demonstrate once again that you have the best willpower in the neighborhood. Tell yourself you do not feel deprived. You feel *empowered* by your food choices.

That she-devil Maria Pagliano will be insanely jealous when she sees you, making it all worth it. Right?

CHAPTER 19

Monday night, Maria stood in the Stop & Shop on Tremont Street, ready to admit defeat. She'd spent the weekend and today, her day off, reliving the horror of her date with Antonio. She'd managed to avoid the phone, her mother, and life in general.

For the first day, sticking to her diet had been easy because she'd been battling a hangover and a queasy stomach. On Sunday, willpower had been a little harder to come by. By Monday, it was nearly nonexistent. She'd finally ended up moving a chair in front of the door to prevent herself from leaving the apartment for Guido's.

But now, caught between aisles four and five, there was no barrier to her desires. No scale to climb on as a visual reminder that every calorie counted.

Just the aisle markers, whispering their wares. Aisle Four: Cookies, Ice-Cream Toppings, Peanut Butter. Aisle Five: Granola Bars, Canned Fruit, Wheat Germ.

The proverbial devil and angel choices.

Go left. Or right? Temptation or salvation. Fat or thin. Satiation or—

"Maria? Is that you?"

She pivoted and nearly missed the pencil outline of a woman pushing a cart that held less calories than a Diet Coke.

Mary Louise Zipparetto. In an A-line skirt and perky little sandals. Her minimal bust was covered by a white stretch cotton top that didn't have anywhere to stretch, given that Mary Louise had dieted away her breasts. "Mary Louise. What a pleasant surprise."

Not.

"I thought that was you, but from the rear, well, I wasn't so sure," Mary Louise said. With a smile, no less.

Bitch. Maria forced a smile to her face and tightened her hands around the cart's handle instead of Mary Louise's throat. "I'm sure you have a lot of shopping to do," Maria said, gesturing at Mary Louise's bare-as-Mother-Hubbard's-cupboard cart. "It was nice to see you." She started to roll her cart away.

"Oh, no, I'm all done. This is all I'm buying for the week." Mary Louise let out a little, self-deprecating laugh and waved at her twelve-items-or-less. "I don't eat nearly as much now that I'm thin."

Maria bit back a nasty comment about birds and how they'd make tasty treats for fat cats. "Congratulations on the weight loss. You look . . . great," she ground out. Mamma hadn't raised an impolite girl. Once again, she tried to escape.

She'd head for the lottery line and play the Mass Millions. She didn't have time to wait until Wednesday for the Megabucks drawing.

"Did I hear you were going to the Chubby Chums, too?"

Maria stopped in her tracks and pivoted back. "Me?" She clasped a hand to her chest. "What gave you that idea?"

"I ran into Stephanie at the movies the other day and

she mentioned someone new had joined. We got to talking and she said her name was Maria." Mary Louise's eyes zeroed in on Maria's face.

"Well, I better get going—"

Mary Louise's gaze narrowed. "I could swear my mother said your mother had talked about you joining a group—"

"Mammas love to gossip, don't they?" Maria interrupted. If she didn't get out of here now, she'd be spending the rest of her life at Cedar Junction for murder by shopping cart. "I really have to go." She turned her cart away.

"Oh, wait! I almost forgot! I'm getting married!" She squealed the words like a pig that had taken over the trough. She thrust her hand forward and dangled a perfect marquise full-carat under Maria's nose. "I'm going to be Mrs. Joey Pantaloni."

Maria forced a polite smile to her face. "From Zipparetto to Pantaloni, huh? Well, that has a nice . . . ring to it."

Mary Louise sighed. "Oh, it does, doesn't it?"

Despite the close proximity of all her favorite comfort foods, Maria had to fight the urge to deposit her lunch on Mary Louise's new joy. God. The woman lost some weight and became a complete pain in the left hand.

"Anyway, I'm having a bachelorette party and I'm inviting all my friends. I want you to come. It's on Saturday night, at that hot new restaurant in town."

A sense of dread filled Maria's throat. "What hot new restaurant?"

"You know, the one the *Globe* just went nuts over a couple weeks ago? La . . . La something." Mary Louise waved a hand at the forgotten syllables. "You practically have to be a Kennedy to get a reservation, but my father knew someone and got us a table."

There was only one restaurant the *Globe* had raved about recently.

Vita.

Mary Louise grabbed Maria's hand. "Please say you'll come. I just can't imagine celebrating without all my friends."

The thought of Mary Louise in Vita—whisper-thin, lording her engagement over the free world—was too much for Maria to handle. "I really don't think I can. You have a good time. Vita's a great place to eat," Maria said. "But watch the pasta. It'll undo the best of any woman's intentions."

Then she left, before she ended up in jail for throttling Mary Louise in a jealous-thin rage, or worse, accepted the invitation to the bachelorette party from hell.

Since she hadn't won Mass Millions, Maria went to work on Tuesday morning. Self-pity wasn't keeping her full any longer. So she headed into the shop. There, she had friends. And cookies.

"What happened to you?" Candace asked when Maria entered. "You look terrible."

Maria took a seat at one of the kitchen stools and dropped her head into her hands. "I had the worst date of my life this weekend."

"Worse than Harvey the Exterminator?" Rebecca asked.

Maria nodded.

"What about Gerry the Pipe Fitter, who kept trying to get you to change your plumbing?"

"Worse than that."

"Nothing would beat Dirk the Destroyer. Remember why he earned that nickname?" Candace asked Rebecca.

She laughed. "Because he liked to pretend he was Jean

Claude Van Damme all the time. Didn't he start kick-boxing his way through the line to see *Lord of the Rings*?"

Maria nodded. "It was a gruesome sight. Popcorn carnage everywhere."

"That would be humiliating." Candace shrugged off her coat and hung it on the hook. "I don't think anything could top that Kung Fu Ken doll."

"Oh, I managed," Maria said. "I spent the whole weekend going through the nightmare."

"What did you do?"

"Regurgitated on Antonio."

"Eww." Rebecca made a face. "I take it he didn't call for a second date?"

"Oh, he called all right. Made up some bullshit about flying back to L.A. early. Probably took a one-way to the dry cleaner's and met a woman with an iron stomach."

"Well," Candace said. "Look at the bright side."

"There's a bright side?"

"Well, no. I can't think of one. But I thought I'd toss that out there because it sounded good."

Maria laughed. "Give me some cookies. And let me wallow in my misery."

Rebecca laid a hand on hers. "You aren't going to blow your diet over this, are you? I thought you were doing so good."

Maria tossed her head back and let out a sigh. "I think I need to change tactics."

"What do you mean?"

"I'm going to get the biggest turkey baster I can find. And stuff Mary Louise Zipparetto until she's four sizes larger than me." Maria grinned. "It'd be a hell of a lot easier than this diet crap."

Her cell phone rang. Maria dug it out of her purse and answered it before the last stanza of Bach finished on the ringer. "Hello?"

"You'll break your mamma's heart if you don't come

to dinner on Wednesday night," Mamma said. "Shatter it like glass."

"Mamma, I just saw you three days ago."

"You are my only child." On the other end of the phone, Maria could almost see her mother clutching at her chest, to add to the drama of the statement. "All I have."

"You have Papa, Nonna and Nonno. Plus, the North End is practically a Pagliano family reunion every time someone hangs out their laundry."

Her mother ignored her. "We always have dinner together at least one time each week. You come, no?"

"No."

The sigh that traveled over the phone line was filled with years of disappointment. The kind that came from a daughter who had never married. Never produced grandchildren. And had yet to live up to the Italian woman tradition of going forth and multiplying.

She had no intention of getting married because of parental pressure. The last thing Maria wanted to do was turn into a baby producing machine like Cousin Paulina or a shrieking, crying drama queen like Paulina's older sister. Marriage made women dependent on men. They'd lay down their lives so they could crank out babies in between raviolis.

No, thank you.

"You come Wednesday," Mamma declared, as if Maria hadn't refused.

"Mamma, I'm on a diet." Rebecca was right. It was crazy to ruin all those weeks of hard starvation over a little barfing incident.

"You still need to eat," Mamma said.

"Not what you cook."

"You don't like my cooking?" Now her voice held hurt and shock. Guilt would be next. Maria knew her mother's repertoire by heart.

Even though she did, the song still tugged at her heart-strings and made her feel bad. "It's not your cooking, Mamma, it's the type of food. I can't have all that cheese and pasta on my diet."

"I make something else. You come. You eat. Be with your family."

"Mamma—"

"You come. I cook. We eat together." Mamma's words were definite, not to be argued with.

"Mamma, I shouldn't." How could she tell her mother being around that food was temptation enough? That she could barely walk past a man with a box of dough-nuts without getting homicidal?

"Mary Louise Zipparetto eats with her mamma. She loves her mamma."

Damn that Mary Louise. And damn her own soft heart for caving. She heard the loneliness in Mamma's tone, the twinge of need that said she missed her only child. "All right. I'll be there."

"Good." Mamma's voice had softened. "You bring the bread. The kind your papa likes."

And with that, Maria knew all was forgiven between her and her mother. Ah, the power of food. A little gluten and a mother-daughter relationship was back on track.

And a diet was sent careening off a cliff.

Sal's Love-is-Sweet-and-Sour Onion Salad

1 pound baby onions, peeled
1 tablespoon minced prosciutto
1 clove garlic, minced
½ cup wine vinegar
3 tablespoons sugar
3 tablespoons olive oil, divided
3 tablespoons tomato paste
1 bay leaf
2 sprigs parsley
½ cup raisins
Salt and pepper

Mince one onion and set aside. Heat 1 tablespoon of the olive oil, add the prosciutto, garlic and minced onion. Cook until onion is translucent and flavors are melded like the beginning of a good marriage. It's not all wine and roses forever. Hell, no.

Now comes the hard years when there's a little sour and a little sweet. Add the wine vinegar, sugar, remaining olive oil, paste, bay leaf, parsley and raisins. Season with a bit of salt and pepper—the seasonings of life. Give the woman you married a kiss on the cheek and remind her she is your angel on earth. She may swat you, but call it a love tap.

Heat all to a boil, like a good argument. Then turn it down to a simmer—the same as the ongoing heat between those who have been married for many years.

Cook uncovered, so all can see the beauty of your dish, for 45 minutes. Remove the bay leaf and parsley, then serve at room temperature to a woman who still has a little bite left in her.

CHAPTER 20

"You're going to need more than a big *ciabatta* to win her heart," said a gruff voice from behind him.

Dante turned around, the loaf of herb bread in his arms. The late Tuesday afternoon sun peeked through the glass windows, causing Dante to squint a little against the glare. "Excuse me?"

The old man nodded his white head toward the baked goods. "My granddaughter, she can get *ciabatta* anywhere. You'll have to do better than that."

Then the voice and the face connected in Dante's brain. He'd seen him briefly the day he'd stopped by Maria's mother's house. Salvatore Pagliano, Maria's grandfather. "This isn't for—"

"I remember you now. You, I'm sure, don't remember me." He pressed a hand to his chest. "I come into your father's restaurant all the time years ago. Your father, he was a good man. Proud of his job, and of his son."

Dante blinked. "He loved Vita."

"A good man often raises a good man." He wagged a finger in emphasis. "Are you a good man?"

"I like to think of myself as one."

Salvatore Pagliano nodded, considering Dante and the bread in his hands for a second. "I believe you. Giovanni Del Rosso never cheated anyone. Always treated you fair."

"That he did."

"Having a Del Rosso in the family would be good," he said. "Very good. The Paglianos, we like to eat."

"I'm not proposing—"

The old man pshawed him. "You will. You first have to win her, though. She is a tough one. Sing to her. Caress her with your voice." He added a flourish with his hand. "Do it on a full moon and she'll be yours."

"Mr. Pagliano, I'm not trying to—"

"Please, call me Sal. Uncle Sal if you want to be formal, because that's as formal as I get." He laughed. "She likes you, my granddaughter. She's stubborn as an ox in mud, though, and won't tell you. All the women in our family are like that." Sal pointed at him. "Are you made of strong stuff?"

"Uh—"

"You have to be. Pagliano women—hard to woo, but easy to keep, if you are smart. You must be strong, like a lion"—he flexed a slightly shaky arm under his green diamond pattern cardigan—"but whisper like the wind in her ear."

"I'll remember that."

Sal took a step forward, raising a fist to emphasize his point. "Don't you give up on her! Maria, she's worth it. She's worth ten men, but the church only lets her marry one."

"I'm not marr—"

Sal shook his head, cutting Dante off. "I'm an old man, but not a stupid one. I have the same wife for fifty-two years. She can make a man scream when she wants to, but she has the face of an angel."

"She sounds, uh, wonderful."

Sal waved a hand at him. "No, she sounds like a wife. But a good woman. And the only one with a leash big enough for me." He gestured to the loaf still in Dante's arms. "You come for dinner. Tomorrow night. But don't bring bread."

"Wednesday? But—"

"Bring dessert," Sal went on, as if he hadn't heard a word of Dante's protest. "Sweeten my granddaughter's tongue first, then her heart." Sal tipped his hat at Dante and gave him a grin. "I tell Biba to expect you." Then he left, moving surprisingly fast for a man of his age, getting out the door before Dante could even formulate an excuse to get out of the dinner.

Dinner at the Paglianos? Surely, Maria would kill him if she saw him there again. She'd made it clear she didn't want anything to do with him. And yet, when she'd kissed him—

When she'd kissed him, his entire world had come to a screeching halt. When was the last time he'd felt that way? When was the last time he'd been so distracted by thoughts of a woman that he'd ended up writing "Maria" instead of "marinara" on his menu? When was the last time he'd found himself watching the clock, wishing he were anywhere but at Vita?

Never.

Dante looked at the *ciabatta* in his arms. Sal was right. This was no way to win a woman.

Dante was just going to have to sweeten the deal.

Maria opened the back door to her mother's house, took in a high-calorie breath and let it out in a sigh. "Mamma, why do you torture me like this?"

Mamma retied the bow on her rooster apron and put on her best innocent face. All Italian mothers, it seemed, had mastered this "who-me?" mask that managed to look both blank and hurt at the same time. "It's not torture to feed my child. It's love."

Maria placed a focaccia bread on the counter, then leaned over and gave her mother a kiss on the cheek. "Love can smother you if you eat too much of it."

"You have a beautiful figure. And my food is good for you." Her mother waved a dismissive hand at her and ratcheted up the hurt in her brown eyes. When Maria didn't cave on the guilt trip, Mamma pivoted toward the stove, picked up a wooden spoon from the rooster spoon rest and gave the risotto a stir. "Dante seemed to like it."

"Mamma, I don't care what Dante thinks. I'm not dating him." Maria crossed to the refrigerator, opened it and pulled out a two-liter Diet Coke.

The spoon circled along the metal pan. In the pattern of a noose. "Just kissing him, hmm?"

Maria paused, her hand halfway to the cabinet for a glass. "You saw that?"

"What, you think I'm blind? You and he, in my yard that day, right by the roses. I look for new buds and I see you."

"To see the roses from the kitchen window . . ." Maria withdrew a glass and filled it with Diet Coke, "you have to stand on a chair and peek around the corner of the window."

Mamma shrugged. "I'm eager for spring."

"It's March. Much too early for roses," Maria said. "Mamma, I love you, but you're nosy. You were hoping to catch him down on one knee."

"The soup, it works."

Maria replaced the soda in the fridge. "He didn't propose."

Mamma busied herself with stacking dirty dishes in the sink. "He will."

"No, he won't." She paused a moment, leaning against the counter and sipping from the glass. "I'm not going out with him. I haven't even seen him in days."

Well, technically, she already had gone on a sort-of date with him. If she counted the dance in the North End street. Oh, yeah, and the chess game at her apartment. The ride to the Chubby Chums. The conversation— hell, that wasn't a conversation, that was mouth soccer—outside on the church steps. And the order he'd placed at the shop on Friday.

But, well, she wasn't going to see him anymore. Or think about him. Even though she had been, every day since he'd walked away with that half-finished kiss between them.

She wasn't going to think about him ever again. Starting today.

Somehow, that resolution didn't sound any stronger than her vow to stay away from snack foods.

"Why not? He's a nice boy," Mamma said, as if reading her thoughts.

Maria sighed and settled into one of the maple kitchen chairs. Across from her, two six-inch high, ugly white porcelain roosters stared back from a wooden shelf perch, their faces blank and stony. "You wouldn't understand."

Mamma turned away from the sink and crossed to the kitchen table, taking the seat across from Maria. "Then tell me, *cara*."

"There's nothing to tell. He's not my type."

Mamma's eyes zeroed in on Maria's, the Italian mother lie detector clicking away. She pursed her lips and gave a little nod. Whether that meant Maria had convinced her or not, would remain to be seen.

"When you were little, you dream of being the ballerina. Remember?"

"Yeah. And the dance teacher always put me in the

back so I wouldn't ruin her "Swan Lake." Or break Prince Charming's back."

Mamma let out a gust. "You too good for that class."

"Oh, Mamma." Maria shook her head, smiling at the same argument she'd heard for years. "I wasn't too good. I was too heavy. You never saw the truth."

"Maybe it's not me who doesn't see the truth."

"And maybe you're just biased because you're my mother." But Maria's voice was soft. Despite her match-making, Mamma loved her and that alone was comforting.

From the front of the house came the sound of the doorbell. Maria glanced at her mother. But she'd already slipped into her "who-me?" outfit again.

No one in the Pagliano family rang the doorbell. Only company announced their presence at dinner. And there was only one person Maria could imagine her mother inviting over for Wednesday night dinner.

"We have company tonight?" Maria asked. "Anyone I know?"

"The veal. I think it's burning." Mamma got to her feet and hurried to the stove.

"Mamma—"

"What?"

"You invited him, didn't you?"

"Who?" Mamma shrugged, like she had no idea who Maria meant. From the front hall, the evidence in question could be heard greeting her grandfather.

"Dante. He's here. I can hear him, so don't deny it."

"He likes my cooking. His own mamma, she so far away."

"Dante can cook for himself. He's a *chef*."

"I also like to be spoiled once in a while." Dante's deep tenor seemed to fill the small, bright kitchen, and reminded her that she'd been talking about him behind his back.

Good thing she hadn't said anything too stupid.

She turned around and saw him standing there, holding a bottle of the same Chianti Classico. Immediately, her mind rocketed back to the night in her apartment. The chess game.

And the unanswered game between them.

Something hot uncoiled in her gut at the sight of him. Damn, he looked good. If there was ever a *Survivor* for dating, Dante would win, hands and corkscrews down.

"Sit, sit," Mamma said, ushering him in like he was the king of England. "You work so hard. You need a woman to fuss."

Dante cocked his head at Maria and grinned. Spoiled as Zsa Zsa Gabor's poodle.

"I'll set the table," Maria said.

Dante started to rise.

"Oh, no, don't get up," Maria said sweetly, giving him a condescending pat on the arm. "Wouldn't want you to tucker yourself out before dinner. Just let the women wait on you."

"If you insist . . ."

"I do. You are, after all, a guest." Then she grabbed the stack of plates on the counter and stalked out.

She'd been right. He was like every other Italian man she'd vowed to stay away from. Next he'd be parking his feet on the coffee table, the remote under one thumb and her under the other.

No, thanks. She didn't need that. Been there, done that, and didn't need a repeat history lesson.

Mamma's Joining-of-Two-Hearts
Double Cheese Risotto

4 tablespoons butter
1 small onion, minced
1 ¾ cup Arborio rice
1 cup white wine, a good vintage from a lucky year
4 cups boiling chicken stock, ready and waiting to
make the rice perfect and hot
1 cup Gorgonzola cheese, chopped
1 cup Fontina cheese, chopped
Salt and pepper
Walnut halves for garnish and extra fertility

Melt the butter in a pan, add the onion and cook until softened like your daughter's heart. Her resistance to him is weakening, so don't let this opportunity go.

Add the rice and stir, until the grains are ready to burst, like *his* heart. Add the wine for a little sweetness from the vine. Now pour in a little of the stock, stirring and stirring until it's absorbed.

Risotto requires tending, just like a new love. So add a little stock, then stir more. Add and stir until the risotto is al dente and creamy. Now it's time to marry the cheeses. Bring in the sweet Gorgonzola with the nutty Fontina and stir together, until they have completely blended. Taste for extra seasoning and add if needed.

Sprinkle with walnuts, which the Romans say bring fertility to all who eat them. Then serve quickly to a couple who needs a good shove in the right direction—

The direction of the altar, of course.

CHAPTER 21

Mamma was clearly on Dante's side. She seated him beside Maria. Before dinner, he noticed her pushing their chairs a tiny bit closer when Maria wasn't looking, too.

Taking the night off from Vita had been a damned good idea.

Dante poured the wine for everyone at the table. He noticed, however, that Maria didn't sip from her glass. Did she not want to bring back the memories of that night? Or was she afraid of a repeat performance?

Maria brushed by her grandfather on her way to her seat, giving him a kiss and a hug. Sal Pagliano gave Dante a wink from across the table, mouthing, *Give her time.*

Time didn't seem to work with Maria. The more Dante stayed away, the more distant she became. If he wanted her, he'd better put a plan into fast forward.

Of course, that would presume he *had* a plan. Between the restaurant's insane schedule and dealing with the problems of Vinny, Rochelle and everyone else, he couldn't remember the last time he'd had five minutes to think about his own life.

All he did know was that Maria intrigued him more than any woman he'd ever met. She had the perfect combination—brains, sass and a talent for chess. Every time he saw her, his desire for her multiplied. All he needed now was a way to steal her heart before she knew what hit her.

That required a plan, which he didn't have. Damned good thing he could improvise.

Sal cleared his throat and introduced Dante to his wife Ada, a diminutive white-haired woman sitting to Sal's right. "Pass the zucchini, *ma petite*," he said loudly to her when he finished the introductions.

"You old fool. I haven't been petite since you married me." But Ada passed the vegetables anyway.

Sal scooped some zucchini onto his plate, grinning at the woman across from him. "In my eyes, you are but a beautiful rose."

"You're legally blind."

"I can still see my heart's true love."

She scowled and reached for a slice of bread. "That's the cataracts."

"You have lost your romance. Where's the little butterfly I married?"

"She got old. Now pass the risotto."

"Are they always like this?" Dante whispered into Maria's ear. Her dark brown hair curled against her earlobe, and for an insane moment, he longed to toy with the springy tendril.

Probably not a good thing to do at the family dinner table.

"Pretty much." She shrugged, smiling at them. "Wait till they really get going. My grandmother's a little hard of hearing so they sometimes end up practically screaming at each other by the end of a conversation. Nonna and Nonno would give the best presidential candidates a run for their money at a debate."

"I think it's wonderful." He'd always craved that kind of family. That kind of life for himself. This exact kind of setting.

Maria turned and looked at him, fork hovering over her plate, big brown eyes catching his. God, she had gorgeous eyes. Like deep pools of mink he could settle into, and be comfortable there for a million years. "You need mental help," she said.

"Oh, come on, look at them. Still in love, still flirting."

"That's not flirting. It's verbal combat." But her voice was soft and admiring, full of love for her grandparents.

"Ah, *ma petite*," he whispered, his voice a much sexier version of her grandfather's, "where's your romance?"

Her eyes widened and filled with something that simmered hotter than the steam coming off the veal. He clenched his free hand in his lap to break the urge to reach out and touch her, to draw her to him and taste her ruby lips again.

"So, Dante, what are your intentions with my little girl?" Maria's father leaned back in his chair, one arm draped over the back.

Dante straightened and coughed, tearing his attention away from Maria. Out of the corner of his eye, he saw her smirk. The grilling had begun. "To drive her crazy until she finally says yes and goes out on a date with me."

"He's a smart man, that one," Sal said to his wife, emphasizing the point with a fork. "Comes from strong stock. I know his father. Good man."

"What?" She cocked an ear at him, cupping her hand around it.

"I said he's a smart man."

"A smart-ass? You shouldn't say those kinds of things at the dinner table. There are young people present."

Maria's father turned his attention toward Dante again. "You have a good job?"

Dante cleared his throat. "I own a restaurant."

"A what?" Ada asked. "A rest stop? How can you make a living at that?"

"A restaurant," Dante repeated, louder.

Her father raised a brow. "And?"

"And that's it. It keeps me pretty busy."

"In my day, a man worked three jobs," Sal said, nodding. "Supported his family in style."

"What style?" Ada snorted. "I drove an Edsel. We lived in a two-room walkup with three kids for fifteen years. Style, my—"

"Mamma!" Maria's father cut her off. "There are young people present. Remember?"

She went back to her zucchini, muttering about Edsels under her breath.

Biba bustled in from the kitchen, depositing additional bread onto the table and then hurrying from place setting to place setting, refilling the wineglasses.

"Sit, Biba," her husband said. "You never eat with the rest of us."

"My kitchen—"

"Will not burn down if you stop to eat." He grabbed her wrist and tugged her toward the chair beside him. "Maria's boyfriend is here. We need to make sure he's the one."

Dante grinned at Maria. She let out a sigh that said her parents had visited this territory more often than Lewis and Clark. "He's not my boyfriend. And he's not the one."

He thought about holding up a sign saying he was interested in the position, but figured Maria wasn't taking applications.

"Good for you," her grandmother said, adding salt to

her zucchini. "Don't settle down. Men are a pain in the ass."

"Mamma!" Biba gasped.

"What? It's true. They're about as useful as a dead elephant in the freezer."

Dante stifled a laugh. Maria choked back one of her own.

Sal grabbed his wife's hand and brought it to his lips, giving it a loud kiss. "Later, I'll show you *useful*."

"Don't you dare." She jerked her hand back. "I took that self-defense class at the community center last year. I know how to use a fist."

Sal chuckled. "There's no defense against *amore*."

Ada let out a chuff of disgust. "Are you sneaking those Viagra pills again? I swear, that Sonny is a terrible friend, giving you those things. Make you act like an animal."

"Mamma!" Biba said.

She dug into her plate again. "I'm old. I can say whatever I want now."

Biba started in on her plate at a furious pace, her cheeks pink. Dante cast an amused glance at Maria, who made a concerted effort to ignore him. He could see the amusement in her gaze, though, and knew as much as she wouldn't admit it, her family and all their quirks were dear to her heart.

The ringlet was back around her ear again, teasing at him, making his fingers itch to brush it back.

As soon as she finished eating, Maria leapt to her feet to help clear the table. Biba got to her feet as well, like a rising chorus of the Rockettes.

Dante stood. "Mrs. Pagliano, please sit. Maria and I will clean up."

"But—" Mamma was half out of her seat.

"You work hard," Dante said. "Let us spoil you for once."

"Suck-up," Maria muttered to him.

"Smart man," Sal said.

"Don't call him a smart-ass," his wife said, swatting him from across the table. "He's a nice boy. Look how he helps."

Clearly, Dante had won over everyone at the Pagliano table. Except Maria. He now had a whole team rooting for him to win her stubborn heart. Dante smiled at Maria's mother. "Let Maria and I do the dishes," he said again.

Confusion flitted across Biba's face, as if she didn't know what to do with herself now. "Well, if you're sure . . ."

"I know my way around a kitchen." Dante laid a gentle hand on her shoulder and she slowly retook her seat. "And I promise to leave yours exactly as you would."

"I changed my mind," Ada said, grabbing Maria's hand. "Marry him. Even if he is a smart-ass."

Dante's Winning-a-Stubborn-Heart
Sicilian Ricotta Cake

2 cups ricotta cheese, sweet and tempting
½ cup heavy cream
2 tablespoons vanilla sugar
Rind of one orange, finely grated
5 tablespoons orange-flavored liqueur
¼ cup semisweet chocolate, chopped (the way to a
girl's heart)
5 tablespoons candied orange peel, chopped and
divided
1 pound sponge cake, sliced into ¼-inch slices
1 cup whipping cream, sweetened, like she is

Combine the ricotta and heavy cream, beating until smooth and creamy, just like you wish everything was between the two of you. Add the sugar, orange rind and orange liqueur. Fold in chocolate chips and all but one tablespoon of the candied orange peel. Now you've made the filling completely irresistible.

Line a five-cup loaf pan with parchment paper. Layer sponge cake, then ricotta mixture, finishing with sponge cake. Try not to imagine you and she layered together after she tastes this creation of yours, or you'll end ricotta-ing yourself.

Press down lightly, wrap with wax paper and plastic wrap, then refrigerate overnight while you dream about her eating that first delectable bite.

Before serving, invert the cake onto a plate and ice

it with the whipped cream. Decorate with candied fruit.

Or, better yet, you can frost each other with the whipped cream and forget the cake altogether.

my old maid status over a bowl of wedding soup." Maria laughed.

"I don't think either of our Cupids would put down their arrows that easily." He noticed she'd managed to avoid answering him about the marriage question. Was he wrong? Or had he been right and she didn't want to admit it?

She'd called him a study in contrasts the last time they'd seen each other. But that wasn't true. She was the one who said she wanted one thing yet seemed so clearly meant for another.

Maria took the clean bowl he handed her and dried it, then placed it in the cabinet. She put a hand on her hip and looked at him. "You look like you're having a blast with the bubbles. Is there something I should know?"

He laughed. "I told you, I like doing dishes. It's a stress reliever." He leaned in her direction and whispered in her ear, lowering his voice into a sexy, teasing range, hoping to coax her back to the intimacy they'd had before. "Sometimes I even do them at home. Alone."

She moved back a few inches, but not before he saw her let out a staggered breath. "I hate anything to do with washing dishes. Paper plates were invented for people like me."

"I like getting my hands into the dough, so to speak. Sometimes, I miss the little stuff in running the restaurant. I get so busy with phone calls, bills, employees fighting like two-year-olds."

"I know what you mean." She moved to his left to load clean glasses into the cabinet. "There are days at the shop when we're so wrapped up in the business end that it feels like we lost the fun somewhere."

Dante's ears perked up. What was this? Détente? A common ground, built on business?

"So your dad started the restaurant?" she asked.

He nodded. "My father opened Vita when he came here from Italy. He loved the place, but he was never very successful with it. He could cook better than Wolfgang Puck and Julia Child rolled into one and he taught me how to cook, too, but he had no head for business."

"Not everyone does," Maria said. "When the three of us started Gift Baskets, we divvied things up according to our skills. Clearly, I didn't get kitchen duty." She laughed and gave him a slight jab in the arm.

Dante wanted to smack himself in the head. Why hadn't he thought of it earlier? Maria was part owner of a business; he owned a business. Right there was the bridge he'd been looking for to cement the connection between them.

Besides the sex connection, of course.

"How'd you three end up in business, anyway?" He started in on one of Mamma's rooster-decorated serving platters.

"We all went to Suffolk and ended up meeting in business class. We were assigned together as a team for one of those projects where you have to invent a business. Being women, our idea involved cookies and chocolate." She laughed, turning the dish towel around and around in her hand. "We must have all been PMSing at the same time. But it worked and *we* worked. After college, we made the leap into business together. Never looked back. Never had second thoughts."

"So you *do* take risks?"

"With things I can control."

He handed her the clean platter, but didn't let go of his end. Yet. "You never really control anything. Not in business and not in life."

"I like the illusion."

"Another thing we have in common." He grinned, then gently released the platter into her grip. "There are a lot of days when it seems the employees run me, rather than the other way around."

She laughed. "All you need is a good manager. And a great business plan."

Dante returned to the sink and worked his way through the silverware. "For that, I'd need time. And in my business, it's the one thing I can't order off the menu."

She sighed, picking up a handful of the silverware he'd washed and began drying the pieces. "It's been a long day. I don't really feel like talking about work. Let's just do the dishes."

Plan A—shot down with a torpedo before it got a chance to do much more than leave the battleship. Guess he'd have to resort to Plan B. The sex connection.

Gee, pity.

Before he could do anything more sexy than suds a plate, Biba Pagliano entered the kitchen. She stopped at the window and pulled back the curtain. "Oh, would you look at that," Biba said. "It's raining. Maria, you can't walk home in that. You'll get sick."

It was, indeed, raining, Dante saw. Not hard, but strong enough to require an umbrella and a fast walk.

"Mamma, I walk in the rain all the time. I won't drown. And, I only live four blocks away."

"You'll catch a cold." Biba let go of the curtain and stepped back, directing a hinting look at Dante. "You don't even have a raincoat with you."

"Let me drive you," Dante said. It would give him some moments alone with her. Maybe he could build that bridge he'd been trying to work on all night. He wasn't winning the war with Maria yet.

But he wasn't a man who gave up easily, either.

"You don't have to."

Dante squeezed out the sponge and put it on top of the sink, then pulled the plug and let the water drain from the now-empty sink. "It would be my pleasure."

"It's not a long walk. Really. You don't have to go out of your way."

"Maria, hush." Biba waved at her. "If the man wants to drive you home, let him be a gentleman."

Maria shot her mother a glare. Mamma and her matchmaking had leapt up notches unknown now. She'd gone way beyond grocery clerks. Now she was blatantly asking Dante to make a pity drive.

"It's not out of my way at all." Dante grinned. "Besides, I've learned it's wise to always take a mother's advice." He gave Mamma a wink.

And Mamma blushed, actually blushed like a schoolgirl smitten by his charms.

Maria glanced out the window and saw God had taken Mamma's side, too. The rain had started pouring down in sheets. Clearly, Maria was outnumbered. "All right, you both win." She gave her mother a hug as an apology for the way she'd been acting.

Mamma beamed. Probably calculating the cost of catering in her head. "Go, go," she said, shooing them out of her kitchen. "I finish drying." Mamma took the dish towel right out of Maria's hands and bumped her with her hip, sending her stumbling toward the door.

A second later, Dante and Maria were outside the house, under Mamma's bright pink umbrella, dashing toward his car. "I want to apologize," Maria said once they were inside.

"For what?"

"For my family. They're a little . . . overbearing at times. And beyond obvious in their attempts to get me married off."

Dante smiled. "I thought they were great."

"Have you been drinking?" He might find them entertaining for a one-meal performance but over time, her family was like the Ringling Brothers without the ringmaster.

"Only the wine at dinner." He turned the key and the engine revved to life. "Even when my dad was alive, my family was nothing like yours."

"There are days I'd love to have a 'normal' family. One you can actually introduce to friends without being afraid they'll have them fill out a marriage license at the dinner table." She pointed at the street sign ahead of them. "It's shorter if you take a right here."

He obliged. "They only have your best interests at heart."

"They don't listen to what I want." She sighed.

"What parents do?"

She laughed. "Maybe the ones on Mars. Certainly not the ones that live in the North End."

He chuckled softly at that. The wipers on the Honda swished back and forth, sluicing the rain from side to side. Dante reached up a hand and rubbed at the back of his neck. He sighed. "What a week."

"Long days at the restaurant?"

"They all are. It's part of the business."

"You need a vacation."

He let out a short, dry laugh. "I gave those up for Lent. And Easter. And Christmas."

"The rewards of entrepreneurship, huh? It's the same for us at Gift Baskets."

"Yeah. Being an owner isn't all it's cracked up to be." He pulled into a space two cars up from her door. "Here we are."

"Listen . . ." She let her voice trail off and considered him in the dark. Beyond his looks, he was a man who understood a part of her no one else did. She'd never talked business with a man before and been listened to. Like an equal.

She'd enjoyed it. Though she'd rather eat pine bark for a year than tell Mamma that.

"Did you want to ask me something?" Dante said.

She took a breath, then went against her own plan not to think about him or see him again. "Why don't you come up for a little while? Have a cup of coffee? A glass of wine?"

One drink didn't constitute a date, she told herself. Or a prelude to marriage.

His smile seemed ten times more intimate in the soft light cast by the street lamps. "A little dessert?"

She put up her hands. "I'm not having any of that. I've sworn off desserts."

"A bit of sweets isn't always a bad idea," Dante murmured.

Oh, damn. When he used that low, sexy voice of his, thoughts of business fled her mind like dirt at a Hoover convention. Her gaze met his and she stopped thinking about anything with calories. "I'm not the kind who can stop at just one bite."

Dante leaned forward, and for a second, she held her breath, until he reached into the backseat. "Are you sure? I've got a box of Sicilian ricotta cake here. I meant to bring it to your mother's house for after dinner. But I forgot it in the car."

"I . . . I shouldn't." The white box of delight in his hands teased at her.

If he came up, with that dessert, she wouldn't get one word of business conversation out. Hell, she'd be lucky if her mouth connected with anything other than him and what was in that box.

"Shouldn't? Or won't?" He untied the string on the box, with slow, sensual movements. As if he were slipping off her dress.

Oh, shit. There went the last of her resolve.

"Can't," Maria gasped. She scrambled for the door handle and hopped out of the car. The rain poured down on her head. She raised an arm to block it, but it did little good. With her free hand, she dug through her purse for her keys.

Damn, that had been close.

Inviting him in had been a bad idea. The kind that came from late nights and cloudy thinking. Maybe she'd been inhaling those soap bubbles. Or maybe the aroma of the risotto and veal had gone to her head. She had to get into her building before she turned around and grabbed him, begging him to end her misery once and for all.

But too late, he was already out of the car. An umbrella extended over his head and the cake box under one arm. He crossed to her, tipping the umbrella to cover her, too. "You're getting wet."

"I'm looking for my keys."

"We don't have to eat a single bite," Dante said. "We could just . . . talk."

"Cows have better bullshit than that."

"I'm serious."

She found her key and inserted it into the lock. Then she turned and took in his face. He wasn't looking at her breasts. He was looking into her eyes. Like he cared about her, not just her body.

But then she remembered last fall when her heart had been broken by David as surely as a Christmas ornament smashed by a Mack truck. Never would she let a man get that close again.

No matter what he had in his little white box.

"Good night, Dante," she said and started to turn back toward her door.

In one swift movement, he dropped the box and umbrella to the ground, then gathered her up against him and kissed her with the force of a summer storm. His hands tangled in her hair, his lips roamed over hers.

The entire thing was sudden and . . .

Wonderful.

Dante murmured against her mouth and cupped her head with hands that seemed to treasure her like a piece of china. When he did, something she'd thought had been dead for months sprang to life again. Emotion. Feeling.

Connection.

To hell with not getting involved, with keeping her heart protected as if it were a rare statue of the Virgin Mary. Dante's hands came around to cup her chin with a feather-light touch and for the first time in a very long time, Maria stopped feeling twenty pounds overweight. Stopped thinking if she was thinner or prettier, no one would ever cheat on her again.

Dante had done the impossible. Made Maria feel beautiful and desirable.

And ready to rumble.

Maria's Dating-Is-a-Chess-Game Mussels and Clams in Wine Sauce

2 pounds fresh mussels, in their shells
2 pounds fresh clams, in their shells
6 tablespoons olive oil
3 cloves of garlic
½ teaspoon dried red chilies, more or less to taste
1 ½ cups of dry white wine
Chopped fresh parsley

Scrub, rinse and debeard the mussels and clams. Discard any with broken shells. Imperfect partners may be allowed in real life, but not in seafood.

In a large saucepan, heat the oil, garlic and chilies. Add the wine, then the shellfish. Cover and steam until the shells have all opened and the shellfish are ready to be honest about what's really inside them. Discard any unopened shells.

Sprinkle with the parsley and serve with the sauce on the side, as well as toasted bruschetta for dipping. Now that the mussels and clams are being open, maybe it's time for a little removal of the shell on your end, too.

CHAPTER 23

She scrambled into her building and unlocked her door faster than David Blaine could make a quarter disappear.

"I believe I owe you a massage," Dante said when they entered her living room.

The thought of having a massage from those strong, thick fingers of his sounded like ten orgasms at once. She pictured him standing over her naked torso, palms working magic. Bringing the flesh to heated life.

Setting off fires in parts of her body that hadn't been inflamed in way too long.

Damn Harvey and his disappointing performance. Damn her hormones for working in reverse whenever Antonio was around. Maybe it was some weird kind of perimenopause. Mr. Right turned her off while Mr. Wrong made her pant like a St. Bernard in St. Tropez.

"Let me guess what you want," Dante whispered, moving into position behind her, his hands now on her shoulders. The fabric of her shirt became a semiconductor, transmitting the heat of his touch directly to her brain.

His fingers didn't just rub. They danced along her

collarbone, her shoulders, along her neckline, doing the rumba and the tango, with a little waltz added in. Everything inside her sprang to life, dancing in time with his touch.

This wasn't any ordinary massage. And her reaction was going beyond hormones. A surge of fear ran through her.

"We shouldn't—"

"Shouldn't what?"

Fall in love. Get married. Make plans beyond today.

"Do—" and then the thought was gone, lost in a heated rush of anticipation as his hands moved to her shoulder blades and then slowly down her spine.

Inch by inch. One vertebra at a time. Caressing and heating, easing every ache that had ever existed in her back.

And a few that didn't.

"You're so good." The words came out in a half moan, half whisper.

"You have no idea," he said softly, then leaned down and pressed his lips to her neck.

An electric thrill coiled through her, whipping against her nerve endings, as if she'd just touched a downed power line. She should—

Stop thinking, that's what she should do. Because if she thought about one more reason why she shouldn't kiss Dante, she'd be—

Oh, God. Now he was kissing the hollow of her throat. The T-spot. That one little secret place they never wrote about in *Cosmo*.

Maria groaned and collapsed onto her love seat, placing one hand on each side of Dante's face and hauling his mouth down with hers before she could think twice about it.

And then *she* kissed *him*. Her mouth wide against his, her tongue seeking more than the tease he'd given before. In bed, she was a woman who took what she wanted—and gave even more in return.

And right now all she wanted was him. For Christmas and her birthday and Flag Day in Aruba.

Dante pulled her to his chest, his arms wrapping around her back, pressing her breasts tight to his torso, the feel both agony and pleasure. She hauled him closer on the sofa, so his entire body now lay across hers.

He was hard and he was hot. His mouth roamed across hers, nipping and tasting at one time, then consuming the next. She rode a roller coaster of sensuality, her senses careening around corners, escalating her desire for him like a shaken champagne bottle about to be uncorked.

He pulled back, an inch, maybe two, from her mouth. "I want you, Maria."

"I want you, too."

"But not like this."

She blinked. The air in her apartment seemed to become very still and heavy. "What?"

"*When* we make love," and he emphasized the when with a gentle swipe of his finger across her lips, "I want it to be because you are madly in love with me."

She drew back. "I don't fall in love."

Not anymore.

"You're a terrible liar."

"I don't fall in love," she repeated. "So don't hold your breath waiting."

"I intend to prove you wrong." He grinned, his face so close to hers the smile seemed like it could be her own. "And that's going to be damned fun."

She swallowed. His argument made sense—and that's what scared her. Would her mind sabotage her as easily as her body had? She *couldn't* fall in love with him. He represented everything she didn't want in her life. Everything risky she couldn't take a chance on again. Her heart couldn't do that a second time. "This isn't a game, Dante," she said, as much to herself as to him.

"Everything between a man and a woman is a game of sorts."

"In games, there's always a loser. And I don't intend to be the loser."

"Sometimes, everyone wins."

She scrambled off the couch and got to her feet. "That's a bunch of crap. That's why they call them 'fairy' tales because the only people they come true for are imaginary little sprites who live in the woods."

He rose and crossed to her, his touch now a tender one on her shoulder. "What's made you so bitter?"

"I'm not bitter. I'm realistic." She turned to him. "What made you such a dreamer?"

He shrugged. "I believe in happy endings."

"Then why don't you have one of your own?" She took a step closer. "You work a million hours a week and from what Franco has said, barely date at all. How were you going to get that fairy tale? Were the mice going to deliver it to you?"

Dante heard the harshness in her voice, springing from some well of past hurts. Some other man had put that sound into her words. Not him. So he didn't take offense.

And he didn't walk away.

Instead, he grinned. "No, an angel was going to stand under a streetlight across from my restaurant and make me realize I'd been working way too much lately."

Maria pivoted away from him, crossing to the windows at the rear of her apartment. Below her, the narrow streets were dark and empty, shrouded by the rain.

In a month or two, the neighbors would be out there, sitting in their lawn chairs, enjoying the warm nights. The men would be smoking and gesturing wildly as they argued politics or sports. The pigeons would dart in and out, hoping for a crumb. Life in the North End would go on, as it had for centuries, as if nothing had ever happened to break her heart in this second-floor one-bedroom apartment.

Maria swallowed. "I've heard that line before."

"From who?"

When she didn't answer, he came closer and wrapped his arms around her waist. How she wanted to lean into that embrace. To trust. To believe in him and everything he'd said. "Who hurt you, Maria?"

"It doesn't matter. A man. Men." She bit her lip and shook her head. "Men who think they can talk a sweet game, make me think they believe in that forever and ever ending. Then it turns out they have a little extra something on the side. A backup plan."

His hand moved to her hair, the caress soft and agonizingly tender. He leaned down, his mouth again at her ear, soft, quiet. Teasing. "With you, the only backup plan a man needs is a way out of checkmate."

Despite herself, she laughed. She turned to face him, finding an answering smile on his lips. Damn him for making her laugh. He'd broken the tension and somehow jerked her out of a damned good pity fest with one sentence. "What am I going to do with you?" she said.

"Let me win my dignity back."

"Dignity?" She grinned. "After that pitiful loss to me, you might as well give up any hopes of dignity."

He trailed a finger along her chin. "I was distracted."

Hell, *she* was distracted after that touch, but she kept her cool. Barely.

"And you aren't now? After that?" She gestured toward the love seat.

"Oh, no. I'm *much* more focused now."

"Right."

"Come on, let's play again."

The way he said it didn't imply a chess game. He meant more. Much more. After all she'd just said and felt, she should say no. She had made her position clear. If she wanted to stick to her love guns, she'd push him out the door now and—

Go to bed alone. Frustrated. Cold. And sans one orgasm.

"I'll just beat you," she said, hedging.

"I don't think so." He grinned. "I've been studying."

"What? *Chess for Dummies* in your spare time?"

He grinned. "Actually, *The Kama Sutra Pop-Up Book*."

That particular title brought up mental images that would add a tinge of blush to the *New York Times* bestseller list. "You're kidding."

"Play me and find out."

The double entendre set off the electrical storm in her gut again. She shouldn't.

But damn. She had even less willpower when it came to sex—and that deep, tempting voice of Dante's—than she did against manicotti.

For a second, she wanted to believe he was different from David and all the other men she'd met. That the words he'd said were real. That after she'd changed her life to accommodate him and started believing in forever, he wasn't going to turn out to be some cretin who ordered her around like a Merry Maid on retainer. Or a nympho who kept a stable of women on the side so he could ride a different pony whenever his saddle got itchy.

Maybe . . . Dante was different. Or maybe she just wanted to think he was for tonight. Because it was raining. And she was cold. And lonely.

And he had made her laugh.

"One game. No more." The words were out of her mouth, as if her brain didn't have anything to do with her voice box.

He took her hand and led her to the chess table. "This time, let's make it *really* interesting."

"How do you propose we do that?"

The corners of his mouth lifted up into a devilish smile. "Naked chess."

Dante's Hurry-Up-and-Get-Naked Broiled Shrimp

24 large shrimp, peeled and deveined
3 cloves of garlic, finely chopped (use a damned food processor; it's faster)
3 tablespoons chopped basil
1 tablespoon fresh parsley
½ tablespoon pepper
Juice of one lemon
4 tablespoons olive oil

If you don't have time for deveining the shrimp, have it done at the fish store. All you need is a quick snack, not a two-hour detour from what you were doing. Mix the shrimp with all the ingredients in one bowl, throw it in the fridge and leave it to marinate for *at least* eight hours.

Preferably overnight.

When you come up for air again, preheat the broiler, then slip the naked shrimp onto skewers and brush with remaining marinade. Cook for about three minutes, then turn and cook for three minutes more. Eat in bed.

But be very careful where you leave your skewers.

CHAPTER 24

Dante saw Maria's reaction and knew as much as she said she didn't want him—

She did.

Everything in her eyes and her body language belied her words. Like a mutiny against her mind.

Good. For a minute there, he'd been worried. And he wasn't a man who'd ever worried before about what a woman thought—or whether a woman would be interested in him. But this time it was different.

Because she was different. Feisty, yet kind. A woman who said she didn't care, yet loved her family with a fierceness that spoke of volumes of love somewhere deep within her. A smart woman who ran a successful business and had been able to save his own butt once already.

"What exactly is naked chess?" she asked.

"Well, one of us gets naked." He'd proposed the idea, not quite sure what the hell he meant, only knowing it sounded damned good.

"Oh, gee, let me guess who." She shook her head. "Men are so predictable."

"If you want, you can get me naked instead." He gave her a suggestive smile, which she waved away. "Okay, here are the rules. Every time somebody calls 'check,' the checked person has to remove a piece of clothing."

"That's not naked chess."

"It's not?"

"No. It's strip chess." She grinned and set up her own pieces. "You know I'm going to beat you again."

"Not necessarily."

"And take great delight in seeing what you look like beneath that apron."

"I'm not wearing my apron right now."

"I was speaking rhetorically."

"I know." His gaze teased her. "Your move first."

She slid a pawn forward; he did the same. This time, though, Dante studied the board and didn't let her distract him.

A few moves later, beneath the table, she crossed one leg over the other, her shoe dropping to the floor with the movement and her foot drifting up against his leg. "Oh, sorry."

He grinned. "Sure you are." He slid his bishop forward. "I believe that's check."

"No. Not already. It can't be."

"Yes, it is." His grin widened. "Take something off."

She studied the board, then him. "You've been boning up."

He arched a brow. "More than you know."

She looked at the board once more, then finally conceded that he had her king in a corner. "Fine. I'll strip. But it will just make it more distracting for you."

"Oh, I don't think so."

"Wanna bet? Watch me." She reached down to her waist, tugged on the stretchy dark pink shirt and then yanked it up and over her head. She flung the shirt away to the left but Dante didn't bother to look where it went. His eyes had never left her chest.

He gulped. Holy Mother of God. Her breasts perked above a lacy red bra, the nipples teasing beneath the delicate floral material. Perfect round globes, begging to be touched. Her skin was like honeyed milk. And all he wanted to do was drink.

She wiggled a little in her seat, clearly enjoying the effect she was having on him. In concert, her breasts did a tiny little jig.

Why had he thought this was going to be a good idea? What hormone-induced frenzy had cooked up this idea in his mind?

"Now, let's see who gets checked next," Maria said. And she moved her king out of the reach of his bishop.

Dante swallowed hard and tried to go back to the chess moves he'd had planned out in his head.

His brain was a blank.

"Your move, *Dante*," she said, placing special emphasis on his name.

Stare at the board. Not at her. Or you'll be down to your boxers quicker than Warren Beatty in his heyday.

He redoubled his concentration. Kept his gaze on everything but her. And two moves later was rewarded with another check.

"No way. That's impossible! I was just about to do that to you."

He smirked. "Beat you to it. Again."

"On purpose?"

"Maybe."

Now he did allow himself to look at her again, his eyes drinking in her skin, her sweet generous chest, her full, open mouth. His breathing escalated. He wanted to groan. To leap across this table and tell her to hell with his stupid little rule about her falling in love with him first. To just have her now. And end this agonizing want that curled within him like a lion in a too-small cage.

She glanced up, caught him looking. "Distract you enough?"

"I barely noticed." He made a big show of peering over the table and pretending he was taking his first look at her. "Oh, I see now. What color is that . . . red? I can barely see."

"Liar."

He just grinned. "You, my dear, need to strip again. Sorry, but them's the rules."

She bit her lip, considering. "I could take off the bra—"

Oh, God, yes.

"But no." She put a finger to her lip, mocking serious thought. "I'm sure that wouldn't work because you said you barely noticed my chest."

I noticed, I noticed. It's imprinted in my memory.

"Or, I could do something a little more . . . devious." Beneath the table, she moved her hand and lifted her hips, then sat down again and tossed another, much smaller piece of clothing to the left.

Something lacy. And the same color as the bra.

Oh, God.

Her panties.

"That's ever so much more comfortable." She smiled right at him before moving her king out of conquering range. "Your move."

"Uh, yeah." He cleared his throat. Directed his attention away from her breasts and back down at the board. But it didn't work this time. All he could see was what he imagined beneath the table. The image of what was hidden, or rather, no longer completely hidden since she'd tossed the panties onto the chair in the corner.

It was worse. Envisioning what could be, rather than what was right there.

He moved a rook, without thinking of the consequences. Maria pounced on it with her queen and took the piece away. "Check," she said.

"Damn." The tables weren't just turned, they were spinning.

She grinned. "Your turn to strip."

"What do you want me to take off first?"

She perused him, her gaze teasing. "Oh, it's all good. You choose."

He began to unbutton his shirt but his fingers stumbled because he couldn't seem to redirect his gaze on anything but her.

Maria's chest heaved with her intake of breath. She swallowed, watching him. Then, in one graceful, feline movement, she got to her feet and came around to his side of the table. "Let me," she said, her voice deep and husky and full of everything that was churning within him, too.

Her fingers slid along the buttons, slipping them through the holes with a deftness that belied the desire surely coursing through her. If her hormones were operating at even one tenth the level of his, she'd barely be coherent, never mind able to work fastening products.

When she was done, she slid her hands across his chest, warmth against warmth, skin on skin, up and over his shoulders, releasing the cotton from his body in one fell double swoop that puddled it on the floor. She took a final step closer, joining their torsos, and kissed him, her mouth hot against his.

The lace of her bra awakened every nerve on the bare skin of his chest. She tilted her pelvis, her skirt pressing against his pants. Her mouth opened against his and her tongue darted in, taking from him and demanding everything he had to give.

He leaned forward and with one hand, swept the

game to the floor, the pieces plinking against each other as they tumbled to the carpet. Then he scooped her up and onto the small gateleg table, fitting himself into the space between her legs, feeling her skirt ride up those hips, knowing she wore nothing underneath and wishing he were naked, too.

To hell with his idea. To hell with falling in love. To hell with everything but Maria and now and hot, passionate sex.

Their mouths were on fire against one another, teasing and nipping, pulling and giving. His hands reached up and tugged the silky straps of her bra down her shoulders, allowing her breasts to spill forward against his chest.

She leaned back and he paused in his kiss long enough to look at the glorious figure before him. "You are incredible," he said. "A perfect woman."

"I'm not—"

"Going to negate my compliment," he interrupted, a finger to her lips. "Everything about you is beautiful and perfect and pleasing. And if I don't make love to you right now, I think I will regret it for the rest of my life."

"If you don't make love to me right now, I'll make sure you regret it," she said with a grin.

Then she reached for his belt buckle.

And his brain turned to mush.

Maria's Too-Sweet-to-Be-Good-for-You Mascarpone and Berries

1 pound raspberries
¼ cup confectioners' sugar
8 ounces mascarpone cheese
6 ounces plain yogurt
1 pound strawberries, hulled

Anything this delectable has to be bad for you. But it looks too good to resist, so why not make it better? Puree half the raspberries with the sugar and set aside. Mix the cheese and the yogurt until your willpower is completely gone and your conscience has fallen silent.

Spread the raspberry sauce on a plate, then top with a mini-mountain of mascarpone and a pile of strawberries. Be careful . . . this is the kind of indulgence that leads to many, many more.

CHAPTER 25

Maria woke up to regrets and mascarpone cheese on toast, with plump, ripe strawberries on the side.

Dante stood beside her bed, a tray filled with the breakfast delight in his hands. "Good morning."

In the light of day, she should know better. He wasn't the kind of man she should involve herself with. For one, he was clearly domesticated. Domesticated men tended to like commitments, women who waited at home, with a smile on their faces and a dinner in the oven.

"Where'd this come from?" she asked, indicating the breakfast.

He lowered himself to the space beside her and she rolled a little to the side, clutching the sheet to her naked torso. Dante kicked off his shoes and laid his legs down the length of the bed. "Not from *your* kitchen," he said with a laugh. "You have the emptiest refrigerator I've ever seen."

"I'm on a diet."

He shook his head. "You're crazy. You were already perfect when I met you."

"So what'd you do? Call some strawberry delivery service?"

"No. I woke up before you, got dressed and ran down to the corner market. It's not much, but I figured you wouldn't be all that hungry." He grinned. "Yet."

"It looks delicious. But . . . I shouldn't."

"There you go again, resisting me."

"You're the type of man I should resist."

"And why is that?"

"Because you want everything I don't want."

"Oh, yeah?" He leaned closer, a strawberry in his hands, inches from her mouth. "And how do you know what you really want unless you've tried everything on the menu?"

She swallowed the breath in her throat. "I've done the sampler platter. That's enough for me."

"Ah, you must have had a bad chef."

"The worst."

"Maybe one who can actually cook would change your mind."

She shook her head. "I'm pretty stubborn."

"Last night didn't sway you at all?"

"Last night was . . . last night. It's morning now and—"

"That changes nothing. Except . . . it's time for replenishment." He grinned and swiped the strawberry in his hands across the mascarpone, then dangled the cheese-dipped treat over her mouth. "Try this."

She put up a hand. "Oh, no."

"Why not?"

"It's too good."

He arched a brow. "Too good?"

"I eat one bite of that and before I know it, I'm standing in Guido's, devouring the entire counter."

"Kind of like when you got one look at my chest, huh?"

"You are too full of yourself."

"You weren't too full of me last night." He teased along her lip with the strawberry. "Not the first time. Or the second time."

"The third time was all your idea."

His laughter came from deep in his gut. "So it was. Well, after all that, you need some sustenance."

The mascarpone smelled heavenly. She licked her lips and caught a dab on her tongue. Oh . . . it tasted like sweet paradise. One bite wouldn't kill her. And strawberries *were* healthy. She opened her mouth and took a nibble.

Then another. Then a third. And with that, the succulent berry was gone.

It was always like this when she was around Dante. One bite led to a second and before she could stop herself, she was in too deep.

"Wasn't that good?" he asked, and before she could respond, he had another berry at her mouth.

"Uh-huh," she said. "I hear, though, that eating alone is what ruins diets."

"Oh, I didn't plan on you dining alone." Dante put the tray on the nightstand, stood and pulled off his shirt. Damn. He looked good topless. She'd barely noticed yesterday. The minute her hands had met his chest, every neuron in her brain began firing on high, like a machine gun stuck on obliterate.

He unbuttoned his pants and tossed them onto the armchair. Damn. He looked good bottomless too, but before she could drink it all in, he'd climbed under the sheet with her. His body against hers was warm and comforting, like a blanket she'd had for years.

And yet, there was something else, something intensely sexual that built in intensity the minute his skin touched hers.

"You know," Dante said, nuzzling at her neck. "I like nice, round numbers."

Maria tipped her head back, giving him better access to her neck. Well . . . if she was going to do something bad for her, she might as well do it right. She'd think about all the reasons why he was wrong for her later. Much, much later.

"Me, too," she murmured. "And four is a nice, even number."

"It is, indeed. You have a little—" He leaned forward and kissed the cheese off her lips.

By the time she came up for air again, she and Dante had eaten all of the mascarpone and tasted every inch of each other.

She'd managed to blow every resolution she'd made in the last few weeks in a thirty-minute time span. But for once, she wasn't as worried about the calories as she was about what Dante was doing to her heart.

Rebecca's Get-Yourself-Out-of-a-Jam Cookies

4 ounces bittersweet chocolate, sort of like those
morning-after thoughts
3 cups flour
½ teaspoon baking soda
½ teaspoon salt
⅔ cup butter, softened
¾ cup sugar
2 eggs
2 teaspoons vanilla
Raspberry jam to taste

Whatever you've done, the best way to forget it is with
cookies. They are amazing in helping you block out memories of bad choices. Preheat the oven to 350 degrees.
Now you're ready to melt the chocolate in a saucepan,
then combine the flour, baking soda and salt in another
bowl.

In another bowl (don't worry about the mess; that's
what dishwashers—or hunky men who like to wash—
are for), beat the butter and sugar. Get it fluffy, like your
thoughts will be once you clear your conscience.

Add the eggs, one at a time, then the vanilla and chocolate. Beat until blended or until you've worked that man
out of your system.

Divide dough, wrap in plastic wrap and refrigerate
for two hours. Just long enough for a shopping trip or a
good confession among close friends.

When the dough is ready, roll it out to a quarter-inch
thickness on a lightly floured surface and cut into two-

inch circles. Cut center circles out of half of them. Bake the cookies for nine or ten minutes.

When the cookies are cool, assemble them. A full cookie on the bottom, topped with jam, then a cut-out cookie on top. Let the jam peek out and tempt those who might want to taste.

These work wonders—just ask Candace. But be careful. They can be used against you, if they fall into the hands of a man with commitment on his mind.

CHAPTER 26

When Dante came into work humming on Thursday afternoon, Franco jumped on him like a cockroach on a sugar crystal.

"Oh, you got it bad, Boss," Franco said. "Someone has your heart."

Dante smiled. "Maybe."

"The woman, she is the one, isn't she?" Franco practically hopped with joy at the thought of being right.

"Maybe."

He cupped a hand over his ears. "I hear the bells of the church. They are ringing for you."

"Don't go renting a tux yet, Franco. We're just dating." Dante went back to his song, heading into his office, Franco trailing along, nipping at his heels.

"I know true love. And this is true love." He nodded. "You marry this girl. Fast. Before another man does."

He'd been having exactly the same thought ever since number four with the strawberries. But he wasn't about to tell Franco that.

"I'm not rushing into anything. Besides, she's not interested in marriage."

"Yet," Franco said.

"Yet," Dante agreed.

"And you," Franco indicated Dante with a flourish of his hand, "you change her mind?"

"With a little help from some mascarpone." He grinned.

"That's what I tell you." Franco wagged a finger at him. "You win her heart with your cooking. You such a good cook. Always know the right foods. A woman, she likes a man who can make magic in a kitchen . . ."

Only half listening to Franco, Dante picked up Thursday's *Globe* and turned the page to the restaurant review section.

And there, staring back at him, was the headline he'd hoped he'd never see . . . but knew would come eventually. NEW RISTORANTE IS DIVINE, screamed the top of the section in forty-eight-point bold type.

Followed by five gold stars.

Five stars. The impossible. Achieved by the new kid in the North End.

Dante slammed the section down on the table, startling Franco into silence. "Did you see the paper today?"

"No, *perche?*"

"Seems we have some competition." Dante slid the review over to Franco. "This isn't good. Not good at all."

"The phone, it has been quiet today," Franco said, scanning the review. "Now I see why. This baby place," he jabbed at the paper, "they steal our people."

Dante ran a hand through his hair. "Reservations are down?"

"Vita will be okay," Franco said, laying a hand on Dante's shoulder. "She is a survivor."

"I don't want okay. Okay is what we've had for two generations." Dante shook his head. "I want more than that."

He shook his head, then took in a breath. Franco was right. Vita had dealt with competition before and survived. The new customers wouldn't desert them that quickly. "Well, it's only Thursday. It's always slow on weeknights. By the end of the weekend, people will forget this new place exists."

Everything else in his life had finally slipped into place. The restaurant was doing well. He'd found a woman he could love. And he actually had a life outside of Vita.

He wasn't going to let anything change that. Not over his fresh fettuccini.

It had gotten pretty ugly in the past thirty-six hours. The dalliance with Dante had sent her flying off the deep end.

She hadn't stopped with the mascarpone. Or the strawberries. Or the Sicilian ricotta cake he'd left behind and they'd forgotten to eat between orgasms. She'd moved from one indulgence to the next, ordering in pizza after he left. A *large* pizza. With every topping offered by the pizzeria.

Then she'd eaten the cannoli in her fridge. And the Cheez Whiz in the cabinet. Moved on to polish off the chips, the lone package of snack cakes she'd found in the back of the cabinet.

And if that hadn't been enough—and it hadn't—she'd headed down to Krispy Kreme for three cream-filled doughnuts and an extra-large cappuccino.

It had gone on from there, every meal a craving excess unmatched in her previous diet-disaster binges.

Six pounds up in two days. And the regrets had multiplied with the digestion of every calorie-laden bite.

Now, on Friday night, Maria sat with Candace and Rebecca at Guido's. The three of them had opted for dinner out after a long day at the shop, completing a rush order for a regular customer.

"Are you okay?" Rebecca asked, laying a hand over Maria's.

"Sure I am. Why wouldn't I be?"

"Uh, because you just ordered the manicotti *and* the lasagna."

"Not to mention, you also preordered dessert," Candace added. "I know the signs, Maria. I've been there myself. I have the Hershey's wrappers in the bottom of my purse to prove it."

Maria laughed. "You were different. You were marrying Mr. Wrong. I just . . ."

When she didn't finish, Rebecca touched her hand again. "Just what?"

"Fell for Mr. Wrong."

"Antonio?"

"No." She shook her head. "Guess I haven't been sharing much in the way of details lately." She told them about Dante and the multiple orgasm marathon they'd had two nights ago. "He's left me a couple messages. Well, more than a couple. And sent me flowers."

"And you've ignored him."

"I do that pretty well when I want to." She stirred her virgin piña colada and took a sip. No way was she going to drink alcohol again. All it created was bad situations.

"I don't get it. I met Dante and he seemed like a normal, non-homicidal man. With a good job and a really cute butt. What's there not to like?"

Maria sighed. "Nothing."

"So *why* are you depressed about it?"

"Because he's all wrong for me."

"He's not gay, and he doesn't have a hamster fetish." Rebecca squeezed some lemon into her water. "And you find him very attractive, I gather. So . . . why the hesitation?"

Maria let out another sigh. "He's everything my mother wants for me."

"Oh . . ." Rebecca said, nodding. "And that's the problem?"

"Yeah."

"He's *too* traditional?" Candace asked.

"More than Martha Stewart at Christmas." Maria pushed the drink to the side. "He believes in falling in love. And getting married."

"Dump him. He's definitely dangerous." Rebecca grinned.

"What's so wrong with getting married?" Candace asked. "I've been thinking about it myself."

"Has Michael asked?"

"No, not yet. But he's been hinting around at it. Asked me how busy the shop is in June and if I was doing anything special next Saturday night."

"All good signs." Rebecca nodded. "You do already have the dress. And the guy. All you need is the ring."

Candace smiled and sipped at her Diet Coke. "Maybe I should ask him. Turn the tables. Keep him on his toes."

Maria laughed. "Now *that* would be the new Candace."

"So why not you, Maria?" Rebecca leaned forward. "Come on over to the dark side. Get married."

Maria chuckled. "No. It's not for me."

"Are you still thinking of . . ." Rebecca's voice trailed off.

"What? Go ahead and say it. I know you want to."

Rebecca let out a breath. "David. You laughed the whole thing off when it happened, but you seemed pretty hurt underneath it all. And, well, ever since then, you haven't really been the same."

"David was a jerk." Maria took another sip.

"A jerk who said he wanted to marry you." Candace set her empty salad plate to the side of the table.

"And then cheated on you. On your own dining room table, no less." Rebecca's face softened with sympathy.

Maria played with the toy sword holding her slice of pineapple. "I was stupid."

"No, he was," Rebecca said. "Any guy who doesn't see what a great person you are is an idiot who doesn't deserve you."

"You're just saying that because I'm your friend. And you need my help packing those baskets tomorrow."

"I'd say it even if you didn't own a third of the company." Rebecca smiled.

Candace reached for a slice of bread from the bowl in the center. She buttered it in neat, precise strokes. "Not all men are like David, you know."

Maria sighed. "I know that in my head. But then a little part of me wonders how I'll ever know the difference. How can I trust a guy? I mean, usually I'm the one who's smart. Who ends the relationship before I get hurt. But that time"—she toyed with her straw—"I was blind to everything."

"No, he was blinded by Bambi the Stripper's butt."

Maria laughed. "Yeah, he was."

"You used to be quite the workaholic before you met David." Rebecca stirred her drink. "Then once he mentioned marriage, you went the other way, sort of a—"

"Bride-a-holic?" Maria finished. "I'm Italian, what can I say? I do things in extremes."

"A little moderation . . ." Candace began gently.

"I know. I'm just afraid I can't balance both. Have a career and that. I know you have it, Rebecca, but you don't understand Italian men. At least the ones I know want their women in the kitchen and not running a business."

"Dante could be different. He's a business owner, too. Maybe your Mr. Wrong isn't really wrong." Rebecca gave Maria's free hand a quick squeeze. "Maybe you need to give him more of a chance."

The waiter arrived with the food. Maria put both

plates in front of her. The aroma wafted up to her nose, reawakening her stomach with a vengeance. "He can't be that good for me. He's got my appetite running like a car on high octane. Any man who makes me blow my diet is bad for my heart."

"He might not be good for your waistline, but your heart could probably use a little of that Italian love." Rebecca smiled. "Try the other side of the menu. You might just like it."

"No way," Maria said, diving into the manicotti. "I'm sticking to the one man I can depend on to always please me."

"Who's that?"

She held a bite of the luscious treat aloft. "Guido."

Arnold's It's-Not-Deprivation-It's-Love-on-a-Plate Salad

1 head romaine lettuce
2 tomatoes
2 hard-boiled eggs, just like your determination to be a Thin Chum
1 avocado
2 ounces provolone cheese, cubed
6 leaves fresh basil
Juice of one lemon
2 tablespoons extra-virgin olive oil (whew, sounds kind of sexy, don't it?)
1 tablespoon good, flavorful mustard
Salt and pepper

Tear the lettuce and cut the tomatoes. Mix in a bowl. Easy as pie, but without the calories. Peel and chop the eggs, then the avocado. Add those, along with the cheese and basil, to the bowl. Simple and yummy. The best kind of meal for a Chum.

Whisk together the lemon juice, oil and mustard, seasoning with the salt and pepper. Nature's dressing, without all that extra fat and calories. Serve on the side for dipping to reduce the calorie count.

Think of every bite as love for your width and height. This is a meal that helps you stay on track, while a good Chum will help you pick up the diet slack. And remember—Chubby Chums can be as fruity as plums!

CHAPTER 27

On Saturday morning, Maria was redeemed. And she didn't even have to go to confession to be forgiven.

Antonio called, his voice a low purr over the phone line. "I'm in Providence today, finishing up a trade show. What do you say I drive up tonight and see you?"

Oh, damn.

"I-I-I didn't know you'd be in town so soon," Maria mumbled around a Twinkie.

"Do you have a cold? Your voice sounds funny."

Cream filling dotted her fingertips but Antonio's voice held more power. She grabbed a napkin and swiped it off before it ended up accompanying the pound cake down her esophagus. "No, just, ah, finishing up some . . . painting on the walls. The fumes, you know."

"Ah, yes. Well, back to tonight. Do you have any plans?"

She glanced at her refrigerator calendar. On Saturday, she had penciled, "Mary Louise Zipparetto Bachelorette Party at Vita. Avoid at all costs."

"No, not a one. Until you called."

He chuckled. "That's my girl. I'll see you soon." Then he clicked off.

* * *

Mary Louise had the determination of a lioness hunting a wild boar. She had left three messages over the past week with the who-what-when-and-where of her "I'm getting married and you're not" party. Each time, she'd ended with additional begging for Maria to come. Probably wanted to make sure she had a full audience for bragging rights to the biggest diamond in the neighborhood.

"It would be good for you to go. Maybe you'd meet a man," Mamma said Saturday during her daily lunchtime phone call when Maria mentioned Mary Louise's annoying invitational frequency.

"You don't meet men at a bachelorette party, Mamma."

"Cousin Carlotta met her Tony at a party for girls."

"That was a birthday party for a five-year-old and Tony was the hired clown."

"Same thing," Mamma said.

"I'm still not going." Maria stabbed at her salad. Fat-free dressing, a pile of lettuce and a couple of lone cherry tomatoes. It wasn't a lunch. It was plate décor.

But it was better than the Twinkies, which were permanently in the trash. She'd run down to Paulie's Grocery after talking to Antonio and raided the fresh vegetables, narrowly missing an offer of a pity date from Gerry as he put the tomatoes carefully atop the romaine in her paper sack.

"Mary Louise's mamma said the party was going to be at Vita tonight," Mamma said. "Maybe Mary Louise will see Dante there."

"I don't care. I'm not seeing Dante."

But she'd yet to tell Dante that. He called and she didn't call back. He sent flowers, she ignored them. When had she lost her backbone? Why couldn't she just end it?

He had too many ideas about futures and commit-

ments. Those things suited her about as well as anchovies did ice cream.

Still, she didn't want to hurt him. She'd begun to
care about him. A lot.

And that was the whole damned problem.

"If you go to the party, you see him." Mamma's logic
made perfect sense only to Mamma.

Maria speared a piece of lettuce and ate it, thinking
and avoiding an answer. One of these days, she thought,
someone would actually create a diet that tasted like it
was bad for you.

"Mary Louise, I bet she like Dante. And his cooking," Mamma said.

"She won't eat it. She doesn't eat anything. I saw her
grocery cart."

"A girl who isn't busy eating will keep busy another
way," Mamma mused.

Maria toyed with a tomato, ignoring the flare of jealousy in her gut. She had no claims over Dante. "She's
engaged, Mamma."

"Not married. Yet."

"Like I said, I don't care. Dante isn't my boyfriend."

"No, no, of course he isn't." On the other end of the
phone, Maria could hear Mamma rolling out pasta. "But
that Mary Louise, she get her teeth in Dante, she not
gonna let go."

Maria stabbed at the tomato. It exploded under the
force of the fork, squirting red juice everywhere. What
if Size Two Mary Louise *did* wrap Dante around her bony
finger?

He'd hate a woman like that—one who didn't eat.
Who had all the personality of bad wallpaper and who
was only after a starter home and a Volvo. She'd ruin
him. And leave the pickings for the vultures.

Why did she care, anyway? Tonight, Antonio was com-

ing into town. She had a date with a gorgeous, no commitments guy. She didn't need any more complications
than that.

The empty feeling returned to her stomach. Damned
salad. What she needed was some lasagna to make it
taste better.

That's all.

"If you go and Mary Louise see you with Dante, I bet
she be so jealous, she eat her ring."

That idea held merit. Making Mary Louise Zipparetto
jealous of *her* for once was something to consider. Antonio
was in town. Convenient jealousy fodder.

And if he showed up at Vita, she could take the cow-
ard's way out in ending things with Dante. Certainly not
the way to be nominated for heroine of the year, but she
had yet to come up with a way to tell him she couldn't
see him anymore.

Because every time she thought about doing that,
her cravings for pasta intensified a hundredfold.

"I'll go," Maria said.

"Ah, I knew you would." She could practically hear
Mamma grinning on the other end. "Mamma is always
right. You listen to me about men and soon, there will
be babies, too."

Maria hung up the phone before her mother could
start picking out colors for a grandchildren-to-come
quilt. *That* was the last thing she needed right now.

Mamma's The-Surprise-Inside Meatballs

1 cup fresh bread crumbs
⅓ cup milk
4 tablespoons olive oil
1 medium onion, finely chopped
½ cup each ground beef, ground pork and ground veal
1 egg, lightly beaten
4 tablespoons freshly grated Parmigiano Reggiano
4 tablespoons chopped fresh parsley
3 tablespoons chopped fresh basil
24 2-ounce fresh mozzarella balls
Salt and pepper
6 cups marinara sauce

Even Mamma has a few surprises up her sleeve. She's not the boring old Mamma her daughter always thought. First, soak the bread crumbs in the milk for ten minutes. Meanwhile, heat the olive oil and cook the onion for a few minutes, then let cool.

In a large bowl, combine the meats, soaked bread crumbs, onion, egg, Parmigiano, herbs and salt and pepper, just like they did in the Old Country. Use your hands. Get in there, mix well. Don't be afraid of it. Shape into 1 ½-inch balls.

Now for the twist of Mamma. Stuff a mozzarella ball into the center of each meatball, making sure none of them peek out and spoil the surprise.

Fry the meatballs in a little more olive oil until browned

on all sides. Add the marinara sauce and simmer another ten, fifteen minutes. Serve them to a daughter who thinks she knows her mamma—

But really doesn't.

CHAPTER 28

Not only did she need something waterproof this time around, but she also needed to double the *Wow* factor on her next dress selection. It had to completely wipe out Antonio's memories of their last date and make her desirable again.

Not an easy feat for a piece of material.

Thanks to her three-day eating frenzy, she'd bumped herself back up into the twelve range. That afternoon, she'd stepped on her scale after getting naked, removing all jewelry, going to the bathroom and letting out all the air in her chest.

The needle gleefully pinged upward again.

Which meant she needed to move upward in the clothes closet, too.

Maria walked up to Mamma's house and tried the door. Locked. No one home. She checked her watch and remembered it was Early Bird Potluck Bingo night at the Sons of Italy hall. Mamma wouldn't be back until she'd exhausted her red stamper and her pull-tab funds. Nonno had probably been smart enough to head down to the corner bar for a few pops before Nonna dragged him back home and chewed his ear off for getting drunk again.

She unlocked the door with her key and headed up to her old bedroom. At the top of the stairs, the linen closet door was ajar. Maria went to shut it, in case the cat climbed in there and shed all over the towels, and noticed a box sticking out of the top shelf.

Had it always been there? Plain cardboard, it sat there like a lonely Christmas gift, unwanted and unopened.

Maria flicked on the hall light switch to read the writing on the side. Her mother's script, in Italian: *Save for Maria.*

It was probably an early birthday gift. Except Maria's birthday was seven months away and Mamma never shopped early. She was one of those people who seemed to love the scattered rush of last-minute gifting, charging through the mall like an army commando with no intentions of failing his mission.

She should shut the door. Leave it alone. Let Mamma tell her what it was in her own good time. With Maria's luck, it was probably an entire wedding trousseau.

Except the box was too small. And something about the handwriting seemed . . .

Old. Like Mamma had packed that box years ago and set it away, with the intention of giving it to her daughter years down the road.

Maria turned away, shutting the door. But it didn't quite latch. The skinny oak door drifted open again, as if inviting her in.

She hesitated, then continued past the door and went into her old room. It took some searching, but she found a red wrap dress in a forgiving twelve that came to a daring V at the neck. A nice match for the Ferrari. And for her second date with Antonio.

With the dress over her arm, Maria headed out of

her room and past the linen closet again. Her gaze went to the box.

Save for Maria.

Save what? Probably Mamma's wedding veil. Or some handkerchief from a great aunt that had been handmade in the Old Country. Or maybe one of those roosters her mother collected, meant for Maria's kitchen someday.

She reached for the door handle. *Shut the door. Don't look.*

She reached for the box instead. The dress slid to her shoulder, the hanger banging against her back. She slid the cardboard forward, now on her tiptoes. It wasn't a rooster. Too light to be anything ceramic.

She pried back the lid.

Staring back at her was a college degree with Biba Pagliano's name on it. A bachelor's degree in art history from UMass Boston, just a few T stops away on Morrissey Boulevard.

Mamma? In college? After she'd married Papa?

She'd never said a word. Never held a job at a museum. Never even bought a Picasso, not that there'd ever been money for something like that.

The only collection Mamma had was those silly roosters. They'd become her hobby, her only thing outside Maria, the quilting club and bingo.

Maria ran her finger over her mother's name on the degree. She'd never known. Had no idea her mother had any ambitions at all. Instead, she'd always thought Biba had been pouring her own goals into Maria by pushing her to go to college, to finish her own dual degrees in business and marketing.

"*Cara?* Is that you?" her mother's voice carried up the stairs. "I win the bingo!"

Maria shoved the box back into the closet, shut the

door and hurried down the stairs. "Mamma! I just stopped by to get a dress." She held up the evidence.

"Ah, another date? With Dante?"

"No. Antonio."

Mamma pursed her lips. "I don't like him. He not treat you right when you know him before."

"Mamma, that was years ago. He's a grown man now."

Mamma wagged a finger at her. "That makes them worse, you know."

Papa came trundling into the house, heading straight for the recliner and the remote. "Mamma won," he told Maria.

"I know. I heard."

"She's the big spender now. She keeps winning like that, I can quit my job." He added a shake of the remote for emphasis.

"And do what?" Mamma said. "Sit around my house and get dusty?" She swatted at him with an imaginary feather duster.

"Keep you happy all day." Papa caught her hand, pulling her into his lap for a loud, dramatic kiss.

Mamma laughed, the sound of it tinkling like wine-glasses at a party. "Oh, you old fool, you already do."

Maria dove for Arnold like a drowning woman after a life preserver. "Arnold, I need help."

She'd stopped by the Chubby Chums meeting before she went over to Vita to face the mother of all temptations. There was nothing she could do about her weight tonight, but she could change the future and get an extra dose of willpower before heading into the restaurant. Arnold had thankfully been outside on the stairs, talking to a new member.

He turned now and beamed at her, giving her a tight

one-armed squeeze. A few of the others were milling around, discussing the merits of tofu in meat loaf. "What's up, Chubby Chum Maria?"

"My scale. By about ten pounds in the last week."

He waved a hand at her figure. "Oh, honey, you'd never know it."

Always count on Arnold to be nice. "Lycra is a gift from God."

"Oh, don't I know it." He patted his stretch jeans rump.

She drew him to the side as Bert and Audrey filed in. Bert carried a bag of Burger King contraband that he scooped from regularly as he walked. Audrey was lecturing him about the cholesterol level in a single French fry.

"Listen," Maria said, "I can't seem to stick to my diet no matter what I do. And I really need to. I have this class reunion coming up in a month. I need to lose weight fast. I have to fit my dress."

Arnold wagged a finger at her. "You know what Stephanie says. If you lose weight for your attire, it won't improve your inner fire."

"Arnold, I really don't want a platitude. I want some real help. Advice. Support. Anything. I'm desperate." She grabbed the front of his shirt and gave it a little shake. "I ate an entire Sicilian ricotta cake yesterday."

"Oh, wow." Arnold blinked. "You have strayed, Chubby Chum."

Maria closed her eyes for a second, releasing Arnold. "More than you know."

"Why are you asking me?"

"Frankly, you're the only normal person in this group."

He laughed and drew her into a second hug, nearly suffocating her this time before releasing her for oxygen. "I don't know about that, but I'll support you if you'll be my Chubby Chum, too. I need a little help getting off my plateau." He patted his stomach. "Right now, it's one big cliff."

"You've got a deal."

"Chubby Chum Maria, you are my rainbow," Arnold said, stepping back to beam at her. "You take my blue and make it into yellow."

Dante's The-Only-Thing-That's-Simple-is-the-Fettuccini Alfredo

12 ounces fettuccini
2 tablespoons butter
1 ¼ cups heavy cream
1 cup Parmigiano Reggiano cheese
¼ teaspoon freshly grated nutmeg
Salt and pepper
2 tablespoons chopped fresh parsley, for garnish

When everything else is going wrong, cook something simple like fettuccini. Anything more complicated, and your brain will go into overload, because it's working so damned hard trying *not* to think about her.

Cook the pasta in boiling salted water until it's al dente. Meanwhile, melt the butter, add the cream and Parmigiano, nutmeg, salt and pepper. Stir until the cheese has melted and the sauce has thickened. It really doesn't get any more basic than that. Stir in the drained pasta, add the chopped parsley.

Eat the whole damned thing and ignore the thoughts of the woman sitting right outside your kitchen, breaking your heart with the precision of a ball peen hammer.

CHAPTER 29

Franco's smile of satisfaction would have put a well-fed cat to shame. "She returns."

Dante tasted the Alfredo sauce the new line chef had made. Not quite Vita material. Not yet. He scooped in some more Parmigiano Reggiano. Then he sprinkled in a dose of nutmeg and whisked the ingredients into the cream sauce. When Franco didn't elaborate, Dante turned to him. "They do better puzzles in the Sunday *Globe*, Franco. Who do you mean?"

"Maria. Your intended."

His hand stilled for a second like the whisk had a stutter, then went back to work. "She's not intended for anything with me."

She'd made that damned clear. Why had he ever been stupid enough to think differently?

"Then why is she here again?" Franco pointed toward the swinging door that led to the dining room. "And she brought her friends. Maybe to show her prize stallion to the herd?"

The whisk skipped against the pan, spattering Alfredo on his apron. "I am not her stallion."

"Hey, Franco. Did you say there's a whole table of women out there?" Vinny asked.

"All *bella donnas,* too," Franco said with a nod.

Vinny abandoned his pasta making and dashed over to the swinging doors. "Hey, Boss, come here. You gotta see this."

Only for curiosity's sake, Dante crossed to the oval glass on the kitchen door. He *didn't* want to see Maria. She was clearly done with him and he was definitely done with her. She'd given him the message—by not returning his calls.

Then why did he peer through the glass, anyway?

"That one with the tiara's quite the looker, huh?" Vinny said.

"Which one?"

"You know, the bride-to-be." Vinny gestured through the window at a woman wearing a rhinestone crown. "Hot as a butane flame, that one."

"I hadn't noticed." Dante supposed, looking at her now, that the woman at the head of the table could be considered pretty. If a man liked his women as shapeless as a stick of angel hair pasta and with a face that had the pinched look of someone who needed a good meal and a good laugh.

Maria, on the other hand—

She looked as she had the last time he'd seen her. Like she enjoyed everything. Her life. Her body. Her food. She sat at the other end of the table from the bride, her face animated, full of expression. She laughed at something the blonde woman beside her said and something in his gut reached out, as if he could taste that laughter. Bottle it for later.

For those nights when he came home after a long, draining day to an empty, silent apartment.

He missed her. Damn it all. More than he wanted to acknowledge. She'd been avoiding him since their night together. It had to be fear. Because he knew—he *knew*—she'd had a damned good time.

He'd heard how good in his ear. Many times over.

But there'd been more to it than that. The way she curled into his arms that night and slept there, as vulnerable as a hummingbird. When Maria Pagliano let down the barriers between herself and the world, she became a woman filled with more dimensions than perfect Waterford crystal.

She was smart, funny, beautiful. What had Sal said about Ada? The only one with a leash strong enough to keep him in line. And that leash was wrapped right around his heart.

Too bad she'd left the other end flapping in the wind.

Rochelle pushed through the opposite door with a tray of dirty dishes in her hands. "If you two gawk any more, you'll harden into salt. Just like in Sodom and Gomorrah."

"Hey, I don't get into that kind of kinky stuff," Vinny said.

"It's busy out there again. Not as busy as last week, but good for a Friday night."

"Busy is good for tips," Dante told her. He stepped away from the door, and reluctantly brought his attention back to his kitchen. Rochelle was right. It was busy. He had a restaurant to run. He couldn't stand there staring at Maria all night like a teenager with an unreciprocated crush. With that new restaurant garnering the elusive five-star review, he couldn't afford to take his eyes off Vita for a second.

As she left the kitchen with two salads, Rochelle muttered something about men and their inability to function when a few pheromones were in the air.

Dante dragged Vinny back to the pasta and returned to his Alfredo sauce.

"Why is Maria here, I wonder," Franco said to no one in particular.

"Don't look at me for the answer," Dante said. "She hasn't returned any of my calls. If I didn't know better, I'd say she was trying to dump me. But then, she shows up here?" Dante shrugged. "Women speak a whole 'nother language."

Franco shrugged. "I go out there. Talk to her. Find out her intentions."

Dante dropped the whisk to the counter with a clatter. "You'll do no such thing. I'll go."

Franco's smile widened.

He'd been had. "Damn you, old man. You're good."

"When it comes to *amore*, Franco is always right." His maître d' bustled around him, removing the apron, patting at a wrinkle in Dante's shirt.

"I'm not meeting the queen of England, you know."

"Ah, no. Someone more important and with a nicer—" Franco made the outline of an hourglass with his hands.

Rochelle swung into the kitchen again, clipping a new order onto the stainless steel board above the counter. She turned and began loading a tray with finished meals marked table twenty-eight.

"Here, let me help you," Dante said, grabbing a second tray and putting half the plates on it.

Rochelle stopped what she was doing to cock a hip in his direction. "I can handle this. I'm no wimp like those new waitresses you hired. They cry if they have to carry more than one glass of wine."

Dante grinned, "No one is as good as you, Ro."

"You know it." She hefted her tray onto her shoulder, then directed a glance toward the tray in his hands, pretending she didn't care one way or the other if he helped. "If you insist on helping, you better keep up with me." She wagged a finger at him. "And no flirting with the women at table nine."

"I had no intentions—"

"Don't bullshit me. You never help carry out orders. A dozen pretty women come in and boom, you're busboy of the year. Just keep your eyes on the tray and head straight for twenty-eight."

He put up one hand, three fingers extended in the hand movement he'd learned back in grade school. "Scout's honor."

Rochelle snorted. "I saw you and Vin mooning over those women like a couple of mutts at the poodle show. And I could hear Franco concocting some matchmaking scheme all the way in the dining room." She headed toward the door, pushing it open with her hip in a practiced move that said she'd done it a hundred times before. "Table twenty-eight. No detours."

Dante chuckled. "I should make you manager. And give you a whip."

Rochelle grinned at him over her shoulder. "Now that just might make this job fun."

Dante followed behind her, laughing.

"Uh, Boss?" Franco said.

He pivoted back. "What?"

Franco patted his head.

His chef hat. Dante removed it and sent it sailing Franco's way. "You're in charge of the kitchen while I'm out there."

Franco beamed, then sobered and eyed Vinny. "You. No funny business with the matches or Franco will put you out."

"Boss! Don't leave me with him. Last time you did, he hosed me down—"

But Dante had already left.

Together, he and Rochelle placed the dinners before the customers at table twenty-eight. Dante introduced himself, staying a few minutes to chat, then turned back toward the kitchen. Rochelle had already picked up the trays and the tray stands, disappearing back into the kitchen.

He had every intention of going back to work. The restaurant couldn't run itself, after all. But then, from across the room, he heard the throaty sound of Maria's laughter. And he stopped.

He pivoted and saw her, sitting at table nine in a red dress with a daring V-neck that set off her hair and made everything about her seem more vibrant.

God, he wanted to kiss her. To pull her to him and pick up where they'd left off, to taste the warmth of her skin, the hollows of her neck, the tender flesh along her belly. He wanted to smell the sweet perfume of her hair, feel the light caress of her hand against his skin.

He wanted, quite simply, as many parts of her as he could have. Again.

He should go over to table nine. Make sure everything was up to par. It was one of the tables one of the new waitresses was handling. She could be falling down on the job. Keeping the guests undersupplied with water. The last thing he wanted was to be a disappointment to—

The customers.

Yeah, that was it. He didn't want to go over there to see if he could turn—what had Vinny called it?—the butane flame in his gut from simmering to scorching.

And set off a four-alarm inside her, too. Once and for all.

Mary Louise's How-to-Be-the-Center-of-Attention Zabaglione

4 egg yolks
½ cup confectioners' sugar
½ cup dry Marsala wine
Biscotti or butter cookies, to serve

First, sit at the head of the table and wear a crown so everyone knows it's your party and you are queen for the day. Be sure you have had your diamond polished and your nails done. Wouldn't want anyone to miss the gleam of the new jewel.

Second, have someone in the kitchen because you are far too busy with gifts and well wishes to do it yourself. Whoever the kitchen person is should whisk together the egg yolks and sugar. Then they need to carefully put the bowl over a saucepan of simmering water (but don't let the bowl touch the water or you'll get scrambled eggs instead and that will ruin everything). The kitchen person has to beat with a handheld mixer until the eggs and sugar are pale and creamy. Add the Marsala, and beat until it reaches 160 degrees. About the same temperature as everyone's jealousy that you are getting married and they are not.

Have the kitchen help bring out the zabaglione in one big bowl with little bowls and biscotti so you, as queen, can dispense to the others. It is, after all, your party. You must remain the focus of the gathering.

No matter what it takes.

CHAPTER 30

"Oh, look, here comes the chef," Mary Louise said.

Oh, no, not him, Maria thought. *Not yet.*

"How do you know it's him?" Carla Romano asked. "He's not even wearing the pork chop hat."

"My father thoroughly checks out every eating establishment before we dine anywhere. Food poisoning and all that," Mary Louise said. "He downloaded all the past articles about Vita off the Internet. One of them had Dante Del Rosso's picture with it."

"I can see why." Carla sighed. "He's a hunk."

"Ladies," Dante said, arriving at the table, looking as good—no, better—than he had the last time she'd seen him. His blue button-down shirt and gray slacks were a perfect compliment to his dark brown hair and eyes. She busied herself with her Diet Coke instead of looking at him. "I hope you are enjoying your meal?"

"Oh, yes, very much," Angela Renaldi piped up from the corner seat.

"Even more so now," Mary Louise added. With a smile. Maria noted Dante ignored the obvious flirt from

Mary Louise. Instead, he turned all his attention on Maria. "It's nice to see you again, too."

She gave him a polite smile. "You, too."

"I've been trying to reach you."

Every woman at the table fell silent, watching the exchange between her and Dante. Mary Louise's mouth dropped open.

Apparently not everything about Dante could be found on the Internet.

"I've been . . . busy."

"Busy? Or avoiding me?"

She swallowed. "Busy."

From the look in his eyes, it was clear he didn't believe her. "You look beautiful tonight."

The air hung between them, heavy and still. For a moment, Maria wanted to chuck her plan out the window and reach out, ending the agony of wanting and resisting Dante. She raised her hand to grasp his and—

"That's my Maria, always the prettiest one at the party." Antonio swooped into the area, laying a proprietary kiss on Maria's cheek. "Hello, *bignole.* Sorry I'm late. I-95 was a mess."

When she'd concocted this idea, it had seemed so smart. Meet Antonio here and kill two relationships with one bachelorette party stone—she'd finally send a clear message to Dante that she wasn't interested and broadcast to Mary Louise that twenty pounds didn't make a woman a hippo.

But when she glanced at Dante's face, she didn't see resignation. Or anger. Or giving up on her.

She saw hurt.

Oh, God. What had she done? All she wanted to do now was undo it. Take it back. Turn the clock around and erase that look in Dante's eyes. The regret inside her became a heavy, burdensome thing she couldn't seem to shake.

"Hi, Antonio," she said, because she knew she had to say something.

He reached behind him, stole a chair from a nearby table and pulled it up to sit beside Maria, draping his coat over it. Then he rested his arm over the back of her seat, clearly conveying possession. Antonio's gaze went to Dante's. Two wolves, squaring off over territory.

"I have a kitchen to run," Dante said. "I hope you enjoy your meal," he said to Maria. She got the feeling he hoped she'd choke. "Ladies, I'll be sure to whip up a special treat in honor of the bride." He sent a smile Mary Louise Zipparetto's way, then left.

Maria sat back in her chair. She needed some stuffed shells. Immediately.

So she could shove them in her mouth and stop herself from ever doing anything so stupid again.

Mary Louise had finally started on her gifts. This torture event would come to an end soon. Maria itched to be out of her seat, but with Antonio's arm over her shoulders, she was pinned to the cranberry cushion.

"Oh, thank you, Maria, for the . . . uh, what exactly is this?" Mary Louise said.

Maria smiled. "Edible underwear."

"Edible?" Mary Louise's eyes widened. "You . . . *eat* it?"

"I figured you, or Joey, might need a little sustenance on the honeymoon."

Mary Louise turned strawberry red, shoved the package of Popsicle-flavored panties under the table and reached for the next gift. Quick.

"I wanted to talk about that plan," Antonio said, his voice low so the oohing and ahhing Mary Louise Zipparetto Fan Club couldn't overhear. "We can talk business now and get down to a little 'other business' later." He nibbled at her neck.

His kiss felt like the overzealous welcome of a sloppy uncle. What had happened? He used to set her skin on fire. She couldn't blame her lack of reaction on a wine-glass because this time, she hadn't been drinking.

It had to be the built-in audience. Mary Louise and her friends, all talking about the gifts and her upcoming marriage and in between, how cute Dante was. She knew they were all speculating about her and just salivating for an opening so they could grill her for more information. After all, a gorgeous man had shown up and was now nuzzling at her neck, right after the owner of the hippest restaurant in the North End had made it clear he had a little unfinished business of his own with her.

Maria forced herself back to Antonio, drawing her neck out of kissing range. "So, what's this plan?"

Maybe if they talked, she'd rekindle the flame from high school again. Because it sure as hell seemed to have gone out since that dinner.

"I might have told you, I work for a securities firm in California?"

"Yes, you mentioned it."

"Well, there's this great opportunity that I came across. Remember those tan-through swimsuits that were on the market years ago?"

"Yeah. They were practically transparent." And tiny enough that only a mouse could wear them.

"Well, I've found someone who has an idea for tan-through Speedos. It's the wave of the future for men's beachwear. No more white butt cracks on your plumber."

Maria blinked. "Tan-through *Speedos?*" She didn't even want to try to wrap her mind around *that* mental image.

Antonio nodded, his eyes full of excitement. "It's brilliant. And I want in. In fact, I don't just want in, I want to own the company."

"That sounds . . . great."

"But here's where I need a little help." He toyed with

the back of her hand, trailing a finger down slow and easy. "The banks, they're picky. You know how they are."

"Yeah. I've been in business with Rebecca and Candace for a few years. We deal with banks all the time."

"And they want all these papers." Antonio let out a gust. "A mountain of them."

"It's a necessary part of getting financing. I'm sure you deal with that all the time, working in the securities industry."

"Well, I'm more an adviser than a pencil pusher. But you"—he pointed at her—"you really seem to know about this stuff."

She nodded, sipping at her Diet Coke. "I did the paperwork for Gift Baskets when we first went into business and handled most of the financials. Rebecca and Candace and I each have our own strengths and mine is in the business end of it."

"You were always so smart," Antonio said, smiling at her. "Smarter than me."

"I got better grades than you, that's all."

"You gave me almost every grade I ever got." He started up on her hand again, his gaze watching his index finger tracing a slow circle around her knuckles. "So I thought, since you were so smart, you could help me."

"I'd be glad to give you some advice."

"I don't really need advice," the finger traced a smaller circle, "more . . . help."

Maria shifted in her chair. "What kind of help are you talking about?"

"Well, yours, of course."

"You're hedging. Why don't you spell it out?"

"I need a business plan. And I know you're the *perfect* one to write it for me." His smile was wide and full of good orthodontia.

"A business plan?" Maria eyed him. "Do you have any idea how much work goes into one of those?"

"Well, yes. That's why I'm asking you." He covered her hand with his own. "I'm so busy. I don't have time to do it."

"You want to buy the business. You should be able to find the time to do this yourself. It's part of being an entrepreneur, Antonio."

He squeezed her hand. "I just want to be an owner of a good thing. Get in on something that's going to make me millions."

"In other words, you don't want to do any of the hard work."

He grinned. "Not if I can help it."

She yanked her hand away from his. "I'm not going to do this for you."

"Why not? It's a chance to help me and in turn, I can make you very happy." His voice was deep and full of innuendo.

Innuendos that no longer held any appeal whatsoever. "I don't think so, Antonio."

"What, don't you want to be my cheerleader anymore?"

"No, I don't. And frankly, I think you're an asshole."

He drew back. "What? Why?"

"Because you're lazy and you're using me. And those two things aren't worth half an orgasm. Even on that, you cheated me back on prom night."

His gaze turned steely. "Well, maybe I'd have been more inclined to work harder if you looked a little more like my ideal woman."

Maria got to her feet, her chair teetering for a minute before falling back into place. The women swiveled to look at her and eavesdrop, but she didn't care. "What is that supposed to mean?"

"Well, you are a little"—his gaze roamed over her form—"pudgy. Not my type at all."

"Pudgy? *Pudgy*! How dare you!" She jerked his coat off the back of the chair and shoved it into his chest. "Get the hell out of this restaurant, out of my life and out of my city."

He rose and draped the black leather over his arm. "What, you can't take a little constructive criticism?"

"What I don't take is bullshit from jerks like you. Now get out." She gave him a little push.

He stumbled backwards two steps. And actually looked surprised. Apparently, not many women rejected Antonio.

"Is there a problem here?" Franco asked, hurrying over to the table. "I bring a special treat, for the bride." He hoisted a large dish of zabaglione with a smile, then laid the bowl and a tray of smaller serving dishes and biscotti before Mary Louise.

"No, not anymore. The *problem* is just leaving," Maria said.

Mary Louise had also hurried over. "Oh, don't go," she said. "Why, you're the only man at our party." She gave him a bright smile.

Five minutes ago, Mary Louise had been too wrapped up in her thong panties and edible underwear to hear the exchange between Maria and Antonio. Now, when he was clearly being a jerk, she was trying to play hostess?

"Mary Louise, I don't need you to interfere. Antonio and I—"

"Were just ending things," Antonio interrupted.

"You broke up? At my bachelorette party?"

Antonio gave a somber nod, as if it were the most tragic event in his life. Just as he had in high school, Antonio capitalized on every bit of female sympathy he could find.

"He—" Maria began.

"Oh, I'm so sorry," Mary Louise said, cutting Maria off. She laid a hand on Antonio's arm. "Why don't you come over here and keep us girls company? Maria's got another friend in the kitchen, anyway." She gave Maria a jealous, catty look.

"That's not true. We—" Then Maria stopped trying to explain. Why waste her breath with these people, anyway?

"Antonio's right," Mary Louise said, looking down her skinny nose. "You *are* pudgy. And I think you should leave my party. You're causing a disturbance."

"Oh, I haven't caused anything yet." And before she could think about what she was doing, she picked up the bowl of zabaglione and dumped it onto Mary Louise's head. "You could use a few calories."

A collective shriek went through the restaurant crowd. Maria picked up her purse and turned away from the table, leaving Mary Louise gasping through custard and Antonio crooning over her, offering to help clean it off.

Too bad there hadn't been two bowls.

She'd almost reached the door when Franco hurried up to her. "Oh, don't go," he said. "Stay. Have a glass of wine."

Maria paused, closing her eyes. She let out a sigh, regret replacing the air in her lungs. "Franco, I'm sorry about the thing with the dessert back there. Sometimes, my Italian temper takes over and I act without thinking."

Franco shrugged. "I would have done it if you didn't. That woman, she is a thorny stick waiting to be broken by the right foot."

Maria laughed. "You're right about that."

He nodded toward the lounge area, separated from the restaurant by a glass door. "Go in there. Enjoy yourself."

All she wanted to do was go home and retreat into a lump of self-pity. Consume as many calories as she could and sob over the fact that all her work had been for nothing. Antonio saw her as a fat, unattractive woman who was only good for one thing—to do his homework. Nothing had changed since high school.

But if she walked out that door right now, she'd look like she was going off to do exactly that—sulk. And the last thing she wanted any of them to think was that Maria Pagliano was bothered by one damned word they'd said.

"You're right, Franco." She turned on her heel and headed toward the bar.

"I'm always right." He held the door for her. "Franco is one smart cookie."

When Franco came hurrying into the kitchen, Dante knew something was up. "You, go out. Get a drink," Franco said.

"You know I don't drink when I'm working."

"Get a Coke. At the bar."

Dante looked at the bustling kitchen. "I really—"

"The kitchen won't explode if you leave for two minutes." Franco gave him a little push. "Now go."

"No. Not until you tell me who is in the bar."

Franco shrugged, doing his Marcel Marceau interpretation.

"Maria is in there, isn't she?"

He shrugged again.

"I have nothing to say to her."

"No?"

"No."

Franco busied himself with straightening a pile of forks in a plastic bin. "Always there are words to say. Sometimes only three words."

Damned if he'd *ever* say those three words to her. Not after she'd torn his heart better than the best Cuisinart on the marketplace. He was through chasing after her.

Sometimes the hunter needed to let the damned deer get away. And go after some slow-moving elk instead.

"Didn't you see what she did?" Dante said. "She met another man here. After all we—" He shook his head. He wasn't going to finish that sentence. He wasn't even going to *think* about how that sentence ended.

He was done with Maria Pagliano. Done. Done. *Done.*

"She gave him the boot." Franco nodded. "Good thing, too, or Franco might have had to throw him out. He no good."

"I don't care."

Franco peered into Dante's eyes. "You can never lie to Franco. I know you since you were little boy. Your lies, they show in your eyes, right there, by the dot." Franco pointed, nearly blinding Dante in his show and tell.

"You have a job to do. And if you want to keep it, I suggest you get out there and tend to the customers."

"I go nowhere until you tend to your heart."

Dante let out a curse. "Fine, if it will make you feel better, I'll grab a soda and come back. But I'm not talking to her."

"Uh-huh. Two lovebirds in the same tree, they cannot help but chirp."

Dante shook his head and left the kitchen before Franco came up with another twisted homily.

She sat at the bar, the red dress riding up a little on her thighs, sipping at a soda. She crossed one leg over the other and his pulse accelerated.

Apparently, his hormones hadn't gotten the message from his brain yet. Oh, damn. This was a bad idea.

He turned to go back into the kitchen, but she saw him before he could go.

"Dante." Her voice was soft, not full of any message at all.

He nodded toward Sonny, the bartender. "Coke, please." If Sonny was surprised to see Dante in the bar in the middle of the evening getting his own beverage, he didn't show it. He merely pushed the button on the dispenser to fill the glass, then slid it over.

Dante didn't sit on one of the bar stools because he didn't intend to stay. He looked at her, waiting for her to say something.

"I know you're mad at me," she said after a moment. "You have every right to be. What I did was wrong and stupid and—"

"I should have known better going into this thing. You warned me, after all." He took a sip of the Coke. It could have been water for all he tasted. "You don't want a man who comes with expectations you might have to deal with. You want some Rico Suave guy who's going to treat you like shit and then dump you for someone else."

She glanced away. "That's unfair."

He took a step forward. "Is it? I saw you with that guy. Antonio, was that his name? He had jerk all over him. You think by dating guys like that you can protect your heart. But all they do is help you build the wall around it."

The quaver in her lips told him the last sentence had hit home. But then she straightened and went back to being all Maria again. Tough cookie, right to the end.

"Dante, you don't understand."

Sonny had quietly slipped to the opposite end of the bar, busying himself with drying glasses and tending to the other customers. Dante lowered his voice so he wouldn't be overheard.

"I understand everything," he said. "You told me you like the illusion of control. And you know what? That's all you have. An illusion. You don't control a relationship because you aren't putting anything into it. You have to *feel* something, Maria, to have something to control. And you never felt anything for me at all."

"That's not true."

"It isn't? Then tell me what you felt. When you kissed me. When you made love with me. When you turned to another man in my restaurant."

She looked at him. A long moment passed and then she looked away, without saying anything.

"You're afraid to tell me what you feel. Because then you'd have to deal with it." He let out a half-laugh. "You're not in control of a damned thing, Maria."

"Walls keep you from being hurt, Dante. They stop people from getting in and breaking your—" She shook her head, as if she couldn't find the words she wanted.

"They also stop you from letting anyone who really cares get close. I like you," he said. "In fact, up until tonight, I thought I was falling in love with you." Her eyes widened and something lit inside them, then went out when he continued. "But I am not a masochist. I'm not going to keep throwing myself against a wall that isn't going to budge."

And then he left before he started listening to his foolish heart.

Mamma's Not-Everything-Is-as-It-Seems Ravioli

2 pounds fresh spinach
½ pound ricotta cheese
2 eggs
2 cups grated Parmigiano Reggiano cheese
½ teaspoon grated nutmeg
Salt and pepper
Ravioli sheets

Sauce:

½ cup butter
7 to 9 fresh sage leaves

You expected meat in my ravioli, no? Well, Mamma has another surprise up her sleeve. Wash the spinach well, then cook in boiling salted water until tender. Drain, let cool, then squeeze out as much water as you can. Use your muscles or ask your big strong man to use his.

Chop your spinach, then add the ricotta, eggs, Parmigiano, nutmeg, a little salt and pepper. Now, take your pasta sheets, one at a time. Don't let them dry out. Work fast. Your daughter is not getting any younger. You need to teach her these lessons before she's old and gray and bitter.

Put a teaspoon of the filling on your pasta, two inches apart. Cover with a second sheet, then press down to form little pockets. Cut out squares with your pastry wheel, then let ravioli dry for half an hour. Long enough to talk with your child about her future.

Heat the butter and sage over low heat and do not let it burn. Then drop the ravioli into boiling salted water and cook for just a little bit, a few minutes. Drain and serve with butter sauce before your daughter can escape out the back door. Show her with these raviolis that even Mamma sometimes has something a little different cooking in her kitchen.

CHAPTER 31

At the end of the day Tuesday, Mamma walked into Gift Baskets, a woman with a purpose. She had on her two-inch pumps that she usually reserved only for Mass, her purse under one arm, locked into place by her hand on the clasp, as if a mugger might come out of nowhere and snatch the Lillian Vernon personalized faux leather handbag.

"I want to speak to you," Mamma said.

"Mamma, what a surprise! You hardly ever come by the shop."

"I come now. My daughter tells her father to tell me to stop interfering. Why you do that?"

Maria let out a breath. She was afraid it might come to this. "Because you're always fixing me up with every single man in the North End. I wish you would stop trying to marry me off."

Her mother stood there for a second, saying nothing. A long second passed before she spoke again, her voice soft and sad. "All I want is for you to be happy."

"That's all I want, too." Maria sighed. "Listen, I have

to close up the shop. Do you want to walk home together?"

Mamma nodded. "I come to see you. In the shop. On the street. No matter."

Maria turned off the lights and locked up the doors, then grabbed her purse before setting the alarm and leaving Gift Baskets.

They started down the sidewalk, heading toward home in the early April evening. "You are not happy, *cara*," Mamma said.

"I was, before all this happened."

"No. No you weren't."

Maria let out a gust. "How do you know that?"

They stopped at a crosswalk and waited for the light to change. "I see your eyes, *cara*. In them is a lonely heart. You say you not want a man, but . . ."

"I don't *need* a man. That's different from wanting."

The light changed and they crossed the street, walking at the brisk pace that came from living in Boston all their lives.

"You don't need a man, maybe. But you need someone to love you."

"Mamma, I don't. Really."

Her mother tsk-tsked her. "Everyone needs love. It's food for the soul."

"My soul is well fed, believe me." She patted her hips. "Too well fed."

Her mother didn't say anything for a while, just kept up her steady pace, those shoes making a steady click against the sidewalk. A few minutes later, they reached the entrance to the North End. "Why you hate marriage so much?"

"I don't hate it. It's . . . it's not for me."

They went on again in silence for a while and then crossed onto the street that led to her parents' house. "You don't want what your mother has?"

How to answer that and keep her mother from disowning her, or worse, going into cardiac arrest right here on Hanover Street? No matter what she said, there were bound to be hurt feelings. And truly, the last thing Maria wanted to do was hurt her mother. "I want different things in life. That's all."

"You think your mamma live a life so bad?" she asked as they turned the corner.

When Maria didn't answer, Mamma waved toward the entrance to her house. "You, come with me. I show you something." They entered the back door and Mamma waved her toward a kitchen chair. "Sit."

Maria sat. She'd already disappointed her mother today, no sense disobeying her, too.

Mamma took one of the blank-faced white roosters off the shelf and put it into Maria's hand. She tipped her chin, indicating the six-inch bird. "How much you think that's worth?"

Maria tried really hard not to wrinkle up her nose at the ugly porcelain farm alarm. "Uh, ten bucks?"

"*Madonn!*" Mamma threw up her hands. "On eBay, this one is two thousand, five hundred dollars."

"eBay?" Maria shook her head. Had she heard her mother right? "Since when do *you* know about eBay?"

"You think I live in a can of Franco American? I know more than you think."

Maria's gaze dropped to the rooster in her hands. "He's worth over two thousand dollars?"

Mamma nodded, beaming. "That one there," She pointed to a multicolored rooster sitting on the shelf above the stove. "Seven hundred. And that one over by the window, nine hundred."

"Your roosters are worth that much money?"

"How you think you go to college? Papa and I gave you that money. Where you think it come from?"

At eighteen, she'd never thought about the ten thousand dollar check her mother had handed her at graduation. She did remember being glad a few roosters were missing from the kitchen and vaguely thinking something about some sucker at a garage sale getting them all.

And now it turned out they were priceless art?

She knew who the sucker was. And it wasn't Mamma. It was her daughter.

"How do you know these roosters are valuable?"

"I have the degree. I know you see the box in the upstairs closet the other day. And you wonder, why my mamma have that degree and never do anything? Well, I do something."

"But . . . roosters?"

Mamma shrugged. "I like roosters. That Picasso, he was crazy. You put crazy man's art in your house, you go crazy, too."

Maria leaned back in her chair. "I never knew."

"You think I only some married woman. Not so happy, huh?"

"I never said—"

"You not have to. I see it in your face." Mamma swallowed and toyed with the rooster dish towel on the stove. "This is why you think marriage is so bad. You not want to be like your mamma."

She'd never realized that all her protests against marriage would hurt her mother—not because they'd put off Mamma's hopes for grandchildren—but because it made it seem like her mother's life wasn't good enough. Wasn't something to be proud of. To emulate.

Maria had been wrong. Blind and wrong. She'd seen her mother through traditional eyes, never taking off the blinders and seeing her mamma was a woman who had it all.

"Oh, Mamma," Maria said. "There's more to it than

that. I didn't want to depend on a man who'd just hurt me in the end. I wanted to take care of myself."

"You can do both, *cara*." Mamma took the rooster from Maria's hands and put it back on the shelf. "I take care of myself. And my family. And Papa, he takes care of me here." She pressed a hand over her heart.

Maria got to her feet and crossed to her mother, taking her hands, her eyes misting. She looked at the face that was so like her own, but older and definitely wiser. "You did do that. And you surprised me."

"Mammas do that sometimes." She smiled, her eyes misty, too.

For a long moment, the two of them stood there, looking at each other with teary eyes, speaking the silent language of mother and daughter.

Tears stung at the back of Maria's throat. She drew her mother into a tight hug. Mamma's warm arms encircled her daughter back. And with that, the break between them was repaired.

"Are *all* these roosters valuable?" Maria said, when they finally drew apart.

Mamma laughed, catching a stray tear with the back of her hand. "No. Some I buy because I like the way they smile at me."

"Mamma, roosters don't smile."

"Mine do." Mamma patted the head of the white one on the shelf. "They make me happy."

"And rich."

"No, not rich. Just . . . comfortable. I don't need much."

"All these years, you never said anything."

"Why? This was mine. Papa doesn't care." She cupped Maria's chin. "You can marry and still have *you*."

Maria grinned. "Do I have to collect chickens?"

Mamma laughed. "Not chickens. They worth nothing. They not have the pride roosters have."

Maria shook her head, chuckling. "It's always the men."

Mamma nodded. "They are good to keep."

"And to sell."

"Papa, I won't sell him."

"Why not?"

Mamma grinned. "No category on eBay for used husbands."

After a week, it became clear that Vita was no longer the top dog in the restaurant kennel. The phone had fallen silent, with only the regulars continuing to show up. The two new line chefs were hired away, along with two of the new waitresses, leaving Dante—

About where he'd started before George Whitman's magic fairy pen had gifted his restaurant with a few weeks of success.

"Boss, this place is falling apart," Rochelle said. She piled the dirty dishes by the dishwasher and then put the empty tray on the counter.

It had to be a metaphor for his life. The restaurant was going down the tubes and he was unable to rescue it. Maria didn't want him and he couldn't rescue that, either.

"Did the faucet go in the ladies' room again? I swear, that plumber—"

"No, I don't mean the building. I mean Vita itself. Everybody's complaining. No one's getting their work done. Vinny's slow as a turtle on quaaludes getting my orders together. Even Franco isn't his usual cheery self."

Dante sighed and rubbed out the kink in the back of his neck. "I'll talk to them."

"It isn't going to do any good." Rochelle straightened her order pad and pen in her pocket. "Face it. We got lucky once. Vita is never going to be in the 'Top of the

Hub' category. Fate is too busy with other restaurants to bother with this one."

She picked up her tray again and headed off to pick up the order for table eleven.

The kink reappeared in Dante's neck. Twice as tight and three times as large. Maybe Rochelle was right. Maybe Vita wasn't meant to be anything more than it was.

And maybe he was a fool for ever thinking differently.

Monica's Be-Loved-for-Who-You-Are Fruit Salad

Juice of 3 oranges
Juice of 1 lemon
1 banana, sliced
2 apples, sliced
1 pear, chunked
2 peaches, chunked
4 apricots, chunked
⅔ cup red grapes, cut in halves
⅔ cup raspberries
Sugar, to taste (as sweet as you need it to be)

Mix the juices in a bowl, then add all the fruits. Sprinkle sugar over all and stir to mix together. No other decorations or frou-frou needed. This is come as you are—and be loved *au naturel.*

Share with someone who loves you, rain or shine, in Kenneth Cole or Kathie Lee Gifford. Be sure to have a little kibble on hand, too, for the other unconditional love of your life.

CHAPTER 32

"I swear on my firstborn child, this is not some evil matchmaking scheme," Rebecca said on Saturday morning

"Yeah, yeah." Maria grinned. "I wouldn't put it past Mamma to conspire with your OB." She reached out and drew Rebecca into a hug. "Seriously, though, I'm happy for you. Congratulations."

"And here I thought I was so tired because I was working too hard." Rebecca rubbed at her belly. "All the signs add up. I was too stupid to see them."

"You're a mom, a wife, a business owner," Candace said, joining the two for a triple embrace. "I think it's understandable you might not notice a missed period or two."

Rebecca shook her head. "Well, whether I'm ready or not, number two is on the way."

Maria smiled. "I'm going to like being an aunt-by-proxy again. I can now spoil two kids and give them back to you, high on candy."

"Not to mention spoiled with big, noisy presents." Candace grinned.

"You two are all heart." Rebecca's smile edged into a frown and she sat back against the counter. Her face washed from pale to lime green. "Oh, damn. Here's that nasty side effect. morning-noon-and-night sickness."

Maria laughed and grabbed Rebecca's spring jacket and purse off the coatrack. "Go home. Get some rest. Have some crackers. And let Jeremy spoil you for as long as you can get away with it. Candace and I can handle the rest of the day. All of next week if you need it."

"Aw, thanks. Listen, if you don't want to go to Vita, you can take those baskets over to Vogler Adver—"

"Oh, no, that's all mine. I insist on a personal delivery of the Vogler order," Candace said.

"Gee, wonder why you're volunteering." Maria grinned, then tossed her the van keys. "Go. Try not to drool over Michael. I'll go to Vita when you get back."

"Can't help myself." Candace smiled. "I'm in love."

Rebecca groaned. "You make me remember what I used to be like. A hundred years ago. Before"—she pressed a hand to her stomach—"being with my husband made me ill."

Candace laughed. "It's a good ill, though."

A contented smile filled Rebecca's face. "It is indeed."

After a quick stop in the kitchen, Maria walked Candace and Rebecca out of the shop. "Here," she said, handing Rebecca a can of ginger ale and a package of crackers. "For the road. Just in case."

A watery smile crossed Rebecca's lips. "This is why you two are my best friends."

"Oh, I meant to tell you. Monica is on her way in," Candace said. "And I have a delivery to make. What a pity." She dangled the keys.

Maria groaned. "Monica is coming by again? What's the big change this time?"

"I think all she's doing is adding planes," Candace said. "You're getting off easy."

"Do I want to know why?"

"Apparently her fiancé is a member of the Wannabe Mile High Club."

"Wannabe?"

"He's never quite had the guts to do more than turn the bathroom lock to 'Occupied.' "

"That's a start."

"Hey, everyone has a mission."

Maria laughed. "Mine is to get through this diet without killing myself or Mary Louise. The reunion is only three weeks away. But . . . I'm not so sure I want to go anymore."

"Why not?"

"I don't know." Maria shrugged. "Stand around for a few hours, playing one-upmanship with a bunch of people I didn't like much then and I don't like much now. I don't have anything to prove anymore, so what's the point?"

Candace chuckled. "Revenge, of course. Show them you've become a business owner. A success."

"Everyone who is important to me already knows that."

Rebecca cocked her head. "Boy, you're sure sounding different lately. You practicing yoga or something?"

Maria shook herself. "Not enough calories, that's all. Makes me maudlin."

Rebecca laughed. "How's the diet going?"

"As long as I stay away from temptation, I'm okay."

"In the form of one sexy chef?"

Maria made a noncommittal sound.

Rebecca pivoted back toward the store. "Listen, I shouldn't make you take his cookie order over there. You're trying to avoid him. I can handle the trip."

"No." Maria gently turned Rebecca around toward the sidewalk. "You go home. Make a baby. I can handle seeing Dante."

"Who knows," Rebecca said, smiling over her shoulder. "It might turn into a happy ending for you, too."

"Hey, I thought you said this wasn't a matchmaking scheme."

"No, it's not." She winked. "That's just another side effect."

Maria shooed Rebecca on her way. "I'd rather have the morning sickness."

As soon as Rebecca had rounded the corner, but before Maria and Candace could duck for cover, a long black stretch limo pulled up in front of the store. "Toodles!" Monica called, stepping from the car with Aphrodite in tow. "I stopped by to add a few finishing touches to the wedding desserts."

"Any major changes?" Behind her back, Maria crossed her fingers.

Monica laughed. "Of course not. What do you think I am? Flighty?"

Neither Candace nor Maria said a word. They merely smiled.

"I was thinking about adding some planes. Lester is just wild about anything that moves," Monica said, laughing. "Oh, and putting cabooses on the train cookies," she began, walking into the shop. Aphrodite tugged at her leash, in the opposite direction Monica was going. "Oh, puppy, do you need to make wee wee?" The dog barked. "I'll be right back. Aphrodite needs to powder her nose." Monica walked around the corner, praising her dog's manners the whole way.

"Well at least she didn't need to powder it on our front stoop," Maria said.

"Or worse, in our rest room." Candace unlocked the van and climbed inside.

"Do you think she'd actually teach her dog to do that?"

"Anything's possible with Monica." Candace shut the

van door and rolled down the window. "Sorry for leaving you with her."

"Sure you are. Have fun."

Candace grinned. "I always do when I see Michael." She started the engine and pulled away.

For a second, Maria wondered what it would be like to feel that way about a man—and have him feel the same in return. Never had she been loved like that. Never had she felt that secure about another person's feelings.

A twinge of something ached inside her. She refused to call it jealousy. Hunger pains, that's what it was. Not envy for what Candace and Rebecca had.

"We're all done with Number One," Monica said, coming back around the corner. "Now it's time for people business."

They entered Gift Baskets and sat at a small round table in the front of the shop. Maria had pulled Monica's file from the cabinet behind the counter. "Okay," she said, settling into the seat across from Monica, "you want to add planes and cabooses?"

Monica nodded. "In cookies, like the train engines are."

Maria nodded, making a notation. "We can do that. There are still a couple weeks left."

"I just want everything to be perfect." Monica sighed. "You only get married once, you know."

"Well, some people do it many times."

Monica shook her head. "I don't want to be one of those people. I want it to be right the first time."

Maria wrote *caboose* on the order form. Her hand stilled. She twirled the pen between her fingers. "Monica, can I ask you something?"

"Sure."

"How did you know Lester was the right one?"

Monica's smile softened everything about her face,

as if the mere thought of her fiancé made her into a puddle of melted butter. "I didn't at first. It's hard for me. Every man I met always wanted me for Daddy's money. Like I was a bankbook and they only wanted to make withdrawals."

The admission caught Maria by surprise. Monica Thurgood, one of the wealthiest heiresses in Boston, had gone through some of the same dating dilemmas as an average girl from the North End. "I'm not from wealth, but I know what it's like to be wanted for everything but yourself."

Monica stroked Aphrodite's petite head. "Lester was very determined. He didn't quit on me. I quit on him once or twice, though."

"You did?"

Monica nodded. "Even told him I hated trains." She bit her lip. "Almost broke his little engineer's heart."

"But how did you know he was *the one?*"

Monica shooed Aphrodite off her lap and leaned forward on her elbows. "When I finally realized Lester didn't care one bit about Daddy's money. He likes simple things and never cared where we went, as long as he was with me. He's happy racing two H-O scales with me."

"H-O scales?"

Monica blushed under her flawless Estée Lauder. "It's a type of train. Lester has taught me a lot. About . . . well, everything." Her gaze went to some distant place of memories. "But really, I knew he was the conductor to my engine when I realized I was more me when I was with him. Less Thurgood and more Monica." She giggled. "If that makes sense."

Maria nodded, the pangs in her gut ten times stronger now. "It does. Perfect sense."

Maria's Twisted-Apologies Lover's Knots

1 ¼ cups flour
½ teaspoon baking powder
Pinch of salt
¼ cup confectioners' sugar, divided, like your heart
1 egg, beaten, just like your emotions
1 tablespoon rum or brandy
Vegetable oil, for deep frying of pastries and of your conscience

Sift the flour, baking powder and salt, then stir in two tablespoons of the sugar. Incorporate egg with a fork, then add the rum until the dough draws together into one big lump, a lot like the one in your throat. Knead the dough on a lightly floured surface, working out your regrets and creating a good apology speech, until it's smooth. Separate dough into four pieces.

Roll each piece into a rectangle, about five inches long and three inches wide. Cut these into ½-inch wide strips and tie into knots similar to the ones tearing up your stomach with guilt.

Heat the oil in a fryer until it reaches 375 degrees. Fry the Lover's Knots for a couple of minutes, until crisp and golden. Drain on paper towels, then sprinkle with remaining sugar. Serve warm, to someone you want to reconcile with.

Be sure your apology is as sweet as your dessert and everything will be all right with your lover's world again.

CHAPTER 33

"Your sweetheart is here. And she has a gift for you."
Franco practically sang the words.

"Maria? She's here?"

The smirk on Franco's face was akin to a parent with
a Power Wheels behind their back on Christmas Day.

"To see me?"

Franco nodded.

Dante stood, his desk chair rocketing across the tiled
floor and sliding into the wall with a clang. He was out
the door and into the main part of the restaurant in an
instant.

Until he saw her. Then all movements ceased.

She was, as always, gorgeous. She stood there, holding
a big cardboard box, wearing a pink T-shirt, dark snug
jeans and black boots with little heels. Her hair was
back in a clippie thing again, the tendrils determinedly
slipping out of the sides, tickling down her neck.

He shouldn't care she was here. His heart shouldn't
thud at the sight of her. But apparently his brain hadn't
had time to lecture the rest of him since that night in
the restaurant.

Either way, he wasn't going to let her see how he felt. He was done pursuing a woman who had chosen another.

"Hi," he said.

"Here's your—" Maria's mind went blank. On the trip over, she'd planned out a big speech. Twenty reasons why they shouldn't let their personal differences interfere with business. But then—

But then she'd seen Dante. And everything she'd thought about today, all the words she'd heard from Rebecca, Candace and Monica, came tumbling back.

Every word of her argument stopped making sense.

"I brought your—" she tried again. What the hell did she have in her hands, anyway?

"Cookies?" Dante supplied.

"Oh, yeah. Cookies."

"Thank you." He took the box from her. No smile. No expression. A man conducting business, nothing more. "I thought you weren't dealing with my account."

"Rebecca was a little under the weather so I offered to make the delivery."

"Well." He cleared his throat. "If you need payment now—"

"There's an invoice in the box. Standard thirty-day terms."

"Good." He shifted the box into one arm, as if it weighed no more than a paper clip. "Do you need anything else?"

"No. Nothing." She bit back the question on the tip of her tongue. "Nothing at all."

His face hardened. "That's what I thought."

Maria pivoted and turned to go, disappointment weighing as heavy as a ten-pound block of provolone in her gut. What had she expected? That he'd be friendly and happy to see her? That he'd go on chasing after her indefinitely?

She'd been the one to ignore him after their night together, as if pretending it hadn't happened would make it go away.

She'd been the one who had invited Antonio to pick her up at Vita.

She'd been the one to turn dating into an S&M ritual where everyone got hurt.

Two months ago, she'd had a plan. Lose twenty-five pounds, astound her old boyfriend and then go on with business as usual. Staying single. And happy.

But now, her life was as twisted and sticky as a pot of overcooked spaghetti. And she wasn't happy at all.

The pangs in her stomach intensified with every step toward the door. She must be hungry. And yet . . . never had she felt this kind of want for a food.

As she neared the exit, Maria realized the pain in her gut wasn't from hunger. It was misery. Loneliness. Maybe even . . . a bit of love . . . all jumbled into one. Before she could do something really stupid—like leave—she circled back toward him.

Dante hadn't moved. He stood in the same place, still holding the box, watching her.

His eyes held no expression, no clue to how he was feeling. Or if he still felt anything at all for her.

She'd screwed up. A lot worse than when she'd eaten all the Twinkies and an entire margherita pie in one sitting. She'd chosen Door Number Two and gotten the jackass.

When the real hero—with the heart of gold—was right there all the time, waiting for her to wake up. She had, finally, but . . .

Maybe too late.

"I was wrong," she said.

"If you can wait a second, I'll grab the checkbook and—"

"Not about the payment." She took a step closer. The

dark intimacy of Vita surrounded them like a blanket. Beside her, a wall sconce flickered. "I was wrong about us."

He took in a breath. "Wrong how?"

"I was afraid. Hell, I still am. Afraid of commitment, of being hurt. Afraid of love." She smiled at him, a tentative smile, searching for a response. Something flickered in his eyes and she plunged forward. "And most of all, afraid of you."

This time, he moved closer to her. "Afraid of me? Why?"

"I told you. You smell too good."

"Always the diet, huh?"

"My mission in life is to get out of the double digits of dress sizes."

"Why are you so unhappy with the way you look?"

She shrugged, as if the answer was a small thing, but he could see it mattered more than that. "I don't look like other women."

"You *aren't* other women, that's the point. You're already perfect the way you are."

Maria shook her head, a refusal forming on her lips.

"Don't say it. Because I'll just disagree. And I have a lot of disagreements ready." Dante put out his hand, ticking off the reasons. "You're funny. You're smart. You're strong." He raised his hand, pressed it lightly to her heart. "In here, where it counts. When you love, you love with everything in you. I've seen it with your family. And when you hurt, you hurt deeply. Everything about you, Maria, is real and true."

She caught his hand with her own. "I've never met a man who noticed those kinds of things about me."

He reached up, catching a tendril of that misbehaving hair between his fingers. "That's because I've been treading water in the deep end for a long damned time, waiting for you."

The smile on her face wavered, her eyes now misty as a foggy day. "Dante, I—"

"Don't say it. Just say, 'Okay.' " He cupped her chin and tipped her face towards his.

"Okay." She smiled, then sighed. "This is too much right now. I . . ." She took in a breath, let it go. "I don't know where I want to go from here yet. Where *we* should go."

"Simple answer." He grinned. "The kitchen."

"The kitchen?"

"It's lunchtime. Stay and eat with me."

"I thought you weren't open for lunch."

"I am for very special customers." He touched the twin peaks of her upper lip. "You're the most special customer I have."

"But aren't you usually busy right now, getting ready for dinner?"

They hadn't been busy all week. If he told her Whitman's latest review had sent the customers in the opposite direction from Vita, she'd leave now and he wouldn't get a chance to say what he wanted to say. He didn't really need the cookies from Gift Baskets anymore.

But he sure as hell needed her.

"Right this minute the only thing I'm busy with is convincing you to try my tortellini."

"I'm not hungry."

He reached up and trailed a finger along her cheek. She didn't move. Didn't breathe. Just held the gaze, her eyes wide and luminous in the half light of Vita. "Liar."

"I have a shop to get back to."

"Stay, Maria. Not because I'm asking you to, but because you want to." He rubbed his thumb against her mouth. "Because you want *me*."

"I do want you. All the time." She shook her head. "And everything you touch. That's the problem."

"A little of a good thing isn't bad, you know. You never tasted the tortellini that Whitman raved about. How did you describe it?"

"Heaven on a plate." The words came out soft, almost reverent.

"Seems a shame to have such passion for a food you've never tasted." He lowered his hand to take hers. "Come, have just a bite."

"Time . . ." she murmured vaguely, as if she couldn't quite get her mind around the excuse.

He took two steps forward, her hand in his. His heart leapt when she moved with him. "It's already made. An early supper for the staff."

"Just a few bites, no more."

"If that's all you want." He kept moving. And she kept following. When they reached the swinging door to the kitchen, he lowered his mouth to her ear, inhaling the warm, fresh fragrance of her. "But if you want seconds, it will be my pleasure."

Franco was the first to step forward, arms wide, welcoming her into the kitchen like an old friend. "Miss Maria, how nice to see you again. You return for my Dante, no?"

"This is Maria?" said the skinny guy who had peeked through the window that first night. "No wonder you stare so hard at her, boss."

"Shut up, Vinny," Dante said. He turned toward the rest of the kitchen staff. "You all need to get back to work." Vinny made a halfhearted attempt at returning to kitchen chores, but it was clear his attention was more on Maria and Dante than chopping onions and marinating beef.

Dante went to the stove, filled two plates with the tortellini. He returned to the small table in the corner of the kitchen and placed both plates before them on the table.

Maria already knew how good it would be. She'd made the sales job herself. Read the review. Knew it had sold the harshest critic in town. The aroma rose from the pasta and teased at her senses.

"Try it."

It was a normal serving of tortellini. Nothing over the top. No bingeing involved. Thousands of people ate like this every day and didn't turn into Goodyear blimps. Surely she could find a way to balance her favorite foods—her traditions, really—with her figure. "All right," she said, and dipped her fork into the meal before her.

"Do you know the legend about tortellini?" he asked.

She shook her head.

Dante folded his arms. A contented smile filled his face. "When Venus was sleeping naked near the sea of Bologna, a chef saw her and fell in love."

"That's why she was the goddess of love and beauty," Maria pointed out. "Makes it hard for us mortal women to compete."

He grinned. "You have nothing to worry about. Anyway, the chef's favorite part of Venus was her . . ."

"Oh, let me guess." Maria held up a circular tortellini. "Belly button?"

Dante nodded. "He was easily pleased."

"He didn't get far with Venus, did he?"

"Not all the way to the strawberries and mascarpone."

Maria swallowed the bite on her fork. Those words brought up a memory a lot steamier than the ancient tale. "So, what'd he do?"

"He went back to his kitchen and created this pasta as a way to always remember her."

Maria took another bite. Delicious. "There are definitely worse ways to be immortalized."

"Then I'll have to get out my pasta machine and set to work creating a memorial to you."

She thrust her chest forward, knowing exactly which part of her he'd choose to pasta-size. "I don't think your creation would be bite-size."

He chuckled. "My father must have told me that tortellini story a hundred times when I was growing up. He said when he met my mother, she reminded him of Venus and every time he went to work, he thought of her." Dante toyed with the edge of his plate. "They grew apart after he opened Vita, but my father always loved her in his own way. He was a romantic. She . . . is not."

Maria noticed Dante had yet to reach for his fork. He'd been watching her eat, a small smile on his face.

"You aren't having any?" she asked, the fork halfway to her mouth.

"I'd much rather watch you. I never really get to see anyone eat my food."

"Pity. After all that hard work, too." She smiled and put the bite into her mouth.

Her description hadn't done the dish justice. Dante's tortellini was a food fit for a goddess. "This is"—she dipped the fork into the dish again, scooping up another bite, eating it and swallowing before she could formulate words—"amazing."

"You sure it isn't too salty? I have a tendency to be a little heavy on the salt sometimes."

She shook her head. "No, it's perfect."

"And the noodles? Al dente?"

She looked at him. "What's this I detect? A little cooking insecurity?"

"Hey, I'm not perfect."

She laughed. "That's a relief. I was beginning to think you were." She forked up a third bite, gave it a moment to connect with her palate before allowing it to make its sweet descent into her stomach.

"You really like it?"

"Dante, I love it. Honest." She laid a hand over his. "I *never* lie about food."

Excitement lit up his eyes and he scrambled to his feet. "Do you mind trying something else I made today?"

"Are you crazy? Sure I would. I'd eat anything you cook." She leaned forward, lowered her voice to a whisper. "Don't tell Mamma, but your cooking rivals hers. May even be better."

He grinned. "I'll never say a word." Then he turned and hurried to the stove. On a second plate, he served up a slice of lasagna. He paused to grate a little bit of fresh cheese over the dish, then brought it back to her. "Try this."

"What is it?"

"An experiment."

She picked up the first bite. When it settled against her tongue, an explosion of flavor—chicken, spinach, cheeses—ran through her senses. "Oh, God, this is incredible, too," she said after she swallowed, but not before she had another bite at the ready.

"Good." He let out a sigh of relief. "I wasn't sure you'd find it as tasty as the tortellini."

"You have no worries there." She sent a second bite of paradise into her mouth. Around them, the kitchen staff had gone back to work, apparently no longer interested in their conversation. Vinny was preparing food; Franco had gone out front, probably to supervise the readying of the tables.

"At least one thing in Vita is going well." Dante leaned back in the chair and rubbed at his neck.

She paused in eating, caught by his troubled gaze. "Did something happen?"

He hesitated.

"I run a business, too. If anyone understands, it's me."

His gaze met hers. "That's one of the things I like about you. You understand me. The way I think. No one else seems to."

She reached for his hand. "It takes a special kind of person to be in business."

"Yeah, a crazy one who doesn't mind a little bankruptcy." He let out a gust, then sighed. "The *Globe* found a new favorite in the North End."

"Oh, Dante. I'm so sorry." She knew what that meant to his business. She'd seen it happen to other places. Diners could be fickle people, running from one hot spot to another. Now that the focus would be elsewhere, Vita would be relegated to the shadows for a while.

"The thing that bugs me the most is my mother is probably right. This place is an albatross. I'm never going to make it into what my father wanted it to be."

Maria knew then why Dante had valued her family so much. Her mother may be persistent about getting her daughter married, but she always had Maria's best intentions at heart and would never say or do anything that didn't support her only child's dreams.

Mamma had been at Gift Baskets the day it opened and had always been one of the shop's most vocal supporters, spreading the word around the North End better than a tissueless two-year-old with a cold.

"You inherited this, but you also inherited what your father made it," she said softly. "Not everything sits on your shoulders, you know."

"I never thought of it that way." He looked past her, out the small window on the back wall. "My father wasn't much for being a hard-nosed businessman. He was always letting people run up a tab and then never making them pay it, stuff like that. But even though he wasn't a success money-wise, he taught me something."

"What?"

Dante flattened his palms on the smooth metal table.

"After my father died, I was going to close Vita. I had no intention of going into a losing proposition. My mother certainly didn't want anything to do with it. She had already put the house up for sale and booked a flight to Florida. But at the funeral, hundreds of people came. People he'd helped. People he'd given credit to. A meal when they couldn't afford one. Or simply a listening ear on a bad day."

"He sounds like a good guy."

"He was. A better man than me." Dante shrugged, his smile wry. "He wasn't a man who talked much. Or was home much. But yet, everyone else said how kind and generous he was."

"But that generosity cost him. This place. You."

"Yeah. He overdid it a little. Still, I couldn't let go of his restaurant and kill his dream, too. And once I started working here, I fell in love with the place, just like he did." Dante pulled back and ran his hands through his hair. "But with that new restaurant picking up all my business, I don't see how I can ever turn Vita into a success."

"Why? You've survived before."

His shoulders dropped and he shook his head. "I'm tired, Maria. It's hard being the one man behind the show. I've run out of ideas. I can't compete with all the other restaurants in the North End. I mean, we're all doing lasagna. How can Vita be different?" He sighed. "The name means 'Delicious Life' and it hasn't quite worked out that way yet. Especially not for me. This place *is* my life. It isn't so delicious when you work seventy hours a week and still don't see anything for all that effort."

Delicious life.

Maria thought about those words for a second. Wasn't that what she'd been seeking all these weeks? And also trying to avoid? Yet every time she denied herself her favorite foods, she ended up bingeing twice as badly the next day.

"This lasagna," she said, scooping up another bite onto the fork, "do you have it on the menu?"

"No. It's just something I cook for the kitchen staff. I like to experiment with new things and this week it's been low-calorie versions of their favorites." He grinned. "As Rochelle likes to remind me, bathing suit season isn't all that far away and they've been dipping into the garlic bread too often this winter. So they asked me to make something lighter."

"Are you planning on putting it on the menu?"

"This? Nah. It's just for fun. When people come here, they expect a certain type of meal. They want what my father gave them. If there's anything people in this neighborhood like, it's predictability."

Maria laughed. "If there's anything I run from, it's predictability."

"That explains a lot."

"What if"—she cut off another bite and ate it, "you gave your customers something unexpected, yet predictable at the same time?"

He shook his head. "I'm not quite sure what you mean."

"The best of both worlds. Right here in this kitchen. Your father and you, in one."

"You mean . . . *change* how things are done at Vita?"

"Yes."

"No."

"Why not?"

He sat straighter in his chair. "I haven't changed anything in here since my father died. I'm not going to start now."

"Well, maybe you should." She leaned forward, the plate forgotten. Around them, the kitchen hummed with its daily activities, but in this corner, only Dante and Maria existed. "I think I'm not the only one who's afraid here."

"What do you mean?"

"You *say* you want a wife and kids. Yet you work so much, it's impossible to have that. You complain the hours at the restaurant are killing you, but you won't change anything to make it easier on yourself." She arched a brow at him. "What are *you* avoiding, Dante?"

"Nothing."

"Liar." She scooted her chair around the table until she sat on the same side as he. It felt good to be close to him again. Comfortable, like she'd known him for years. That feeling made her get a little more honest. "You were right about me. I don't have control over anything, as much as I'd like to think I do. You, however, control things too much. And it's making you miserable."

"I do not." Dante paused, looked around the kitchen. Thought of all the jobs in the restaurant that he handled himself instead of letting someone else do it. All the stresses he put on his own shoulders. All the choices he'd made that didn't have to be his alone. "Okay, I do. It's easier that way, though."

"Tradition is comfortable, isn't it? Yeah, I may be afraid of getting too comfortable but you are afraid of getting out of the comfort zone."

He got to his feet, a tease in his eyes. "You think I'm afraid?"

She rose, her gaze meeting his head-on. *"Terrified."*

"Hey, I can change. Step out of that comfort zone, as you called it. I'll prove it to you." He looked around the kitchen and as he did, an African-American woman entered from the back door. "Rochelle! Just the person I want to see."

"Me?" She narrowed her eyes, her jacket halfway to the hook. "Why? What'd I do?"

"You've just become my new dining room manager. With a pay raise to go along with the title."

"I . . . I . . ." She blinked at him. "I what?"

"No one can get the waitresses' and the busboys' butts in gear like you can. Hell, they don't even listen to me. But you, you ride them like a rodeo cowboy, but they still like you at the end of the day. And I have to admit . . ." he took a breath, "you'll do a better job than me."

Her mouth dropped open. She stared at him for a long time, before shutting her jaw again. "I don't know what to say."

He laughed. "Now that's a first."

"Okay, I do know what to say. Yes. And . . . thank you." Rochelle stepped forward and threw her arms around him, hugging Dante for a brief second before moving back and thrusting out her hand. "Guess I should start being professional now."

"Be yourself. That's all I expect." He took one of her hands in both of his.

"Hey, Boss. What about me?" Vinny called from across the kitchen.

"You, Vin? You're the . . . head sous chef."

"No way. Really? I was just sous chef yesterday. Now I'm the head. Man, wait till I tell Theresa. She's going to bust a gut."

"Hopefully not before that baby is due."

"Oh, yeah, true. I'll wait to tell her." Vinny jerked his chin in Dante's direction. "And Boss, thanks for the, ah, other day. She said yes."

Dante grinned. "Good. You deserve happiness, Vinny."

Vinny nodded furiously and swiped at his eyes with the back of his hand. "You gotta excuse me." He abandoned his pepper chopping and headed toward the rest room. A second later, they heard the sound of happy sobs coming from behind the door.

"Well," Maria said. "I stand corrected. Maybe you can change." She pushed her empty plate to the side. "I have an idea."

He grinned. "I always like your ideas."

"But you have to trust me." She gestured toward the plate. "Make up a lot more of this and make it one of the specials tonight."

"But—"

"Don't but me. You did the impossible already. You got me to try the tortellini." She leaned forward and pressed a quick, hot kiss to his mouth. "Now listen to me on this. I'll be back later. I promise."

"You promise?"

She grinned. "Yeah. I have to come back. We have unfinished business, you and I."

"I told you I'd pay that invoice."

"Not that kind of business. We never finished our last chess game. If I remember right, I was winning."

He cupped her chin in his hand. "*I* was less naked than you."

Her fingers skipped along the soft cotton of his shirt, promising more than she could do in a busy kitchen. "Maybe. But *I* was the one with my hands on both your knights." She grinned, gave him another kiss, then turned on her heel. "I'm coming back for the king."

After the shop closed for the day, Maria stopped at home to change and freshen up. While she was there, she stepped on her scale. She closed her eyes. After a few seconds, she peeked one eye open. The needle hadn't moved upward at all. In fact, it looked like it was nudging downward almost a half a pound from the weight she'd been three days ago.

She stepped off. Got back on. The needle did the same little downward dance.

Maria ran through her food choices over the last couple of days. Working with Arnold, she'd put together a fairly livable diet. Except for the tortellini, she'd managed to stay on the light side of the menu today, too.

The scale, apparently, agreed.

Her plan could work. Maria got dressed, grabbed her coat and dashed out of the apartment, nearly running the few blocks over to the church for the Saturday night Chubby Chums meeting. Arnold saw her the minute she entered the basement meeting room.

"Maria! How are you?" He pulled her into a hug. This time it felt like an embrace from a friend, not suffocation by human burrito. He stepped back and looked over her form. "You know, I think you're becoming a new animal."

"I am?"

He grinned. "Yep. You're not a chinchilla anymore. You're a mink." He gave her a nod. "Looking good."

"Thanks."

"I don't think you're looking so much like a teddy bear anymore either."

He nodded, his face full of happiness. "I'm down five in two weeks."

"Hey, that's great!"

He flexed out an arm and thrust his chest forward. "I may end up with the body of a bobcat, but I'll always have the heart of a teddy bear."

"I know you will, Arnold." She smiled and patted his chest. He'd held the Schwarzenegger pose too long and the breath whooshed out of him.

Together, they went into the Chubby Chums meeting. The others—Audrey, Bert, Homer, Stephanie, and the rest of the regulars—each greeted her like an old friend. She wasn't an outsider anymore. She was part of the group.

It didn't matter if she was fat, thin, green or purple. The Chubby Chums accepted her regardless.

Maria took her seat and realized she no longer envied Mary Louise. Why the hell had she been trying so hard to look like a woman she didn't even like, anyway?

She liked who she was. Maria Pagliano was a hell of a nice woman. And looking like her wasn't bad at all.

"So, everyone, what have you all learned since the last meeting?" Stephanie asked.

Audrey's hand shot up. "That I really hate tofu. It was a breakthrough for me."

"That's good, Audrey. Glad to hear it." Stephanie turned to the next person. "Bert?"

"That Miller Lite has less calories than regular Miller. That was my freakin' breakthrough." He sat back against his chair, legs spreading in the way only a man could take up room, and scratched at his chin.

"Uh, great. I think. Maria?"

"That I don't have to diet."

The group gasped.

"You don't have to diet?"

"Well, I have to watch what I eat, but I don't have to starve myself. I can have my favorite foods, just not binge on them." She grabbed Arnold's hand and gave it a squeeze. "Arnold has been there for me during a really rough time. Together, we worked out an eating plan that works for me. And lets me keep my favorite foods."

"That's no way to lose weight," Bert said.

"I can't eat the whole box of Twinkies, Bert. Or five cups of fettuccini Alfredo. But I can have a little and eat healthier. If I'm careful, I still come out ahead."

Bert eyed her. "You ain't gonna look like no Cindy Crawford doing that."

"I don't want to be Cindy Crawford. Or Mary Louise Zipparetto. Or anyone else but me." She smiled and realized as the words came out that they were true. "Do you know what I realized when I stepped on my scale this morning?"

Audrey had her pencil at the ready, pad flipped to a clean sheet. "What?"

"That I like *me*. No matter what size I am. And if I never lose another pound, I'll still be happy."

"Oh, Maria," Arnold cried, "you're *my* teddy bear!" He wrapped an arm around her shoulders.

Stephanie smiled. "That's the true definition of a Chubby Chum." She started to clap. "Bravo, Maria!"

One by one, the others joined in with Stephanie, applauding Maria in the lime-green room.

All but one.

Bert crossed his arms, hands cemented in the region of his armpits. "How the hell does that help the rest of us? What kind of support group is this, anyway?"

Stephanie pursed her lips. "Now, Bert, you know frowns are contagious."

"I got something contagious for you." He got to his feet. "I'm heading over to that Italian place across the street. They got the all-you-can-eat-pasta special running again tonight." He jerked his chin in Maria's direction. "That's my new diet. All you can eat until you puke." He pointed toward Audrey. "You might want to write that down."

"Uh . . ." Her hand hovered over the pad.

"The food at Vita is delicious," Maria said. "But the all-you-can-eat pasta special probably isn't the best choice."

Bert gave her a nonplussed look. "You don't say?"

"We're trying to have a support group meeting here, Bert," Stephanie said. "You're not being very supportive."

He shrugged. "I'll support you if you decide to join me. Even hold the bowl while you dish up your spaghetti."

"Me?" Stephanie put a hand to her chest. "Oh, no. I can't go. One bite and . . . Well, I just couldn't."

"Me, too," Audrey said, shaking her head. "I have no self-control when it comes to starches."

"I know the chef over at Vita," Maria said. "He has a lot of great salads on the menu. And he said he'd be glad to accommodate your diets with a few lower-calorie choices." It was a bit of a lie, but she knew she had to show Dante there was a ready and willing customer base before he'd change the menu.

"He'd do that? For us?" Audrey asked.

"Well, yeah. It's good for business. And good for our waistlines."

"A good cook is not a friend for your looks," Stephanie pointed out.

"This cook is a friend, believe me."

"Oh, I don't know," Audrey said. She worried the end of her pencil between her teeth. "I never eat pasta anymore. And never, ever go into real restaurants. They tempt me like that snake with the apple."

"Maria wouldn't steer us wrong," Arnold said. "She's a Chubby Chum. And remember what we always say, Chubby Chums keep us from feeling glum!"

Stephanie got to her feet. "Well, group. We *are* a support group. I think we could handle a field trip, if we stick together. That way, if one of us strays too close to the four-cheese lasagna, we'll remember our Chubby Chum mantra."

"A friend, we reckon, won't let a Chum take seconds," the group repeated en masse.

They all got to their feet, charging out of the door and across the street with the frenzied zealousness of bargain-hunting brides at the annual Filene's Basement sale.

Happy-Ending-for-All Chicken Florentine Lasagna

1 ½ tablespoons butter or margarine
3 tablespoons flour
2 12-ounce cans evaporated skim milk
½ teaspoon salt
⅛ teaspoon nutmeg
16 ounces nonfat cottage cheese
¾ cup reduced fat shredded mozzarella cheese
Cooking spray
7 ounces whole wheat lasagna noodles, cooked and drained
1 ½ cups cooked chicken breast, shredded
1 10-ounce package frozen chopped spinach, thawed and squeezed dry
Salt and pepper
2 tablespoons grated Parmigiano Reggiano (a little of the good stuff can go a long way)
2 tablespoons fresh parsley

Preheat oven to 375 degrees and get ready for a culinary masterpiece that's good for you—and good to eat. In a medium saucepan, melt the butter, then add the flour and cook thirty seconds. Gradually whisk in milk, salt and nutmeg. Cook until thickened, about three minutes. Voila! Low-calorie white sauce. Mix the cottage cheese and mozzarella in a separate bowl. Looking good already, isn't it? And best of all, it's only about ten grams of fat per serving.

Long as you're realistic about portion control, that is.

Spread ⅓ of the sauce over an 11 x 7-inch baking dish that has been coated with cooking spray to prevent a sticky mess. Arrange noodles across sauce, top with half the chicken and spinach, then sprinkle with salt and pepper. Protein, veggies, dairy—what more can you ask? Oh yes, a little fat. Just a little though—nothing too dangerous.

Top with half the cheese mixture, then a little more sauce. Add another layer, same as before. End with noodles, then spread remaining sauce over top.

Cover with foil and bake for forty-five to fifty-five minutes. Long enough to write out a menu that involves plenty of Chum-friendly meals—and a new plan for your life that allows for a true "delicious life."

Remove foil, sprinkle with grated Parmigiano and bake another five minutes. Serve with parsley garnish and a smile because you know this combines the best of all your worlds.

A happy ending. Who knew you could find it on a plate?

CHAPTER 34

When Maria walked in the door, trailed by a baker's dozen of the Chubby Chums, Franco took a step back, blinked, then blinked again. "Miss Maria! You bring friends! Lots of them."

"I did, Franco. And we'd like a table for"—she ran a quick head count—"fourteen."

"Right away!" He hurried into the dining room, grabbing the first busboy he saw and gesturing at him to get a table ready.

Within seconds, Franco was back and scooping menus into his arms. "Follow me, please."

The group filed behind him and took seats at the table. Maria at one end, Stephanie at the other. A moment later, Rochelle came up to their table. "I'll take this one myself, Franco," she told him. "It's my last night waitressing and this table is special." She smiled at Maria, then turned to the group and introduced herself. "I can take your drink orders now and come back for the food orders."

"Actually, if you all don't mind, I'll order for us."

Maria looked at everyone else, most of whom nodded agreement.

Bert snorted. "Just get me a Miller Lite and I'll be happy."

"Rochelle, we'd like six orders of the lasagna special and of the antipasto. And bring us a couple big bowls of the house salad. We're going to try a buffet of some of Dante's lighter fare."

"Lighter fare?" Rochelle's hand paused over the order pad. "Since when?"

"Did you lie to us?" Bert asked. "Probably trying to get us all fat so she looks thin."

"Bert, *shut up*." Audrey gave him a jab in the shoulder.

Bert blinked in surprise. And stopped talking.

"You go, Audrey!" Arnold beamed at her.

She flexed her little arm. "Thanks. I'm feeling assertive today."

"Is this the lasagna we had for lunch today?" Rochelle asked.

"Yep."

"Oh, that's amazing stuff. I've been telling Dante he should put it on the menu. Glad you convinced him." She wrote down what Maria had ordered, then took everyone's drink choices and headed into the kitchen.

Franco bustled in from the opposite direction, leading a group of four more to the table beside them. "Your guests have arrived, Miss Maria," he said.

"You made it!" Maria rose, crossing to hug and kiss Mamma, Papa, Nonna and Nonno.

"Of course," her grandfather said. "The Paglianos, we like to eat." He smiled and embraced her back. "And, we like to see you, *nipote*."

Rochelle had returned with a tray full of diet sodas and water glasses. She looked at Maria. "Let me guess. More lasagna specials?"

Maria glanced at her parents and grandparents. "Is that okay with you?"

Mamma nodded, exchanging a private look with her daughter. "We not so old we can't learn new things." She turned to Rochelle. "Four, *per favore*."

"You got it." Rochelle grinned, took their drink orders, then practically ran back into the kitchen. Before the door finished swinging shut behind her, Dante exited from the opposite side.

Maria's heart sang at the sight of him. Would it always be like this? Would she always feel this little skip of joy every time he came home?

Every time he came home?

That kind of thought implied permanence. Commitment.

Marriage.

Maria sat back in her chair and tasted the word in her mind. It didn't seem so scary anymore. The empty feeling in her stomach had disappeared.

Could she have been filling that feeling with food instead of . . .

Love?

That would make Mamma and the Chubby Chums and everyone else right.

Well, if that were so, Maria would never admit it. Not even if they tempted her with a heaping bowl of tortellini. With Twinkies on the side.

After pausing to greet her parents, Dante arrived at her seat. "You came back," he said, a smile on his lips.

"I keep my promises."

"Good." He looked at the crowd surrounding the pushed-together tables. "And who did you bring with you?"

"Your new demographic."

"My new . . . what?"

"We're the Chubby Chums," Arnold said, spreading

his arms to indicate the group. "And Maria said you've got some great healthy Italian food that can fit on our diets. Best of both worlds."

Dante paused, thinking. Maria tensed. If he didn't go along with this, then she'd read him completely wrong. A long second passed as he looked at her, then the others. Finally, a slow smile spread across his face.

He turned toward her, his dark brown eyes linking with hers, like a connection stretching for miles. Strong and deep, seeming unbreakable. She took in a breath, held it.

"Maria," he said, the word quiet and intimate, "I love you."

The Chubby Chums whooped. Mamma clapped.

"You-you—," she sputtered.

"He loves you, Maria," Arnold said. "Tell him you love him back."

"But-but . . ."

"Those who delay, lose their way." Arnold tugged her out of her chair. "And your way is right"—he gave her a little shove—"there."

She stumbled toward Dante. The room seemed to drop away, leaving only them. That dimple by his smile. Those eyes that saw further inside her than any eyes before. "All I expected to hear was thanks."

He grinned. "Didn't seem like enough. You saved my restaurant. And my heart."

"Your heart?"

"It was going down the garbage disposal fast, until you came along."

She chuckled. "Gee, you're so romantic."

"I've got an audience." He came closer, his voice lowering to a whisper. "When we're alone, *ma petite*, I'll show you romantic."

She smirked. "Nonna taught me some of her self-defense tricks, you know."

His brown eyes twinkled. "Now that could make things very interesting."

She took in a breath and held his gaze until the tease disappeared. "You . . . you really meant what you said?"

In an instant, he had both her hands in a firm, secure grip that seemed like it could hold her forever. "I love you, Maria Pagliano. *You*. Not what's on the outside. Just you."

"Kiss him!" Nonna shouted.

"Kiss him!" the Chubby Chums echoed.

"Kiss him before my damned beer gets warm," Bert muttered.

And so they obliged the crowd for a long, sweet second. Dante's lips on hers felt as perfect as cheese on penne, as delicious as meatballs with sauce. The chef and Venus—but with a much happier ending.

She drew back, pressing her cheek to his. "I love you, too," Maria whispered into Dante's ear. "But don't tell my mother."

He chuckled and motioned toward the Pagliano table. "I think she already knows."

Maria turned. Nonna and Mamma had taken out a piece of paper. Each had a pen in their hands, writing as fast as they could, the names pouring down either side of the paper.

"Is that what I think it is?" Maria asked. "If we don't get out of here soon, they'll be planning our baby shower next."

He grinned. "That's not a bad idea," Dante whispered in her ear.

For just a minute, Maria's heart stopped beating.

Dante's Dreams-Are-Made-of-This
Linguine with Clams

32 fresh-from-the-Cape Cherrystone clams
1 pound linguine
2 teaspoons extra virgin olive oil
1 onion, finely chopped
4 cloves garlic, sliced
½ cup dry white wine
Salt and pepper to taste
½ ounce finely chopped Italian parsley

Steam the clams until they open, begging you to remove them from their shells. Put them into a dish, reserving a few tablespoons of broth. Discard any shells that didn't open. Meanwhile, boil the linguine until it's al dente. Cook the onion in olive oil, stirring often, letting it soften under your tutelage. Just like her resolve and her heart finally have.

Once the onion is translucent, add the garlic, wine, and the strained clam broth to the sauce. Ah, perfection. Almost ready to share with the woman you love. Bring the sauce to a boil, stirring occasionally, until the liquid is reduced by about half. Now add those delicate clams, season with salt and pepper to taste, and stir in some of the parsley. Delectable, just like her.

Bring the yin and yang together by spooning the hot sauce over linguine. Garnish with parsley and a bit of hope for a steamy future.

CHAPTER 35

The lasagna had been a huge success. The Chubby Chums raved about it and promised to tell all the other Chubby Chum chapters throughout the eastern seaboard about the new option in Italian dining. They also made a long-standing reservation for dinner after every meeting. As she walked out, Chubby Chums in tow, Stephanie called Vita the perfect destination for dieters who wanted to have their pasta and eat it, too.

Dante looked around the familiar walls of his father's dream. It had now become Dante's vision, too. A twist on the original.

"You're brilliant," he said to Maria. They'd stolen a moment alone in the lobby while Mamma and Nonna argued about inviting a few cousins who couldn't hold their liquor and their tongues at the same time.

"That's why you love me," she said, grinning up at him. "Meet me at my place tonight when you're done. I'll wait up for you."

"Should I bring the Chianti?"

She tiptoed her fingers up his chest, lingering at the

open V of skin above his shirt. "You don't even have to bring clothes."

He groaned, grabbing her fingers and putting them to his lips. "Oh, Lord, Maria, you torture me."

"You haven't seen anything yet," she said, her voice full of promises she intended to keep. "Wait till you see what I can do with my bishops."

When Dante arrived, he held a plastic container in his hands. Red-and-white roosters danced around the perimeter of the opaque bowl. "I found this outside your front door."

"That's one of Mamma's containers," Maria said. She took a closer look and saw liquid swishing beneath the clear lid. "She wouldn't."

"Let me guess." He held the bowl up to the light and laughed. "Wedding soup?"

"I've told her a hundred times that you aren't going to propose just because I have some meatballs and spinach. Give me that," she said, taking the bowl from him. "I'm going to settle this once and for all."

Maria marched towards the kitchen, withdrawing a stoneware bowl from the cabinet. "I'm going to eat this soup and prove to my mother that eating it doesn't automatically generate a marriage proposal."

"No way could that happen." Dante said as he followed behind her. He stifled a grin and fingered the small velvet box in his pocket. He'd had to call in a hell of a favor to get this ring after hours, but given the timing, it was going to be worth it, just to see the expression on Maria's face after she ate the soup. "No way at all."

Maria's Recipe for Happily Ever After

1 skipped class reunion
1 well-meaning, meddling family
1 sexy chef
1 confident heroine
Chubby Chums, to taste

Take family and add in all their good wishes, charms for grandbabies and muttered prayers.

Mix chef and heroine together. Often. If necessary, dip both in mascarpone.

When needed, sprinkle in Chubby Chums for garnish and rhyming advice. Invite all to the wedding. But banish the words "I told you so" from everyone's vocabulary.

Please turn the page for an exciting preview of
Shirley Jump's next book in this series,
THE ANGEL CRAVED LOBSTER.
Available in August 2005 from Zebra

Travis Campbell was a man who didn't want to be tempted. Now *that* was exactly the kind of challenge Meredith had come to this city to find. It was even better than her original plan—to find a man who was ready, willing, and able.

A man who wasn't willing, wasn't ready but still able would force her to really act like a woman. To try out this new sexy siren persona she wanted to affect.

And help her shed the image of a girl steeped in cow manure and homespun roots once and for all.

"Can I buy you a drink?" she asked, forcing her voice not to shake as she spoke. Never before had she made a pass at a man.

Hopefully she didn't fumble it and end up overshooting the goal line. Like the guy in the blue-and-red uniform on the TV above them just had, eliciting a few frustrated groans and several curses from the male audience in the bar.

Travis turned to face her and rested his elbow on the bar. "I don't drink. Anymore."

Anymore. There was a word that invited questions. Meredith opened her mouth to ask one, then shut it again. Her objective wasn't to form a relationship here, just to . . . complete her education. For that, she didn't need to know what "anymore" meant.

"Meredith Shordon," she said, thrusting out her hand.

He paused, then took her hand in his and shook. He had a firm grip. Long, strong fingers.

Perfect.

"Travis Campbell."

"Nice to meet you, Travis."

"Where do you come from, Meredith Shordon?" He cocked his head and studied her.

"Indiana."

"There are people who live in Indiana? I thought they all left after the finale of *Little House on the Prairie.*"

She laughed. "A few of us hung on in Walnut Grove."

He released her hand. "Well, it was a pleasure meeting you, Miss Indiana."

The beauty queen reference, coupled with the word pleasure, sent another round of heat roaring through her.

Now or never. She only had so much time before she'd have to go back.

Back to Indiana. Back to being Meredith Shordon. The woman everybody knew like the back of their hands. If there was anything Meredith hated about herself, it was her conventionality. All her life, she'd fit into the little square created by midwestern values. No lying. No cheating on her tax returns.

And most of all, no sex.

She'd been a good girl. And what the hell had it gotten her?

A mortician as an ex-fiancé. A job as a waitress in Petey's Pizza Parlor, despite two years of college. An associate's degree instead of a bachelor's because somewhere along the way she'd convinced herself that was good enough.

And most of all, a fear of anything that took her outside that insular environment because that was where the big, bad wolves existed. Too much sin, she'd heard over and over again from Pastor Wendall at the First Presbyterian Church, and she'd be headed on a nonstop highway to hell.

Hell, Meredith had decided, didn't seem such a bad alternative to slogging pepperoni pizzas around and being kissed by a man who smelled of formaldehyde.

Meredith took a step forward and tossed all the rules she'd lived her life by out the window. "I'd like to make you an offer, Mr. Campbell."

He gave her an inquiring look. "You hardly know me."

"Exactly."

His mouth lifted up on one side. "Only because I'm a curious man, I'll ask what this offer is."

She swallowed. "As I mentioned, I come from a small town in Indiana."

He nodded.

"And, well, this is my first time in a city."

"A good city to pick for your first time." He grinned.

She met his dark brown gaze. "Exactly."

The air hung between them, punctuated by a Sheryl Crow song. In the distance, a couple danced in the center of the room, another flirted in a corner booth.

Travis slid onto a stool, propping one heel against the steel circle on the base. "Are you saying what I'm thinking you're saying? Or am I just an idiot guy who's thinking with his lesser brain?"

"You heard me right." Meredith drew in a breath. "I want my first time to be in the city."

"First time?" he echoed again.

She saw him swallow. Who knew two words could

have such an impact on a six-foot-two man? "That's what I said."

"Uh, I'm not what you think I am."

"You're not a man?"

He chuckled. "Oh, I'm a man all right. I'm not a . . . well, a gigolo."

She smiled. "Good. I wouldn't want a professional. I suspect that would be about as fun as a breast exam from a gynecologist."

Travis leaned forward, resting a hand on her arm. "I know you're new in town and all, Miss Shordon, but that isn't the kind of thing you go up to a stranger and offer."

"I may be from Indiana but that doesn't mean I'm an idiot, Mr. Campbell. I know what I'm doing." She took a step forward, placing her own hand on top of his. "Are you interested in the position?"

A hundred emotions flickered on his face. He swallowed, then cleared his throat and considered her again. "I'm really not the right man for what you want."

She frowned. "You can't perform?"

That got his attention. "Of course I can."

"No football injuries or surgeries that prevent you from doing the job?"

"Of course not." He cocked his head and studied her. "But you don't know anything about me."

"I know enough." She'd seen him with Mike. Her gut told her Travis Campbell was a decent man, the kind who wouldn't turn her life story into a TNT special. Meredith collected her courage and drifted her hand down his chest. "I've seen the merchandise and I want to buy it."

He let out a long breath, as if her touch had taken away his resolve. "I'm not for sale."

"Then you can work for free."

"Don't you, ah," he watched her hand make its way

back up his chest, "have a boyfriend back on the farm, or wherever it is you lived in Indiana, that can do this for you?"

She shook her head. "Not anymore."

A fleeting thought of Caleb ran through her mind. She could just imagine his reaction to her propositioning a complete stranger like this. He'd be horrified, unable to understand how she could do something so personal with someone she hadn't known all her life. What Caleb didn't understand was that was *exactly* why she wanted a stranger for this job. So no one would know but her and the whole town of Heavendale could keep their noses out of her sex life.

She sighed and took her hand off his chest. "Listen, I don't want this to get personal. Are you interested in the job or not?"

His gaze skimmed over her again. For the first time, Meredith was sure she had made a mistake. This was a crazy idea. It had seemed so sane when she'd left the farm and boarded a plane.

"Yes," he said after a moment. "I'll take the job."

She gulped. "Good."

"But first, I think you should know what you're getting yourself into."

Then he swooped forward and kissed her.

Travis had only intended to give Meredith Shordon a taste of her own medicine. But when his mouth met hers, an explosion of want burst in his brain.

She kissed him back, tentative at first, as delicate as a hummingbird. The innocence of her lips, so tender, so soft, told him to tread lightly. The quiet fragrance of spring flowers drifted off her skin, a sweet contrast to the salty taste of margarita on her lips.

He cupped her chin with his hand, tracing her jaw with his thumb. She opened her mouth to his and in one hesitant, gentle move, tasted him with her tongue.

Holy shit. What had he done?

He'd only meant to teach her a lesson. Instead, he found himself quickly drowning in desire.

As if she felt the same, Meredith pressed forward, her breasts brushing against his chest. She tangled a hand in his hair and again brought her tongue into his mouth.

Travis jerked back, ending the kiss before he jumped off the cliff and into bed with her. This was *so* not the plan.

"Still want to honor that deal?" he asked, hoping she'd say no. Praying she'd say yes.

Eyes closed, she nodded her head. "Uh-huh."

Oh, damn. He didn't need to be getting involved with this woman. She was too sweet, too naive, too much of a—holy crap—a virgin.

Was he nuts? Any man with more than one functioning brain cell would leap at this kind of opportunity.

The little voice in the back of his head reminded him that he'd vowed to stay away from all the things that got him into trouble. Namely, alcohol and women. Especially women who had "hurt potential" written all over them.

Travis glanced at Meredith and her wide, open, trusting eyes. When he did, he knew one thing—he needed to protect her from herself. She had no idea what she was asking for—or how another man with less morals than himself would take it.